"[Ian Hamilton is] a lively writer with an attentive eye for the details of complicated suspense." — *London Free Press*

"Hamilton does a masterly job capturing the sights, smells, and sounds of Hong Kong as he charts Chow's struggle to survive." — *Publishers Weekly*

"[Uncle's] rise through the ranks of the Hong Kong Triads makes for fascinating reading… Those fresh to Hamilton's work or simply looking for something familiar but different, meanwhile, will find much to like in the author's new series." — *Quill & Quire*

"A welcome origin story about the man who helped shape Ava Lee." — *Booklist*

"A magnetic tale of intrigue among rivals and cohorts, the early ascent of 'Uncle' Chow Tung within the Hong Kong Triads is exhilarating and utterly convincing. This is the first in a spin-off series that you'll want to keep spinning forever. Jump on at the start!" — John Farrow, bestselling author of the Émile Cinq-Mars series

"Ian Hamilton's knowledge of the Triads and their operations is fascinating — and slightly unsettling. He unwinds his tale of Uncle's origins with such detail that readers will wonder how he grew so familiar without being a triad himself. A must-read for fans of the Ava Lee novels!" — John Lawrence Reynolds, Arthur Ellis Award-winning author of *Beach Strip*

FORESIGHT

FORESIGHT

THE LOST DECADES OF UNCLE CHOW TUNG

IAN HAMILTON

SPIDERLINE

Published in Canada in 2020 and the USA in 2020
by House of Anansi Press Inc.
www.houseofanansi.com

House of Anansi Press is committed to protecting our natural environment.
This book is made of material from well-managed FSC®-certified forests,
recycled materials, and other controlled sources.

24 23 22 21 20   1 2 3 4 5

Library and Archives Canada Cataloguing in Publication

Title: Foresight / Ian Hamilton.
Names: Hamilton, Ian, 1946– author.
Description: Series statement: The lost decades of Uncle Chow Tung ; 2
Identifiers: Canadiana (print) 2019006594X | Canadiana (ebook)
20190065982 | ISBN 9781487003999 (softcover) |
ISBN 9781487004002 (EPUB) | ISBN 9781487004019 (Kindle)
Classification: LCC PS8615.A4423 F67 2020 | DDC C813/.6—dc23

Book design: Alysia Shewchuk
Typesetting: Sara Loos

Canada Council   Conseil des Arts
for the Arts   du Canada

ONTARIO ARTS COUNCIL
CONSEIL DES ARTS DE L'ONTARIO
an Ontario government agency
un organisme du gouvernement de l'Ontario

*We acknowledge for their financial support of our publishing
program the Canada Council for the Arts, the Ontario Arts Council,
and the Government of Canada.*

Printed and bound in Canada

MIX
Paper from
responsible sources
FSC
www.fsc.org
FSC® C103567

This book is dedicated to Laura Meyer,
one of the warmest, kindest, and most professional
people it has been my privilege to work with.

It doesn't matter if a cat is white or black;
if it catches mice it is a good cat.

— DENG XIAOPING, CHINESE COMMUNIST
YOUTH LEAGUE CONFERENCE, BEIJING, JULY 1962

(1)
May 1981
Fanling, New Territories, Hong Kong

FOR ALMOST TEN YEARS, MONDAY HAD ALWAYS BEEN
Chow Tung's favourite day of the week. Now it was a day
he was starting to dread. The reason for this was the piece
of paper in front of him, which contained the results from
his betting shops for the previous day's horse racing at Sha
Tin Racecourse. Recently the results had been declining at
a slow, steady pace, but now they seemed to be accelerating.

"The goddamn Hong Kong Jockey Club," Chow muttered
as he sipped his second instant coffee of the morning.

The Jockey Club had a legal betting monopoly in Hong
Kong. Founded in 1884, it was almost one hundred years
old, and it offered two race meetings a week for nine months
of the year at the Happy Valley Racecourse on Hong Kong
Island. The track could accommodate 55,000 people and was
always sold out, and since the only legal place to bet was at
the track, this meant that thousands — if not hundreds of
thousands — of race-crazy Hong Kongers weren't able to put
down their bets. Under his leadership, Chow Tung's Fanling

Triad gang had opened a number of betting shops in their hometown to cater to this need. The shops were illegal, but Chow had reached an understanding with the local police that allowed them to operate.

The betting shops had been tremendously profitable and, combined with night markets, mah-jong parlours, restaurants, mini-casinos, and massage parlours, had made the Fanling Triad one of the wealthiest in all of Hong Kong and the New Territories. In fact, they were wealthy enough that Chow — more commonly known as Uncle — had been able to eliminate his gang's involvement in loan-sharking, protection rackets, and drug dealing, which had the benefits of reducing police scrutiny and making the triad members more respectable and acceptable in the community. Even if much of what they were doing was still officially regarded as crime, in Uncle's eyes it was victimless: he was simply providing a public service.

But nothing in Hong Kong ever stayed the same. It was a city always on the move, and the Hong Kong Jockey Club was no exception. In 1974 the Club had opened six of its own off-track betting shops. None were located in Fanling, but since the gang's shops drew people from outside the town as well, there was a slight but manageable decrease in business. As more Club-owned betting shops opened, business continued to decrease. Uncle had been hopeful that the Sha Tin Racecourse, which had opened in 1978, would lead to an increase in racing dates, but that didn't happen; the Club assigned only one race day a week to each track. It also kept building more off-track shops, including one in Fanling. The gang had kept many of its customers but lost enough for it to hurt, and with each passing month Uncle knew the loyalties of those who stayed with them would be increasingly strained.

"The goddamn Hong Kong Jockey Club," he said again, slipping on his black suit jacket over a white shirt buttoned to the neck. Then he headed for the door of his one-bedroom apartment.

It wasn't quite seven when he reached the street and turned left to walk to Jia's, a congee restaurant where he ate breakfast nearly every day. It was a splendid morning, the sun rising in a clear blue sky, the air fresh, and the temperature a comfortable twenty degrees Celsius or so. He walked quickly, stopping only to buy a copy of the *Oriental Daily News*.

Reading the newspaper as he ate breakfast was his custom, but the newspaper would have to wait this morning because he was being joined by Xu, the gang's White Paper Fan. Uncle had been the White Paper Fan before his election as Mountain Master. It was an administrative and financial management position, and it had been Xu who had delivered Sunday's business numbers to Uncle the night before.

Like Uncle, Xu had fled China twenty years before, but for different reasons. In Uncle's case, the famine caused by Mao's catastrophic agricultural policies during the Great Leap Forward had killed his entire family. Before starvation could take him as well, he had joined a group of other young people in his village of Changzhai, near Wuhan, and together they journeyed to the Chinese town of Shenzhen, on the Hong Kong border, where they swam four kilometres across Shenzhen Bay to Hong Kong. Four of his companions had died making the swim, including his fiancée, Lin Gui-San. Uncle would forever blame the Communists for her death.

Xu's original home was in Shanghai and, unlike Uncle, he was already a triad when he arrived in Fanling. That gang membership had become a problem when Mao issued an order to eradicate all the triads in China. Xu had been fortunate enough to escape the wrath of the People's Liberation Army, but many of his triad brothers didn't make it out of China.

As Uncle neared the restaurant, he saw a small knot of people at the door, a testament to the quality of Jia's food. He slid past them and saw Jia, grey-haired and sturdy, standing near the cash register. He figured she had to be sixty, but he'd never been in the restaurant when she wasn't waiting tables and her husband wasn't cooking in the kitchen. She waved at him. "Your friend Xu is already here," she said.

Uncle walked to the rear of the restaurant, where Xu sat in a booth with his back to the door.

"Hey, good morning," Uncle said.

Xu swivelled to face him. Uncle blinked. "What's happened to you?" he asked. "I know the numbers aren't terrific, but you shouldn't take them to heart."

"Sit, please," Xu said.

Uncle slid into the booth and looked across the table. Even seated, the six-foot Xu towered over five-foot-four-inch Uncle. "What's going on?" Uncle asked.

"Can we eat first? I might feel better with something in my stomach."

"Sure," Uncle said, holding his right arm in the air.

Jia hurried towards them with a pot of tea and two cups.

Congee is plain, bland boiled rice porridge, but Uncle never ate it by itself. He added soy sauce and white pepper to give it some flavour and ordered various add-ons to give it some heft. "I'm going to have sausage, scallions, a duck egg, and some youtiao this morning," he told Jia.

"I'll have the same," Xu said.

Jia nodded, poured tea into their cups, and hurried back to the kitchen.

Uncle sipped his tea, then said to Xu, "I know something is troubling you, and I don't want to wait until you've eaten to hear about it."

Xu shook his head. "It could be nothing."

"Or it could be something. I won't be able to judge until you tell me what it is."

Xu sighed. "About an hour ago, I got a phone call from the White Paper Fan in Mong Kok. We've developed a good working relationship over the years," he said. "He told me he's been hearing rumours about Fanling and he thought I should know what's going on."

"Was he just reporting rumours or telling you specifically that something is going on?"

"A bit of both actually, but he started by asking how our betting shops are doing. I told him the Jockey Club shops are cutting into our business but we aren't overly concerned," Xu said. "Then he asked if I knew that the gang in Tai Wai New Village is actively going after our customers. When I said no, he told me they've co-opted several of our men to direct business in their direction and are paying them for every new customer."

"Did he have any proof to back up those claims? Any names?"

"No."

"I find it hard to believe that any of our men would betray us like that. Still, we need to look into it. Talk to Wang, and the two of you figure out how to pursue this," Uncle said, referring to his Red Pole, the gang's enforcer and the one who ran the men, called forty-niners, on the ground.

"There's more," Xu said, and then went silent as Jia arrived with their breakfast. He watched, visibly impatient, as she placed their bowls and platters of add-ons on the table. When she was out of hearing range, he leaned towards Uncle. "He also told me that Tai Wai is actively recruiting some of our men to sell drugs in Fanling. Since we're the only major gang that doesn't sell drugs, Tai Wai thinks we're a market that's ready to be exploited. They don't want to send their own men here to do it, because that would be an obvious provocation, so they're trying to use ours."

Uncle looked down at his bowl of congee, sprinkled black pepper over it, added soy sauce, and then dipped a stick of the fried bread known as youtiao into it. He chewed quickly, dipped again, and then sat back. "Tai Wai must believe we are weak," he said.

"I don't understand why they would. Our two gangs are of almost equal size, and Wang is a superior Red Pole to theirs."

"I don't mean weak in that sense, I mean weak economically," Uncle said. "When we cut back on the monthly cash allotment to our men three months ago, we told them it was a temporary measure. Maybe some of them didn't believe us and are looking for ways to augment their income."

"We had no choice. We had to preserve our reserve and we couldn't reduce payments to the wives, children, and parents of the brothers who are no longer with us."

Uncle pushed the bowl away, his appetite gone. "We need to increase our income. We need to restore the allotment."

"I agree, but how can we do that without draining the reserve?"

"We need to revisit the entire situation with the executive committee. The problem is that both Fong and Yu are in Macau doing god knows what, and I have no idea when they'll be back."

"Do you want me to try to reach them?"

"Yes, and in the meantime, get hold of Wang and try to verify what the guy in Mong Kok told you."

"Will you call the Mountain Master in Tai Wai New Village?"

"Not until we're absolutely certain that what you've been told is true. Let's start by finding that out."

"Okay, Uncle, I'm on it."

Uncle looked at Xu's congee. "You haven't touched your breakfast."

"Now that I've told you what's going on, I'm anxious to get to Wang."

"We will sort this out."

"I wish I had your confidence, Uncle."

"Xu, I believe in the strength of our brotherhood."

"I know you do, but I have to say, when it comes to Fanling, everyone believes that our strength flows from one man, and that man is you."

2

UNCLE SAT QUIETLY FOR SEVERAL MINUTES AFTER XU
left the restaurant, trying to gather himself. He had been rattled
by what Xu told him. He had assumed he had the loyalty of all
his men, but money was the strongest of lures, and he couldn't
discount the idea that some of them might be drawn to it. He
hoped otherwise, but he wasn't naive, and he was already certain that cutting the monthly allotment had triggered doubts
about the ongoing strength and future of the gang.

Gang members working part-time for other gangs, or
even switching allegiance, wasn't common, but it also wasn't
unknown. Uncle knew of at least two other Hong Kong–
based gangs that had bled members when their financial
structure weakened.

Ten years before, when Uncle became Mountain Master,
the betting shops had provided enough money to support
everyone. With that no longer the case, and with no hope of
turning that situation around because of the Jockey Club's
aggressive expansion, he needed the other businesses to
increase their contributions. But they could achieve only so
much growth, since they were limited by Fanling's size, his

own refusal to get into loan-sharking, protection rackets, and drug dealing, and the fact that every bit of land that abutted Fanling was controlled by a rival gang.

Uncle hadn't been inactive, though. He had invested gang money in additional massage parlours and a secondary night market, but all that had done was cannibalize their existing businesses. He needed an additional income stream that would bring new money to the table, and right now he didn't have a single viable option.

The Fanling gang had about 160 members, and when Chow factored in their families and the families of past members they were morally obligated to support, close to six hundred people depended on the income generated by the gang. He had hesitated before cutting the amount each gang member received but had decided it would buy him some time to address the larger problem. If what Xu had been told was correct, he hadn't bought much of that.

One immediate option was to restore the allotment to its previous level. That might stop defections or prevent gang members from freelancing, but it would slowly and surely drain the reserve fund he had spent years accumulating, leaving them with nothing to invest if the right opportunity presented itself. With the executive committee's approval, he had been dipping into the fund for more than a year already. He figured that, with no change in current revenues, it might last another two years.

Uncle shook his head, fighting back frustration and a sense of hopelessness. He waved to Jia, and she hurried to the table. "Could you warm my tea, please?"

"You aren't eating. Is something wrong?" she asked, pointing at his bowl.

"I don't have much of an appetite this morning."

"You are too thin to begin with. I can't have you coming in here and not eating, because we can't afford to lose you," she said. "Your congee must be cold by now. Let me replace it with a fresher bowl."

"Okay," he said with a smile.

When she left, Uncle reached for the *Oriental Daily News*, thinking that the paper might offer a small distraction. He opened it to the back pages, which were full of summaries and analysis of the previous day's races at Sha Tin. As was his habit, he had been there and had wagered on every race. It had started badly, but he hit the winners of the last three races and had left ahead by a little.

"Here you are," Jia said, as she reappeared with a small bowl of fresh congee and a pot containing hot water. She poured the water into Chow's teapot and put the bowl in front of him. "I feel like standing here to make sure you eat."

"You don't have to fret so much," he said, picking up a spoon.

He closed the paper, turning it over to the front page. A photo of China's new premier, Deng Xiaoping, stared back at him. The headline declared: "Shenzhen Has Become China's Boomtown." Uncle began to read the article, which was about the myriad commercial and manufacturing activities planned for — and already partially underway — in Shenzhen. The previous year, Deng had named Shenzhen a special economic zone in a bid to attract foreign investors to that region of China. Uncle hadn't paid much attention at the time, just as he hadn't seen any significance in Shenzhen's being given city status the year before, even though it had a population of only thirty thousand. Now he was beginning to realize that Shenzhen's designation as a city had been a prelude to its establishment as a special economic zone. But where was it all heading? Was sleepy Shenzhen really open to investment from the West? Was it already on its way to becoming an economic powerhouse, as the *Daily News* implied?

Uncle hadn't set foot in China since he'd left, even though Shenzhen was just a thirty-minute drive from Fanling. Initially he'd been afraid of being arrested or not being allowed back across the border into Hong Kong. But even when he became a Hong Kong citizen and received his all-important Hong Kong ID card, his memories of China were still too raw and his hatred of the Communists too intense to tempt him to travel there. And then there was the rather important fact that triads were still outlawed in China and, unlike the Hong Kong Police Force, the People's Liberation Army wasn't the least bit accommodating.

The article continued on two inside pages, and as Uncle read further he found his interest in Shenzhen starting to grow. The article praised Deng Xiaoping's vision for a new China, of which Shenzhen was one of the first building blocks. Despite his hatred of the Communists, Uncle was fascinated by Deng Xiaoping. He had tracked his recent career and read extensively about Deng's colourful past. Now, he wondered, what was the little man (Deng was only four-eleven) up to with these special economic zones?

Deng had been born in 1904 and had devoted almost his entire life to the Chinese Communist Party. It had been a life filled with dramatic ups and downs that included the deaths of a wife and two children, various persecutions followed by expulsions from high office, and four years of working as a labourer in a tractor factory when he was in his sixties, a victim of the Cultural Revolution. He was seventy-four when he finally became premier. Deng was a man whom Chow could admire on a personal level for — if nothing else — his persistence and that ability to survive.

One major reason for Deng's erratic political career was his practicality when it came to managing China's economy. He believed that individuals were most productive when they were rewarded with the fruits of their labour. This ran contrary to Mao's ideology, and it kept Deng in constant trouble. Without being critical of Mao, the article in the *Daily News* outlined the changes Deng had introduced since taking power, including the introduction of economic reforms in 1979 that had accelerated the open-market model. While many in Beijing were still mouthing the old Communist rhetoric, Deng had started dismantling the commune system that had taken Uncle's family farm and contributed to the Bitter Years. Deng gave the peasants more freedom to manage their land and allowed them to sell their products on the open market. At the same time, he began to open China's economy to foreign trade. He called his approach "socialism with Chinese characteristics."

What will be Deng's next major step? Chow thought as he finished his bowl of congee. *Is he really a reformer? Is Shenzhen really a crucial part of what he's trying to do? If it is, could we somehow find a way to do business there?* Before he could answer that question, he told himself, he needed to understand what a special economic zone was.

"Ah, Uncle, you've eaten it all," Jia said as she approached the table.

"Thank you for insisting that I eat," he said. "I feel much better for it."

Uncle left the restaurant soon after and, with the newspaper tucked under his arm, began to walk to the gang's offices in the centre of town.

The offices were located on the second floor above a dress shop. A forty-niner and a Blue Lantern — an uninitiated apprentice triad — stood on either side of the door that led to the stairway. The men were sentries and the first line of defence if the offices were ever attacked, although in Uncle's twenty years as a Fanling triad there had been only one threat. That was ten years before, and it had been rebuffed. When he became Mountain Master, one of the first things he had done was ask Wang, the Red Pole, if the men were necessary. "Since I've been here, there hasn't been a Mountain Master willing to take the risk of them not being there," Wang had said. "I don't think you should either." Uncle had followed his advice, and every day when he reached the offices, he nodded to whichever two men were at the door.

Saturday, Sunday, and Wednesday — because of Happy Valley racing — were the busiest days of the week at the office. Mondays and Thursdays were the quietest, and Uncle found the offices almost deserted when he reached the top of the stairs. Xu was speaking on the phone while his assistant in the adjoining office was going over some paperwork. Uncle motioned to Xu to join him when he had finished his conversation. A few minutes later, Xu entered Uncle's office.

"Did you talk to Wang about Tai Wai?" Uncle asked.

"Yes. He said he'll get to the truth by the end of the day."

"Was he angry?"

"Of course, but you know he won't do anything rash."

"I know; we're fortunate to have him," Uncle said. "How about Yu and Fong — any luck in reaching them?"

"I managed to get hold of Fong. He told me he got back from Macau an hour ago and needs some sleep," Xu said. "I had no luck with Yu, but I expect he'll show up sometime today."

"Good. Then it sounds like we can have an executive meeting later."

"Is it because of this Tai Wai situation?"

"Only indirectly, although that has spurred my sense of urgency about creating new income sources," Uncle said. "After you left Jia's, I began to think that the only real, long-lasting option we have is to start creating business outside of Fanling."

"Uncle, we've never poached on another gang's territory," Xu said quickly. "You have always insisted that we respect their boundaries and that they respect ours."

"Relax. I'm not talking about trying to move in on another gang's turf," Uncle said, reaching for the *Oriental Daily News*. "I've been reading about what's going on in Shenzhen. It sounds like things are starting to take off economically over there since Deng designated it a special economic zone."

"What's a special economic zone?"

"I don't know the details, but I want us to find out as quickly as possible," Uncle said. "Deng seems to be opening doors for people to do business in China. It would be logical, given its proximity to Hong Kong and Hong Kong's relationships with the rest of the world, that Shenzhen might be one of those doors. The thing about doors, Xu, is that they let you in and they let you out. Maybe the time is right for us to re-establish a foothold on the mainland."

"But Mao banned us. He turned the PLA loose on us. Has Deng reversed that policy?"

"No, but maybe what Deng has set in motion will give us a way to get back in carefully and quietly," Uncle said, and then paused. "Just imagine the possibilities if we could accomplish that."

"I can't tell you how much I'd love to be living in Shanghai again," Xu said. "I still own a house in the French Concession. For years my wife has wanted me to sell it, but I couldn't bring myself to do it."

"It's too soon to be talking about Shanghai, but Shenzhen is as close as Kowloon — we're practically neighbours. What we need is to understand what's going on there," Uncle said. "I sense that Deng is forcing change in China, and I want us to be out in front of whatever's coming. There aren't many rewards for being second to recognize what the future may look like, and Shenzhen could be at the forefront of that future."

"We do have a connection there."

"In Shenzhen?" Uncle asked in surprise.

"Yes. We're doing business with a small factory making knock-off Lacoste shirts that we sell in our night markets."

"I didn't know that."

"We just started with them a few months ago, and the amount of business is so minor that I didn't think it worth mentioning."

"How did we find them?"

"They found us. The factory owner knows someone who knows Fong. They were looking for a market on this side of the border and contacted him. Fong met with him and brokered a deal."

Fong was the gang's Straw Sandal, the man in charge of communications within the gang and maintaining connections with other organizations, including other gangs. He was as close to Uncle as Xu.

"Then I need to talk to Fong as soon as possible. Call his apartment and tell him I want to see him now."

"He could be asleep already. He may not answer."

"Then send someone to get him."

"If it comes to that, I'll go to his apartment myself," Xu said.

"Thank you."

Xu stood to leave, then hesitated, leaning towards Uncle. "You're really serious about Shenzhen, aren't you."

"I'm serious about growing and expanding our business, and unless you know something I don't, I can't think of how to do that in Hong Kong," Uncle said. "There may be nothing for us in Shenzhen and this special economic zone experiment may amount to absolutely nothing, but we won't know until we investigate it. The one thing I know is that if we can do business there, we won't be bumping into any other triads, at least not for a while."

The gang's office layout was basic: a large expanse of floor dotted with desks and surrounded by seven offices, one for each member of the executive. Uncle watched Xu cross the floor, enter his office, and close the door. He had hoped for a bit more enthusiasm from Xu, but given how suddenly he'd sprung the idea on him, and considering the way Xu had been driven from China, he realized that might have been an unrealistic expectation. *And he might think I'm just grasping at straws,* Uncle thought as he took out a ledger and began to enter the previous day's betting tallies. By noon he'd have the sales figures from the massage parlours and restaurants to add, and unless they were spectacular, once more he'd be calculating how large the week's loss was for the gang.

"Fong answered his phone," Xu said, appearing suddenly in the doorway. "He'll be here in half an hour."

3

FONG ARRIVED AT THE OFFICE DRAGGING HIS FEET AND with his head hanging low. He was as thin as Uncle but six inches taller, and where Uncle's hair was shaved tight to his scalp, Fong's was long and flopped over his ears, reaching his eyebrows. This morning he was unshaven, and that, combined with his downturned mouth, made him look mournful. An incorrigible gambler and night owl, Fong seldom made an appearance before mid-afternoon, but by then he had slept. Being summoned to a meeting so early and without sleep couldn't have pleased him, but still he smiled when he saw Uncle in his office doorway.

"Hey, boss, what's up? Xu sounded like it was urgent."

"Did you really just get home from Macau?" Uncle said. "I'm not accustomed to seeing you smiling after a weekend over there."

"That's not funny," Fong said, the smile evaporating.

"So it was Macau, and from your sour tone I'm guessing it was either baccarat or roulette that did you in," Uncle said.

"Roulette," Fong said with a groan. "I read about this system that's supposedly foolproof. You bet on the first twelve, second twelve, or third twelve numbers where you get odds of two to one if you hit. But you don't bet on any of them until one of them doesn't hit twice in a row. That's when you bet on it, and keep doubling up until it pays off. When it does, you start all over again."

"What went wrong?" Uncle asked.

"I was betting the last twelve numbers. Somehow not one of them was hit ten times in a row. Mathematically that's almost impossible."

"You should have learned by now that there's no such thing as impossible when it comes to gambling."

"You don't have to tell me," Fong said. "I feel stupid enough as it is."

"I'm only expressing a brother's concern," Uncle said.

"I know."

"And regardless of the circumstances, I'm glad you're here, because I need your help with something."

"What?"

"Have a seat," Uncle said, pointing to a chair inside his office and then waving at Xu across the office floor.

When Xu had joined them, Uncle took his seat behind the desk. "I understand that you put together a deal to buy some knock-off Lacoste clothing from a factory in Shenzhen," Uncle said to Fong.

"I did. Is there a problem with that?"

"Not unless you know of one."

Fong shrugged. "The last I heard everything was going well."

"Are we making money with the product?"

"We're selling it for three times our cost. I only wish I could get more of it, but the factory is small and doesn't produce anything in big volume."

"Still, it's a terrific profit margin, and I'm glad to hear that. Because I'd like you to call your contact there and arrange a meeting for us."

"Who do you want to meet with?"

"The guy who owns the factory," Uncle said. "Does he know you're triad?"

"No. As far as he's concerned I'm just someone who runs a night market. But Uncle, both the guy and the deal are small potatoes," Fong said. "And, to be truthful, his clothes are shit. The only things about them that even resemble the real thing are the alligator logo and the label that he sews on."

"None of that is important to me. I want you to set up a meeting anyway."

Fong sighed, knowing Uncle had made up his mind, and that when he did, there wasn't much point in trying to change it. "When do you want to do this?"

"Today, if possible. If not, then as soon as you can arrange it."

"Who would be going from our side?"

"Me, Xu, and you — if you're up to joining us."

"Where do you want to meet?" Fong asked, and then shook his head. "That was a silly question. I doubt the guy would be allowed to cross the border. We'll have to go there. Given how you two left China, are you okay with that?"

Uncle produced a booklet from a drawer. The cover read HOME-VISITING CERTIFICATE FOR COMPATRIOTS FROM HONG KONG AND MACAU. "Xu talked me into getting this a year ago. It's a home-visit permit that will get me into China. Anyone who was born in China but lives in Hong Kong is eligible. I've never used it, and never thought I would."

"That seems perfect," Fong said. "Assuming I can contact the guy, what reason do I have for us wanting to meet?"

"Tell him we want to talk to him about ways of expanding our business together."

Fong looked at Uncle and then at Xu. "But I don't think he's capable of giving us more product. The factory is small and the equipment is old."

"I don't care what he can do right now," Uncle said. "I'm thinking about the future."

"Deng Xiaoping has designated Shenzhen as a special economic zone," Xu said. "Uncle thinks that might offer us an opportunity to expand our business into China."

"How can we do that when they don't permit triad gangs to operate?" Fong said.

"Please stop being negative and make the call to the owner. You can use my phone if you want," Uncle said.

"I'll go to my own office. I could use some tea, and I have some pills there to pick me up."

Uncle waited for Fong to leave before saying to Xu, "I love Fong, but there are times when I worry that his gambling is getting completely out of control."

"We've banned him from betting in any of our shops."

"That doesn't stop him from going to Macau."

"If you want to put a stop to that, you'll have to talk to him directly. You're the only person he listens to."

"I'd feel like a hypocrite. I mean, I don't miss many race days at Happy Valley or Sha Tin."

"There's a big difference between betting on horses and

betting on games where the odds are rigged against you."

"Both are addictions."

"Uncle, pardon me, but what has brought this on? It isn't like you to talk like this."

Uncle shrugged. "I can't help having negative thoughts every time I review the ledger. If our gang can't survive economically, I don't want Fong to end up completely broke."

"We'll survive," Xu said.

"Not if we stand still. We need to be proactive," Uncle said, and then smiled. "I have to say I like the profit margin we're making on those shirts."

Xu nodded but remained quiet.

Uncle looked into the main office. "Here comes Fong. That was quick," he said.

"The factory owner says he'll meet with us whenever we want," Fong said from the doorway. "I told him we want to come this afternoon, and he's fine with that."

"That didn't take long."

"We're a valued customer," Fong said. "In fact, we're his only source of foreign currency."

"And you mentioned that we're interested in doing more business with him?"

"I did. He was very happy to hear it."

"Good. Now, where and when are we meeting?"

"He suggests we take the train to the Luohu railway station in Shenzhen. He'll meet us there with his car. I'm to phone him just before we get on the train in Fanling."

"We could drive ourselves," Uncle said.

"The border crossing is small, understaffed, and usually jammed with trucks. It's a pain in the ass getting through," Fong said. "The train is easier. We can go through Hong

Kong Immigration, get a five-day Chinese visa, and clear Chinese Customs, Immigration and Health in about half an hour at the station. Do you have your Hong Kong ID card and passport with you? You should have both of them."

"I can get them quickly enough."

"I have mine with me," Xu said.

"Then I'm ready whenever you two are," Fong said.

A few minutes later, after locking the previous day's accounts in a desk drawer, Uncle joined Xu and Fong in the office.

"I told everyone we'll be gone and out of touch for the rest of the day," Xu said.

"Then let's get moving," said Uncle.

The three men left the office together. "Taxi?" Fong said.

"We'll walk to the station. It's too beautiful a day to waste," Uncle said.

Despite the fact that he had been living in Fanling for about twenty years, Uncle had never fully acclimatized to the weather. The winters, which ran from November to March, were cold and damp, with temperatures ranging between ten and fifteen degrees Celsius. Uncle's apartment, like just about every other home in Fanling, didn't have central heating, and when the cold penetrated the walls, it got into his bones. The summer months, from June to September, were even harder for him to tolerate. Temperatures ran in the high twenties and might have been bearable if it weren't for the humidity and the rain that came with it. April, May, and October were months with moderate heat and low humidity, and Uncle hated to waste that kind of weather.

"How many times have you been across the border on

this business?" Uncle asked Fong as they made their way to the train station.

"Three. The first time I drove, which is why I know about the mess at the border. And when I finally got across, things didn't get much better. They don't believe in street signs and I got lost. The other two times I took the train and let the owner do the driving."

"What is his name?"

"Ming."

"How did he get into the business of producing knock-offs?"

"I never asked him."

They reached the station after a ten-minute walk and Uncle waited on the platform while Xu bought their tickets and Fong called Ming.

Xu was frowning when he rejoined Uncle.

"What's the problem?"

"The ticket seller grilled me about what we were going to be doing in Shenzhen and insisted I show him my ID," Xu said. "I know we're still in Hong Kong, but it reminded me of why I left China."

"The train company probably gets grief if they let someone on who doesn't have the proper identification."

Uncle saw the train arriving from Hong Kong before he heard it. As it pulled into the station, Fong came running towards them. "We're all set with Ming," he said. "He'll meet us at the station in Shenzhen."

They climbed onto the train. Uncle took a window seat facing China. Xu sat next to him. Fong sat across from them, and the instant his bum hit the seat, he closed his eyes and pushed his head back. "Wake me when we get there," he said.

"I'm surprisingly nervous," Xu said to Uncle.

"Me too. This is what it must feel like when you're about to see a woman ten years after she broke your heart and left it in little pieces," Uncle said.

"Did a woman ever do that to you?" Xu asked.

"My heart was broken many years ago, and it has never mended. But she didn't do it to me," Uncle said, and then turned away.

It was a forty-five-minute ride to Shenzhen, and as they neared their destination, Uncle found himself staring intently out of the window. Had it really been twenty years since he'd been there? How much had it changed? He remembered walking into the town square for the first time with his friends from Changzhai. It was twilight and, in almost an instant, the empty square was filled with people, many in swimsuits and carrying homemade flotation devices of every conceivable construction. They were headed for Mirs Bay, which was filled with sharks and PLA patrol vessels, or the foul waters of Shenzhen Bay, or the land crossing near Wutong Mountain, with its huge barbed-wire fences and army patrols ready to shoot and kill. He had read that as many as 500,000 people managed to escape over a three-year period, and that many more had died in the attempt. Uncle had been one of the lucky ones.

A voice spoke over the intercom: they were approaching Shenzhen station. "Passengers will first have to clear Hong Kong Immigration. If you do not have a visa or permit to visit Shenzhen, you will have to procure one at the station before going through the People's Republic of China Customs, Immigration, and Health Departments. Please make sure you have your documentation with you. If you do not, we strongly suggest you stay on the train."

Fong sat up. "The train isn't crowded today, so it won't be too bad," he said. "Most of these people will run like mad to get in line when the train stops. Let them go. It saves only a few minutes and it isn't worth getting shoved and pushed."

The train slowed to a stop. Uncle saw that Fong was right; people jumped onto the platform and sprinted towards a line of immigration booths. They climbed down and followed the pack at a leisurely pace.

The Hong Kong Immigration Service was its usual efficient self, and in less than ten minutes the three men had passed through and were approaching a group of PRC immigration officers.

Uncle handed his permit to an officer who opened it and then began looking back and forth between the booklet and Uncle. For a few irrational seconds Uncle wondered if his departure from China had somehow been recorded and he was a wanted man. Finally, and with a show of reluctance, the agent stamped his booklet and passed it back to him.

Ten minutes later, the three men walked out of the station and into a time warp. There wasn't a building in sight taller than three storeys, or one that wasn't dotted with crumbling stucco or covered in creeping vines. The street was paved but coated in dust, and Uncle saw that several side streets were dirt roads. There was no sign of a bus and there were no taxis. Aside from one car sitting at the station entrance, bicycles were the only form of transportation in view.

"There's Ming," Fong said, pointing to a grey-haired man of medium height and build standing in front of an aged blue Toyota with a crumpled right fender.

Uncle didn't respond right away. His attention was focused

on the street and the town square. He had been in this exact spot. "I was here twenty years ago. I remember it. And nothing has changed — not one goddamn thing," he said.

"Does it get any better than this?" Xu asked.

"Not really," Fong said. "And don't expect anything great when you see the factory. It's solidly built, but beyond that it isn't much to look at."

"We're not here because of the factory," Uncle said.

"Or the town," Xu added.

"Look over there," Fong said, pointing past the square to lines of cranes visible on the horizon. "That's where they've really started building, and they're building fast. In a few years not much of the old town will be left standing."

Uncle stared at the cranes, his lips moving ever so slightly as he counted. "There are more than thirty of them."

Fong touched Uncle lightly on the arm. "Boss, Ming is starting to look worried. I think we should go meet him."

"Of course. Sorry," Uncle said.

Ming smiled as they walked towards him, and Uncle saw that he was missing several front teeth. He was wearing a blue Mao jacket, trousers, and straw sandals. Uncle guessed he was about fifty, although he could have been ten years older or younger.

Fong introduced Uncle and Xu to Ming.

"Welcome to Shenzhen. Welcome to the new China," Ming said.

"It looks a lot like the old China," Uncle said.

"You won't recognize this square a year from now. They're going to tear down most of these buildings and replace them with high-rises. Even the train station is going to be rebuilt," said Ming.

"You sound very optimistic. Business must be good," said Uncle.

Ming motioned to his car. "Why don't we drive to the factory. We can talk about business on the way."

They piled into the Toyota, Uncle sitting up front with Ming. They drove across the square and started down a road that was littered with potholes. "How far is the factory?" Uncle asked.

"About thirty minutes," Ming said. "There are plans to build a highway from our area to the city. When that's finished, we'll be twenty minutes away."

They drove past a part of Shenzhen that Uncle had never seen. It was a combination of older low-rise commercial buildings separated by small rows of houses and some empty lots. After fifteen minutes, buildings of any type became scarce, and a few minutes later they found themselves in open country, surrounded by fields. Off in the distance Uncle could see clusters of farm structures. "What are they growing?" he asked.

"Most of these are vegetable farms growing things like pea tips, mustard greens, bok choy, celery," Ming said.

"Those buildings look like they're for more than vegetables."

"More than half are for pigs. The others are either dairy or chicken farms."

"How did you come to build a garment factory out here?"

"My older brother owned a hatchery. He never married, and when he died, he left it to me. I was working in a garment factory in Guangzhou, and that was the only trade I knew. But when I inherited the hatchery, I had to do something with it. I tried to sell it but there weren't any takers," Ming said. "When I explained my problem to my boss in

Guangzhou, he asked me how solid the hatchery buildings were. I told him they were well-built, with stone walls. He told me to get rid of the chickens and convert them into a garment factory. He said he had some old equipment he could sell to me cheap on long-term credit. I took him up on it."

"That was when?"

"About ten years ago."

"How many buildings did you convert?"

"I could only afford to do one."

"But it has been a success?" Uncle asked.

"Only recently. Before the SEZ was created it was a struggle to make ends meet."

"SEZ?" Xu asked.

"Special economic zone," Ming said.

"How has that changed things for you?" Uncle asked.

"In every way imaginable."

"Explain what that means, please," said Uncle.

"Well, it used to be I was given an annual quota of material — set by the prefecture — and was told what I could make. If I had my machinery running at full capacity, I'd go through the quota in six months or less, so I had to operate at a reduced level."

"Why not just shut down for six months?" Xu asked.

"My workers wanted full-time employment, so I would have lost them. That isn't a bad thing if you don't need skilled labour, but I do, and I'd spent a lot of time training these people. I wanted to hang on to them."

"What kind of clothes did they have you making?"

"Basic clothes for workers," Ming said. "The government bought them all from me, which was a good thing, but they also set the price, which wasn't so good."

"How has the SEZ changed that?"

"I can get all the material I want as long as I can pay for it. I still have to fill the orders I get from the government, but after that I can make what I want. And I can sell it to anyone I want at a price I set."

"They don't mind that you're selling to Hong Kong?"

"They love it when we sell to Hong Kong. They want foreign money to flow into the SEZ. That's one of the reasons it was created."

"What are the others?" Uncle asked.

Ming shrugged. "I went to a local meeting, and the bigshots of the SEZ explained it's part of a 'geopolitical experiment' that Premier Deng has ordered. I don't really understand what they meant. All I care about is being able to run my factory at full capacity and make some money," he said.

"Are you at full capacity now?"

"Not yet."

"Why not?"

"I don't have enough money to buy the raw materials I need to achieve that," Ming said. He turned to look at Uncle as if to underline his message.

"Having enough money to run and grow a business is a challenge," Uncle said. "It's nice to hear that it's becoming a reality in China."

"Not in most of China, but certainly in the SEZs."

"There's the factory," Fong said from the back seat, pointing to the left.

Uncle looked out the window and saw two identical undistinguished buildings set back about a hundred metres from the road. Their walls seemed to be about fifty metres long and ten metres high and were made of stone and rock on top of cinder-block bases. A row of small windows ran along the top of each wall, but they were so small he doubted they'd let in much light. Metal double front doors were the only visible entrances. Uncle thought they looked more like prisons than factory buildings. "Which one is the garment factory?" he asked.

"The one to the left. I know it doesn't look like much, but it meets my needs," Ming said as he turned onto a dirt track.

"It looks deserted," Uncle said, noticing an absence of bicycles or any other means of transportation.

"We aren't operating today. If I'd known yesterday that you were coming, I would have called in some workers. It's very difficult to assemble a work crew at such short notice."

"Don't worry about that. It would have been instructive to see the plant in operation, but I'm more interested in talking to you than looking at machinery."

"Do you want to go inside?"

"Sure. We're here, and it would be wasteful not to."

Ming parked the car near the door and then led them to the entrance. He unlocked the door and stood back so they could enter first.

Uncle took a dozen steps inside and stopped to take in the factory. The interior was as plain as the exterior, with a concrete floor, grey-painted walls, and several strings of naked light bulbs running overhead. On his right, against the wall, were stacks of various fabrics and spools of brightly coloured thread. On the far left he saw stacks of boxes piled on top of each other. In between were two rows of machinery that Uncle assumed were production lines. The equipment looked old but well maintained.

"You don't have a warehouse?" Uncle asked.

"I've never needed one, and I can use the other building if it comes to that."

"So everything is under one roof?"

"It is."

Uncle nodded and stepped closer to the machinery. "I don't mean to be rude, Mr. Ming, but Fong tells me the quality of your product isn't exactly first-rate."

"I do the best I can with the equipment I have and the materials I can afford," Ming said with a shrug. "Better equipment and fabrics will produce a better product and allow me to expand my production."

"And you can't afford better equipment?"

"That's correct," Ming said.

Uncle turned. "Do you mind if we go outside?"

"Not at all."

They left the factory and walked into what had once been a farmyard. "How much land do you have here?" he asked the trailing Ming.

"Close to five hectares."

"Are there are any restrictions on what you can do with it?"

"I have a permit to operate a garment factory. The original was from Guangdong province, but it was replaced by one from the Special Zone Development Corporation," Ming said. "But I'm not sure if that answers your question."

"What I'm getting at is whether or not you would need approval to turn that second building into another factory."

"I don't know."

"Who would know?"

"When I applied for my permit, I dealt with a man named Peng at the Development Corporation. He was also the one who explained the SEZ at that local meeting."

"It might be a good idea to talk to him to find out."

"Why?"

"Before I answer that question, do you mind answering a few more of mine?"

"Of course not. I figure you're here for a reason."

"Thank you. To begin with, how much more could you produce if you could purchase all the raw material you wanted?"

"I could double what I'm doing now," Ming said without hesitation.

"What if you could also upgrade your equipment?"

"That would depend on how much and what kind of equipment."

"Assume we could replace everything you have with new machinery," said Uncle.

"Not everything I have would need to be replaced."

"That's good to know, but please humour me and give me a rough estimate of the impact new machinery would have on your production."

Ming looked at Fong and frowned.

"We won't hold you to the number," Fong said. "My boss just wants an idea of what you think is possible."

"If I had all the raw material I wanted and some key pieces of new machinery, then I could probably turn out three times the product," Fong said. Then he stared at Uncle. "Where is this heading?"

"Mr. Ming, I'd like to meet with Peng, but before I ask you to make that arrangement, I should make it clear what I'm proposing," Uncle said. "I want to expand our business into China and I want to do it properly and with the right partner. You strike me as the kind of person who could be an excellent partner for us. Do you have any interest?"

Ming looked thoughtful and didn't rush to reply. "What would a partnership involve?" he asked finally.

"We'd invest in your business. We'd put up the money so you could buy all the fabric you need to reach full capacity in this factory. We'd also consider buying new equipment for it, and I'm prepared to discuss turning your other building into a factory."

"What would you want in return?"

"The right of first refusal on everything you produce — at a fair price, of course," Uncle said.

Ming waited for Uncle to continue. When he didn't, he said, "That's all?"

"That's all if we're simply giving you the money to aid in production. But obviously if we start buying equipment and converting the second building, we'd want to be partners, to own part of the action."

"The SEZ has a whole bunch of regulations about partnerships and joint ventures between foreigners and Chinese companies in the zone."

"All the more reason for us to meet with Peng — assuming that you have an interest in what I'm proposing."

"I'm interested," Ming said, and then hesitated, looking past Uncle towards the factory. "But truthfully, I've been running the factory by myself all this time, and I like being my own boss. I don't want to work for anyone else."

"Mr. Ming," Uncle said with a laugh, "I promise you that none of us has the slightest interest in the day-to-day operations of your business. You would still be your own boss. In fact, if you didn't want to be independent, I'd have to reconsider putting our money behind you."

"Then I'll go call Peng right now."

"Where is his office?" Uncle asked.

"Near the train station."

"Perfect. See if you can get us in to see him today, and if not, then the next possible day. We're only a short train ride away."

As Ming disappeared into the factory, Fong turned to Uncle. "Are you serious about doing this? That equipment isn't cheap; it could be a huge investment."

"What I'm serious about is finding out the benefits and limitations for us if we try to do business here. I won't commit to anything that I don't fully understand."

"Sorry, boss. I didn't mean to sound negative again or to second-guess you," said Fong. "It's just that this is a whole different world over here."

"Which is why I want to understand it before making a commitment," Uncle said, and then pointed at the factory. "Tell me, how many garment factories in Hong Kong do you know that still make knock-offs?"

"There are fewer and fewer. In fact, almost none are left," Fong said. "The cops keep shutting them down."

"And how big is the market for products like that?"

"We sell everything Ming can send us, even with his shitty quality."

"And we sell it all in our own night markets?"

"Yeah."

"So suppose we help Ming improve the quality and we increase his production volume tenfold. Do you think we'd have a problem selling the goods?"

"I don't think we'd have any problem at all. What we couldn't sell directly, we'd be able to move into other gang's markets in Hong Kong."

"Exactly. And is there any reason why we need to limit Ming to Lacoste? In fact, is there any reason why we need to limit him to clothes? If we can legally set up shop here, and if the guys who run this SEZ are prepared to tolerate us, then who's to say what we can and can't make?"

"I see where you're going," Fong said.

"We're not going anywhere until we talk to Peng," Uncle said. "Keep your fingers crossed and hope that after we've spoken to him, it will make sense to do this."

"I have to say that I like everything I've heard so far," Xu said.

Several minutes later Ming hurried out of the factory towards them. "Peng can't see anyone until tomorrow afternoon," he said.

"That will have to do. Confirm an appointment for us."

"Who will be going?"

"We three and you," Uncle said.

Ming left and then returned a few minutes later with a slight smile on his face. "We're set for three o'clock. Peng sounded eager to talk to you," he said. "He told me that a lot of the investment money coming into the zone from Hong Kong has been for real estate projects like apartment buildings. They're anxious for more industrial development."

"Thank you for doing that. It sounds like our timing is good," Uncle said. "We'll head for the train station now, if you don't mind, but we'll be back tomorrow. Say, around two?"

"I'll meet you at the station again. We can walk to Peng's office from there."

"Perfect. And in the meantime, could you put together some numbers for me?" asked Uncle.

"Numbers?"

"How much will it cost to buy the new equipment? How much money — say, on a monthly basis — will we have to provide for raw material? How much would it cost and how long would it take to convert the second building into an operating factory? Finally, if we finance everything I've just mentioned, what volume of production could we expect to see?" Uncle said. "Can you have those numbers for me tomorrow, before we meet with Peng? I know it's a lot to ask on such short notice, but I'm assuming you're a man who understands his business."

Ming nodded. "I'll do the best I can. I should be able to come up with something that's closer to what's possible than not. I worked out some of those numbers before, when I was dreaming about expanding."

"We're not typically in the business of making dreams come true, but we are capable businesspeople. If your numbers make sense, then you may get the chance to have yours become a reality."

4

IT WAS MID-AFTERNOON WHEN UNCLE, XU, AND FONG arrived back in Fanling. The train ride had been subdued; Fong had fallen asleep again and Uncle spent most of the trip staring out the window. Xu had tried to start a conversation but quickly recognized that Uncle wanted to be left alone.

When they got off the train, they formed a huddle on the platform. "You need to go home and get some sleep," Uncle said to Fong. "I need you to be alert tomorrow."

"Xu mentioned earlier that there might be an executive meeting today."

"I've decided against it. There are too many issues that need clarification. When we have more information, I'll hold a meeting."

"Are you really as enthusiastic as you seemed about Ming's operation?" Fong asked.

"I need to see his numbers. And I need to be confident that if we increase his production we can sell everything he produces."

"Tonight I'll call the guys who run the night markets in Kowloon and Wanchai. They're the biggest, and if they're willing to buy they'll move volume."

"Don't say a word to them about Shenzhen. If they ask where we're getting the goods, tell them we've found someone in the Territories who has quietly resumed production."

"I understand," Fong said.

"Good. Now take off. We'll meet at the office at noon tomorrow."

"See you then," said Fong.

Uncle stayed put as Fong walked towards a taxi stand. When he was out of earshot, Uncle turned to Xu. "You must think I'm acting out of character today."

"In what way?" Xu asked.

Uncle smiled. "You're always so circumspect. In your next life you should be a politician."

"I'm sure there won't be a next life, so let me stay in this one by admitting that I'm not used to seeing you make decisions so quickly."

"I haven't made any decisions."

"But I sense that you're infatuated with the idea of doing business in Shenzhen, and that it won't take much to get you to commit," Xu said. "This morning when we met at Jia's, Shenzhen wasn't even on our horizon."

Uncle reached for Xu, gripping his forearm. "My friend, the earth is moving beneath my feet. For the past few years I've felt the tremors and ignored them while the Jockey Club incrementally absorbed our best business. But this morning, when you told me about our men deserting, I felt an electric shock. This isn't a time to move slowly."

"But we don't even know if what I was told is true."

"Wang will run it down, and he'll do it quickly," Uncle said. "I'm willing to bet he'll confirm what you heard."

"What makes you so sure?"

"In our world, rumours never exist in a vacuum," Uncle said. "Is he going to contact you tonight or will he call me?"

"You're the Mountain Master. I told him to call you."

"I'll let you know what he reports."

"I hope it isn't what you expect."

"Me too, but it won't change the fact that we can't sit here doing nothing to change our situation."

"But is a garment factory in Shenzhen the answer?"

"It has the potential. What other options do we have that we can say that about?"

Xu lowered his head. "That's a difficult question."

"I know, and my strong feeling is that we don't have much time to come up with an answer," Uncle said. "We either sit and watch others pick us apart or we get aggressive and gamble. If we can get whole, then we can start to grow again."

"I'm not being negative. Whatever course you choose I will support."

"You're a good friend, Xu."

"I'm someone who respects his Mountain Master's judgement, because that Mountain Master has demonstrated over and over that his judgement is sound."

"As I said, you're a good friend." Uncle checked his watch. "The day is as good as done. I think I'll go to my apartment rather than the office."

"And I'll head home. Why don't you join us for dinner?"

"Thanks for the offer, but I'll pass. I don't have much of an appetite," Uncle said. "I'm going to walk home. You should catch a taxi. I'll call you if I hear from Wang."

Uncle took his time walking to the apartment, hoping that slowing down his body would help his mind follow suit. The tactic was partially successful; when he reached his building, his mind was still full of questions and doubts, but at least it had stopped churning.

He climbed the stairs, opened the unlocked door, and stepped into a modest apartment that had one bedroom, furnished with a double bed, a night table, and a dresser. It did have a closet, but it lacked a door and contained only a single row of white shirts and black suits hanging from wooden coat hangers. The bathroom had a bathtub he never used, a glass-enclosed shower stall, a single sink, and a small mirror. His toothbrush, toothpaste, razor, and shaving cream sat on the edge of the bathtub surround. The kitchen was an alcove off the living room. It contained a sink with counters on either side, on which sat a hot-water Thermos, a two-ring burner — which had been turned on so seldom that it looked new — and a small fridge that usually contained nothing more than beer, bread, butter, and marmalade.

When he was in the apartment, Uncle spent most of his time in the living room, sitting in a red leather reclining chair that faced the window, giving him a clear view of the street below. The only other furnishings were two small folding metal tables that flanked the chair. On one was his phone and answering machine and on the other an ashtray, pens, and typically the racing form that he was working on. The only people who had ever been inside his apartment were Xu, Fong, Wang, and Tian Longwei, the man who had mentored Uncle when he was a Blue Lantern. Tian now served as the gang's Vanguard, as well as being the supervisor of the gang's best betting shop, which was inside Dong's Kitchen.

Of the four men, he was the only one with enough seniority and gravitas to be able to comment freely on Uncle's spartan existence. "I know street beggars who live in better conditions than you," Tian had said. "No one is going to think badly of you if you spoil yourself a little. You don't even have a television, for god's sake. If you did — and if for no other reason — you could watch your precious racehorses working out. They broadcast the workouts live."

"I have everything I need," Uncle had replied, although the idea of getting a television to watch training sessions did have some appeal, and he hadn't completely discounted the possibility.

On this day Uncle hung up his suit jacket, got a bottle of San Miguel beer from the fridge, and climbed into the chair. It was in an upright position, but his feet barely touched the floor. He took a swig of San Miguel and then reached for the pack of Marlboros that sat next to the ashtray. He lit a stick with a Zippo lighter covered in faded black crackle and took a deep drag. The lighter had belonged to Gui-San's father. It and a photo were the only things he had left to remind him of her.

"Gui-San, I've been trying to cut back on smoking. That's why I've been leaving my cigarettes here in the apartment. I thought if the pack was out of sight it would be out of mind, but it's hard, especially after a day like today," he said aloud. "It isn't often that I feel things are out of my control, but that's how I feel right now. What makes it worse is that I have only myself to blame for things getting to this point. If you remember, I reduced the amount of money we were giving monthly to our forty-niners and Blue Lanterns. I told them it was only a temporary measure, and I meant it at the time, though I had no solid basis for making that claim. I thought that would pacify them until I found a way to restore the payments they were accustomed to. Well, up to today I hadn't found that way, and it seems some of our men may have lost patience. And if they have, that means they've also lost trust in me.

"What does a Mountain Master have left when he loses the trust and loyalty of his men? There is nothing more important, and the idea that I may be losing that hurts me so much I almost feel ill," he said, stubbing out the cigarette and immediately lighting another. "Wang is poking around trying to find out if the rumours about some of our men doing work for another gang are true, but even if he finds nothing, the fact that there are rumours is warning enough that unless I act, some of them will eventually transfer at least part of their loyalty to another Mountain Master. Once that happens, the entire foundation of our gang will start to erode. So I have to act. I have to do something to restore the men's faith in our Fanling gang, and in me.

"I haven't been idle these past few months. I understood that we need to find new sources of income. I tried to think of some and I've been pushing Xu, Fong, and the others to come up with ideas too. They didn't have many. Neither did I, and those we did have were either impractical or too minor to make a difference. Then this morning, when I read in the paper about what the Communists are trying to do in Shenzhen, it suddenly occurred to me that that's where we have to go. I had no rational reason for thinking that and no facts to support me, but the thought was there all the same, and it was wholly formed. Later I mentioned it to Xu, and he told me about a garment factory in Shenzhen that we are already doing business with. I couldn't believe that was a coincidence.

"So I'm thinking of putting money into a factory I saw for a few minutes and a man I've met once for about an hour," he said. "I don't know how something so impetuous could be less like me. Is this a sign of desperation on my part? Is it simply wishful thinking? Or have I had a vision of what the future might hold? Whatever it is, Gui-San, I'm going to follow my instincts, even if it means going back to China — a place that holds many terrible memories, and that I never wanted to see again."

Uncle slid from his chair and went to the fridge for another San Miguel, standing in the kitchen as he drank from the bottle. As he walked back to the recliner, he stopped to look outside. The street was alive with people heading home from work or hurrying to dinner. There were days when he wished his life could be that simple.

His phone rang. It jolted him, pricking the bubble he entered whenever he spoke to Gui-San. He picked it up. "*Wei*," he said.

"Uncle, this is Wang. I'm following up on the request you asked Xu to make this morning."

"What did you find out?" Uncle asked abruptly.

"It isn't quite as bad as Xu thought, but it's bad enough," Wang said. "Tai Wai certainly has an unhealthy interest in us."

"Are they paying some of our men to divert gamblers to them?"

"Not that I've been able to confirm. I spoke to Tian and two of the other betting shop managers, and they don't think any of our men have been involved in anything like that. They have noticed, though, some forty-niners from Tai Wai hanging around outside our shops and talking to the customers. Some of them even came inside and placed a few bets, but that could have been to throw us off guard."

"What about recruiting our men to sell drugs?"

"I couldn't find any of our men who are dealing, but several of them have been approached by Tai Wai and offered goods to sell. They all claim they said no, and they might have, but you and I know that if enough men are approached, sooner or later someone is going to take them up on the offer."

"I'm going to have to call Wu," Uncle said angrily.

"How long has it been since he replaced Lo as Mountain Master in Tai Wai?"

"About six months, and it seems obvious that he isn't content to honour the agreement I had with Lo."

"Do you want me to call their Red Pole first? I could let him know that we're onto them."

"No, I think it's time I had a heart-to-heart with Wu," Uncle said.

"I've never liked that guy."

"Me neither, but he is the Mountain Master and needs to be respected."

"Is there anything else you want me to do right now?"

"No. I'll talk to Wu."

"Uncle, if push comes to shove I can have our men ready for action in a few hours."

"I know, but that's the last thing we need right now," said Uncle. "Thanks for finding out what you did, and if you don't hear from me again tonight you'll know that Wu was reasonable."

Uncle put down the phone, counted to five, and then dialed Wu's number in Tai Wai New Village.

"*Wei*," a woman answered.

"This is Uncle — Chow Tung — calling from Fanling. Is Wu there?"

"Just a moment," she said.

Seconds later Uncle heard Wu's distinctive cigarette-scarred voice. "This is an unusual event. You aren't a man known for socializing with colleagues outside Fanling."

"Not that I would object to socializing with you, but this is a business call," Uncle said.

"I wasn't aware that we're doing business together."

"We're not. I'm calling because it has come to my attention that someone in your gang has decided that doing business in Fanling is appropriate for someone from Tai Wai."

"I have no idea what you're talking about," Wu said.

"I'm pleased to hear that you don't, because that should make it easier for you to bring it to a halt."

"Bring what to a halt?"

"Some of your men have been loitering around our betting shops, trying to entice our customers to do their gambling in Tai Wai."

"You don't have a monopoly on gambling. And as I remember, when you first opened your betting shops, you were drawing customers from all over the New Territories, including Tai Wai. How can you object now to Fanling customers betting with us?"

"I can't stop them from betting where they want, but we never poached customers from other gangs, and I'd like you to stop your men from doing that in Fanling."

Wu became quiet, and Uncle waited uncertainly for his response.

"If that's been going on, I'll put a stop to it," Wu said finally.

Uncle didn't sense any sincerity but had no reason to challenge him. "Thank you. And there's one more thing we need to discuss that's a bit more serious," he said. "I've been told that some Tai Wai forty-niners have been trying to recruit my men to sell drugs. I need that stopped as well."

"Because you've chosen not to sell drugs in Fanling doesn't mean there isn't a demand for them," Wu said.

"We don't like the damage drugs do. We also don't like the attention they draw from the Hong Kong police, so we stopped selling years ago," Uncle said. "Lo understood our position, and in fact he benefited from it several times."

"How could he have benefited?"

"Over the years I have developed a special relationship with some key people in the Hong Kong Police Force. It isn't something I talk about very often, and I utilize it even less, but it is there, and from time to time I call upon it when I or some friends need help," said Uncle. "Lo had some personal problems he needed help to rectify. At my request, my contacts obliged him. I don't see why it couldn't work the same way for you."

"In exchange for not trying to fill a market demand for our drugs?" Wu said. "You should know that we have the finest-quality cocaine in the entire region, and that I'm supplying many of the other gangs. It bothers me — as I think you should understand — that Fanling has turned its back on us."

"If we permitted you to sell drugs either directly or indirectly into our territory, I'd be going against the promise I made to my police contact. Whatever relationship that now exists would be destroyed. In my eyes, it isn't even close to being worth it. So, with all due respect, keep your drugs in Tai Wai and stop trying to involve my men in that business."

"Or else what?"

"It's been a long time since a brother said 'Or else what' to me," Uncle said, then paused. "Since you are relatively new in your position, I suggest you call a Mountain Master like Sammy Wing in Wanchai and ask him what it's like to take on Fanling. Ask him about Wang. Ask him about how well trained our men are. If you still feel determined to pursue your course, then we'll deal with it in a way that's appropriate to our priorities."

"That is making things clear," Wu said. "Lo told me you can be a difficult man to reason with. Now I see that's true."

"There's no reasoning with me when it comes to drugs," Uncle said. The line immediately went dead.

He had been sipping beer while he spoke with Wang and Wu, and now the bottle was empty. He went to the fridge for his third, opened it, and phoned Wang.

"Yes, boss," Wang answered.

"I spoke to Wu. It didn't go as well as I had hoped," Uncle said. "I'd like you to bring together your men tomorrow and tell them that if any of them as much as think of selling drugs, they'll be gone from Fanling the moment we find out."

"What if we get guys from Tai Wai trying to peddle?"

"Remove them."

"How physical do you want us to be?"

"Physical enough that they won't return, but not so much that they end up in an urn."

"Sometimes that's a difficult line to define."

"If you have no choice and have to err on one side, I'd prefer that there be no doubt about our message."

"Okay, I get it."

"And one more thing, Wang, I want you to tell the men that we're going to restore their full monthly payment, effective immediately."

"Maybe I shouldn't say this, but with everything else that's going on, I think that's a very wise move."

We'll see how wise it is in a year's time, after we've burnt through most of our reserve fund, Uncle thought as he hung up.

5

THE NEXT MORNING FOLLOWED THE USUAL PATTERN
for Uncle: reading the newspapers over congee at Jia's, a leisurely walk to the office, and several hours reviewing the
gang's finances. He had phoned the rest of the executive
the night before to tell them about his decision to restore
the monthly payments. No one had objected, but Yu and
Xu both asked how long they could sustain those payments
before the reserve fund was depleted. Now, as Uncle processed the numbers in front of him, he figured that if their
income remained stable they might be able to stretch things
out longer than a year, but he knew that was a big if.

Fong and Xu arrived mid-morning, and an hour later they
all left the office together to catch the train to Shenzhen. They
left at one-thirty; forty minutes later they exited the station
to see Ming waiting outside with a notepad in his hand.

As the four men converged, Ming pointed to the pad. "I
have numbers for you," he said. "Last night and this morning I worked at pulling something together. I spoke to my
friend in Guangzhou, and he gave me a lot of information
and put me in touch with some equipment manufacturers."

"I'm impressed you were able to do it so quickly," Uncle said, and looked at his watch. "Is there a place near Peng's office where we can go over them?"

"There's a restaurant about two minutes away."

"Let's go there," said Uncle.

It was less than a ten-minute walk to the restaurant, which turned out to be so busy they had to wait at the door for a table to become available. Uncle could tell that Ming was anxious to share his information, but he didn't want to have the conversation in fits and starts. "We'll talk when we're seated," he said. "I want to give you my full concentration."

It was two-thirty when they finally got a table. Ming opened his notepad as soon as they were seated. "I started by thinking about upgrading my existing factory, but I have to tell you I'm just as excited about turning my second building into another one," he said in a rush.

"There's no reason why we can't do both if the numbers make sense," Uncle said. "But the benefit of doing the upgrade is that it would be quicker and it would generate money for us that much faster."

"I know, so here's what I suggest we could do," Ming said, turning the notepad so Uncle could see a list. "I figure that half of my present equipment should be retired. All the replacement machinery on my list is available right now. I've put the costs next to them, in Hong Kong dollars."

Uncle did a quick calculation. "Just over ten million."

"I know it's a lot, but I could improve the quality of my Lacoste T-shirts and polos, and I'm guessing that I could increase my output by at least twenty-five percent just using the raw materials I can currently afford."

"How much would it cost for you to buy all the raw materials you need to operate fifty-two weeks a year?"

"Another five million."

"What terms do you get?"

"I pay in cash."

"So, about half a million a month?"

"Yes, that sounds right."

"How easy is it to acquire raw material?"

"All I need is the money."

Uncle nodded. "Where is the equipment currently located?"

"Most of it is in Hong Kong. A lot of garment factories that used to operate there have closed because they found it too difficult to compete against countries with cheaper labour and overheads. The owners have moved their production to places like Thailand and India."

"So this machinery is used?"

"Yes, but a lot of it has hardly been used. The prices I was quoted are about half of what the machinery would cost new."

A waiter arrived at the table. "Just tea for me," Uncle said. "We don't have time to eat."

Xu, Fong, and Ming all ordered beer. When the waiter left, Uncle looked across the table at Xu and Fong. "Do either of you have any questions for Ming?"

"Yes. I've been wondering what percentage of your current production is knock-offs," Xu said.

"About a third, but if I can buy all the raw materials I need, put in the new equipment, and run at full capacity, it would be more than two-thirds," Ming said. "The one thing I can't do is not fulfill my government contracts."

"I understand why," Xu said.

"I have a question," Fong said. "Some of the people I'm selling to have asked if you can do some other brands. There's
nothing wrong with Lacoste, but they'd like more variety.
Could you make something like Burberry or Adidas?"

"I don't see why not."

The waiter arrived with their drinks. "Good health,"
Uncle said lifting his teacup. After they'd sipped, he checked
his watch. "We need to get going soon, and Ming hasn't told
us his ideas for converting his second building into a plant."

"There isn't that much we'd need to do to the building.
Most of the cost would be attached to acquiring and install-
ing the machinery."

"What's your estimate?" Uncle asked.

"Assuming we could find some that was used but in good
condition, between twenty and thirty million Hong Kong
dollars."

"That's a hefty sum."

"I know, but there's no point in doing it unless you're willing to put in the right kind of machinery."

"I'm not disagreeing with you. I'm just pointing out that
it's a lot of money," Uncle said. "I'm prepared to tell you
right now that upgrading the existing factory is immediately
doable, but I'll want Xu to run a cost and profit analysis
before I commit to the new one."

"That's understandable."

"Good. Now let's go and see Peng and find out what else
we need to understand," Uncle said.

A few minutes later Ming led them from the restaurant
and headed towards a three-storey building with a flaking
beige stucco exterior pitted with small holes. A sign nailed
roughly to the wall near double glass doors read SHENZHEN

SPECIAL ECONOMIC ZONE DEVELOPMENT CORPORATION OFFICE.

"What a dump," Fong said.

"It won't be here in six months. The Corporation is building a new office tower a couple of kilometres from here. It's almost finished," Ming said.

"And don't say anything critical about the office, the town, or anything else for that matter when we're talking to Peng," Uncle said to Fong, and then turned to Ming. "What do you know about Peng? Is he from Shenzhen?"

"He's from Guangzhou. He was an assistant party secretary there."

"Does he have any business experience?"

"Not that I know of."

They reached the office. Ming opened one of the glass doors and stepped into a small lobby that, with its green walls and faded, cracked linoleum, was as shabby as the building's exterior. A young woman sat behind a plain grey metal desk that had a black dial phone on it and nothing else. Sitting about six feet away on either side of her were two men in uniforms that Uncle recognized as belonging to the People's Liberation Army. The men had rifles laid across their knees.

"My name is Ming. My friends and I have an appointment with Mr. Peng," Ming said to the woman.

"May I see your ID, please?" she asked.

Ming pulled a piece of paper out of his jacket pocket and passed it to her.

"I also need to see the ID of your friends," she said.

When Uncle took out his Hong Kong ID card, Fong and Xu followed suit, and they put them on the desk.

The woman took a spiral notebook and a pen from a drawer and carefully wrote their names and ID numbers in the book. When she had finished, she looked up at Ming. "You can get your IDs back when you leave," she said. "One of the soldiers will take you to Mr. Peng's office now."

They climbed stairs to the third floor. When they reached it, Uncle found himself looking down a long corridor with offices on both sides. The soldier marched to the end and then pointed at a closed door with the name Peng stencilled on it in gold. Ming knocked on it. "Mr. Peng, it's me, Ming."

Another young woman opened the door, bowed slightly in their direction, and then stepped aside so they could enter a small outer office. When they were all inside, she went to an inner door, knocked, and then opened it. "Mr. Peng, your visitors are here," she said.

Peng sat at a large wooden desk that had four chairs placed in a row in front of it. Behind him, framed photographs of Mao and Premier Deng hung on the wall. Peng motioned for them to sit. "Which of you is Ming?" he asked.

"I am. And this is Uncle, Fong, and Xu," Ming said, pointing to each of them in turn.

"Uncle?"

"It is a nickname, but everyone knows and calls me by it."

"And you are Ming's potential investors?"

"That's correct," Uncle said, taking a seat and examining Peng as he did so. He was in his forties, Uncle guessed, and in his navy-blue suit, white shirt, and what claimed to be a Dior tie, he looked quite prosperous. He certainly wasn't lacking for food, Uncle thought; even sitting at the desk, Peng's girth was impressive. He had a broad, fleshy face, but it was the small mole on his right cheek, which had three long black hairs curling around it, that drew Uncle's attention.

"And you are from Hong Kong?"

"Fanling, actually."

"Once you're on the other side of the border, it's all Hong Kong to us."

"Whatever you say."

"How did you meet Ming? Or rather I should ask, how did you come to have an interest in his business?"

"We own and manage several businesses in Fanling that sell designer clothes," Uncle said, and then motioned towards Fong. "My partner here heard about Ming's factory, came to see it, and offered to buy the production that wasn't already contracted to your government. We've been his customer for several months now."

"You are obviously pleased with the arrangement or you wouldn't be here," Peng said. "So tell me, what are you proposing?"

"We're thinking about updating Ming's existing factory and perhaps building a new one."

"What level of investment would both of those plans entail?"

"We haven't finalized any numbers or, I have to add, made any commitment yet, but the update could cost as much as ten million Hong Kong dollars. Ming estimates that building a new factory could run as high as thirty million."

"Those are interesting numbers. We exist to welcome investments like yours from Hong Kong and elsewhere, but there are still rules and regulations that need to be followed," Peng said.

"That's why we're here today," Uncle said. "We would

like to understand what has to be done for us to be in compliance."

"To begin with, you'll have to file a proposal," Peng said, reaching for a file on his desk. He picked it up and passed it to Uncle. "There are several forms in here that need to be completed. The guidelines are attached."

"Thanks."

"In essence our goal is to initiate as many joint ventures with foreign companies as we can. Although investment money is important, our government values almost as much the transfer of management skills, production expertise, market knowledge, and product development information that would come with the money."

"We are open to all of that," Uncle said, not quite sure what they had to contribute besides money. "But as I'm sure you can understand, our first interest is in how things would function financially. What are the benefits for us of making an investment, aside from helping Ming increase his production?"

"You won't pay duties on anything going in or out of the factory. There's a flat tax of fifteen percent on profits. Your labour costs will be about a quarter of what they are in Hong Kong — though I hasten to add that you won't have to sign labour contracts or abide by any government employment or salary requirements, so you can recruit and pay your workers whatever you wish."

"Those are very sensible regulations," Uncle said. "But there must be some we won't find as agreeable."

Peng nodded. "This is China, and we do need to protect our sovereignty."

"What does that mean?" Uncle asked.

"As a foreign investor, you aren't permitted to own land, and a condition of all joint ventures is that the Chinese partners must own a majority share," Peng said.

"We wouldn't have a problem partnering with Ming under those conditions," Uncle said.

"Excellent, but there is one other thing that might not please you," Peng said. "Foreign investments are currently capped at approximately fifteen million Hong Kong dollars."

Uncle saw Ming shift uncomfortably in his chair. "That would rule out the possibility of building a new factory for Ming," Uncle said.

Peng smiled wanly and reached towards his cheek. He took hold of one of the hairs sprouting from his mole and rolled it between his fingers. "Uncle, can I assume that you make the decisions for your group?" he asked.

"Decisions are made in concert with my colleagues, but I am, you could say, the first among equals."

"Then perhaps your colleagues and Ming could leave my office for a few minutes so you and I can speak privately."

Uncle hesitated, then said, "Sure. I don't think they'll mind."

Peng sat back in his chair until the three men had left the room. As the door closed behind them, he said, "Your colleagues could have stayed, but I thought it would be rude to ask only Ming to leave."

"You would be the best judge of that."

Peng leaned forward with his hands clenched on the desk. "If there was a way for you to put thirty million into his business, do you have the money to actually make it happen?"

"We have the money."

"Excellent. Then all that leaves is the matter of working around our present investment limits."

"I'm sure there must be a way to make it happen," Uncle said, already quite sure where the conversation was headed.

Peng assumed a thoughtful expression and then said, "There may be a route we can explore. For example, do you and your business colleagues by any chance own more than one corporate entity?"

"We own several, maybe as many as ten."

"That could be the solution to this little problem."

"How so?"

Peng tapped the folder in front of Uncle. "When you make your investment proposal, submit it as a venture that has multiple corporate partners at your end. Each of their investments should be in compliance with our guidelines."

"Will company names be sufficient for these partners, or do we have to identify owners and shareholders?"

"We'll need the names of the primary owners."

"What if the same partners own all the businesses?"

"You don't have to list all the partners for every business. You can pick and choose. As long as there's a different name attached to each business, we should be able to get by."

"Is someone actually going to check?" Uncle asked.

"The proposal will come to me and I have the main responsibility for approval, but there are other eyes that might look at it, so it's wise to be cautious."

"Other eyes?"

"The customs department, the office for municipal border defence, and even some units within the PLA have the right to examine investment proposals," Peng said. "But they usually restrict their interest to those that have a technical component. I can't imagine they'd care about a clothing factory."

"That's good to know. I have to say that I really appreciate your help."

"My job is to make things run smoothly for foreign investors."

"That is much appreciated."

"And it doesn't have to end with your submission," Peng said with a tight smile. "Some other investors have found it difficult to deal with local officials on matters such as building permits. We can help ease and speed up those processes. It does take a bit of persuasion, but we've discovered what they respond to best, and we'll be glad to do it on your behalf."

"What do they respond to?" Uncle asked.

Peng cocked an eyebrow as if trying to gauge Uncle's seriousness. "What do you think?" he said.

"Money?"

Peng nodded.

Uncle shifted in his chair. "Truthfully, I'd be reluctant to pay money directly to an official like that. It could cause problems with the authorities down the line."

"That's why I'm here to help," Peng said. "I can arrange to have it done at arm's length. No one would be able to trace the money back to you."

"So you've done this before?"

"More times than not, our investors use the services that my colleagues and I provide. It's an extra cost of doing business, but when you think of it as a way to ensure that your plans run according to schedule, it's a small and very justifiable cost," Peng said. "I mean, a building permit can take anywhere from one week to six months to be issued, and that's only one example of the power the local officials wield. I'm quite sure you'd rather have them supporting rather than hindering you."

"Of course I would," Uncle said. "But what is the cost?"

"We typically charge three percent, but given the size of your potential investment, I think two percent would be sufficient."

"That's more than half a million Hong Kong dollars if we choose to do everything we've discussed with Ming."

"Yes, or thereabouts, but I can live with that as a round number."

"And how would this payment be made?" asked Uncle.

Peng reached into the top drawer of his desk, extracted a slip of paper, and slid it over to Uncle. "The Shenzhen Research Partnership has this account at Barclays Bank in Hong Kong. You can deposit the money there."

"When would we be expected to do that?"

"Before you send me your submission."

"What if our proposal is turned down?"

Peng laughed. "Believe me, if you've visited the bank, there isn't much chance of that happening."

"And what if it is approved and then we run into problems with permits? What guarantee can you offer that things will run as smoothly as you say?"

"You have my word, and that's all you need."

Uncle nodded. He had other follow-up questions, but he knew some of them might be thought of as insulting. Like it or not, he figured he needed Peng if he was going to do business in Shenzhen. "One last thing," he said, "if we do make the payment, is it the only one or will more be expected?"

"That's all that would be required for this project, but if you decide to start additional businesses here, they would naturally incur additional one-time costs," Peng said. "That's only fair, isn't it?"

"I guess it is," said Uncle.

"So what do you think? Will we be getting a proposal from you?"

"I'll have to discuss it with my partners and we still have to finalize some cost estimates," Uncle said slowly. "But, on balance, I think you can assume that you will."

"Wonderful. Now why don't we invite your partners and Ming to rejoin us." Peng stood and walked to the office door. When he opened it, Uncle saw Fong, Xu, and Ming standing against the wall in the corridor. "Gentlemen, come back inside, please," Peng said.

As they re-entered the room, Peng held out his hand and shook all of theirs in turn. "You have some very fine partners here, Mr. Ming," he said. "I'm sure they're going to have a lot of success with your garments."

A few minutes later Uncle led his team out of the office. As they started down the stairs, Xu said, "What did Peng want?"

"He wanted to demonstrate to me that China is now well and truly open for business," Uncle said. "If he's any indication of what we can expect to find here, then there's even more opportunity than I imagined."

"Does that mean you're leaning towards making an investment in my business?" Ming asked.

"No, there's no leaning," Uncle said. "We are going to put up the money for you to re-equip your current plant and for you to buy all the raw materials you need to run at full capacity. We'll make a decision about the second factory after Xu has analyzed those numbers and Fong has felt out the market at our end, to make sure we have a home for that much volume of product."

Ming stopped walking and grabbed Uncle by the arm. "I don't know how to thank you. This is a dream come true," he said, tears welling in his eyes.

"You can thank me by moving as fast as you can to gear up production," Uncle said. "And my dream is that in three or four months I'll be the one thanking you."

UNCLE ARRIVED AT HIS OFFICE AT NINE A.M. IT WAS A
Thursday, the day after the nighttime racing card at Happy
Valley, and he was anxious to see the returns from the betting shops. Normally he would have waited until Xu had
processed the numbers, but they were scheduled to leave for
Shenzhen at eleven for the official opening of the re-equipped
Ming Garment Factory and the start of work on the second
factory, which would stand alongside it in three months or so,
thanks to the support of the gang's bank. The ceremony itself
would be over by mid-afternoon, but Ming had arranged for
a grand dinner that would start at seven and probably not
end until midnight.

In between the ceremony and dinner, Uncle had scheduled a meeting with two Mountain Masters, Yin from
Kowloon and Tse from Happy Valley, and some of their
key people. They were allies and potentially important customers, and, as important to Uncle, both were sufficiently
forward-looking to understand what he was trying to do
in Shenzhen.

But his immediate attention was on the numbers from the previous night's betting, and he didn't like what he saw. During the summer break from racing, the Hong Kong Jockey Club had opened even more off-track betting shops, and they were now siphoning off an ever-increasing amount of the gang's revenue. "Damn," he said.

"Boss, we have a problem."

Uncle looked up from the papers that covered his desk and saw Fong standing in the doorway. "What's going on?"

"Ming just called me. He wants to postpone the ceremony."

"Why?"

"He doesn't have the materials he needs to start full production, and he doesn't think we should reopen the plant if it isn't completely operational. He says it would make us all look stupid."

"Why doesn't he have the materials? Didn't he order them in time? Is there a shortage?"

"He ordered them ages ago, but they've been sitting in customs for weeks."

"Why are we just now finding out about this?"

"His customs brokers kept telling him there wasn't a problem," Fong said. "I guess he believed them."

"If there isn't a problem, why haven't they been released?" Uncle asked.

"I don't know, boss."

"Has Ming talked to Peng?"

"Peng isn't returning his calls."

"What time does Peng usually get to the office?"

"He should be there now."

"We need to sort this out," Uncle said. "We're paying Peng to prevent problems like this."

"Even if it is sorted, we may not have time to get the materials to the factory in time to begin production," Fong said. "If we can't, do you still want to go ahead with the reopening?"

"Don't forget the meeting I've scheduled, and the dinner."

"No, of course not."

"Because Yin and Tse most certainly won't," Uncle said. "They and their men will be leaving for the border in a few hours, and it's far too late to tell them not to."

"What do you want me to tell Ming?"

"We're going ahead. If the plant isn't fully operational, so be it. I'll think of something to tell our brothers," Uncle said. "Truthfully, I don't think they'll know the difference. What they want to see is that we really do have a footprint in China."

"I'll call him right now."

"While you're doing that, I'll try to reach Peng," Uncle said.

When Fong had left, Uncle searched his Rolodex for Peng's number and then dialled it.

"Mr. Peng's office," a woman's voice answered.

"This is Mr. Chow — Uncle, in Fanling. I need to speak to Mr. Peng."

"He's not available at the moment."

"Then I'll wait."

"I'm not sure how long you'll have to do that."

"Young lady, please listen to me carefully," Uncle said briskly. "I want you to find Mr. Peng, wherever he is, and tell him I'm on the line and that I'm in a very unpleasant mood."

She hesitated and then said. "Yes, sir, I'll do that right now."

What could have happened? Was Peng playing games? Was he angling for more money now that the plant reopening was imminent? Did he think that gave him leverage?

"Uncle, sorry to keep you waiting," Peng said, interrupting his thought process.

"Do you know why I'm calling?"

"I have a very good idea."

"Then tell me why our goods haven't been released by customs."

"I haven't been ignoring your problem."

"From what I've been told, though, you have been avoiding Ming."

"That's only because I had nothing to tell him," Peng said. "I've been trying to get to the bottom of this and this morning I think I finally did."

"Does that mean we can pick up our goods?"

"No, unfortunately. It's a lot more complicated than that," Peng said. "It appears from what I was told that the customs department has decided to go into business for itself."

"I thought you had them under control."

"So did I."

"What has changed?"

"A new director of customs was appointed by Beijing about a month ago. He's younger but he has strong Party connections, including an uncle on the Politburo Standing Committee. The man who had the job originally came from Guangzhou the same time as I did. He and I were close. Now they've shipped him back to Guangzhou and this new guy has appointed his own team. He seems determined to do things his way."

"What is his way?"

"It appears he's set up his own customs brokerage business. It is called the Shenzhen Master Customs Brokerage House. He did it indirectly, of course. The owners of record are M.K. Chen and L.A. Gao. It took a lot of digging, but I finally discovered those are the names of his wife and his uncle's wife."

"So we use them as our broker now?"

"No, he's too smart for that. And besides, he wouldn't want to hire the staff he'd need to process everything coming in and going out," Peng said. "Instead he's set up the business as a clearing house, a conduit. Instead of the brokers sending their paperwork directly to the customs department, now they have to channel it through Master Customs, where all they do is initial it and pass it along to the customs department. It probably takes them five seconds."

"And they collect a fee on every transaction."

"They do. It's actually quite small, so it hasn't caused any real fuss or raised questions, but when you multiply it by all the shipments, it adds up."

"If it's so small, why hasn't our broker paid the fee?"

"He's refusing to do business with them."

"Why?"

"He's from Hong Kong and has his own sense of how business should be done," Peng said.

"What's that supposed to mean?"

"He resents having to do a deal of that nature. He says he won't pay bribes."

"Then how come we had no problems with the equipment we bought for the factory?"

"That was before the new customs director was appointed."

Uncle paused and then said, "I don't disagree with our broker that this is a crap way to operate."

"Neither of you understand how many people the new customs director may be indebted to for his appointment,"

Peng said. "The income from the Master Brokerage may be his way of repaying them."

"In that case, why don't you look after this master broker until I can sort out things on my end?"

"It isn't possible."

"Why not?"

"It would raise too many questions. For example, they'd want to know why I was prepared to pay the fee. They would assume I was being paid to do it. I don't know this new director well enough to risk that."

"So what do you suggest?"

"You'll have to talk to your customs broker."

"I know who he is and we've had contact with him, but we didn't hire him. Ming did," Uncle said.

"But at the end of the day he's working for you."

"Okay," Uncle said, working to stay calm. "I'll talk to the broker, but even if I do, it's going to be too late to do much today."

"I'm sorry about that."

"Well, raw materials or not, we're going ahead with our plant reopening and dinner."

"I think that's the right thing to do. Of course, I'll see you there."

"Good. And could you do me a favour?"

"Of course," Peng said.

"What's the name of the new director of customs?"

"Liu."

"Invite him. If not to the plant, at least to the dinner," Uncle said. "We've reserved what I'm told is the best restaurant in Shenzhen for the evening."

Peng went quiet.

"I'm not going to discuss our relationship or make him some kind of offer, if that's what you're worried about. But since we intend to make more investments in Shenzhen, I want to know what kind of man I'm dealing with," Uncle said. "I'm also, to be honest, quite interested in knowing how close he is to that uncle of his."

"I'll invite him," Peng said.

Next, Uncle called Fong into his office, explained the problem, and told him to contact the customs broker. "Tell him it's okay to have principles, but not at our expense," Uncle said. "He should have told us or Ming that there's a problem. No matter how bogus he thinks it is, he needs to register with the Master Brokerage House. We'll pay the fee and whatever it costs to process the paperwork."

"I'll call him right away."

"And Fong, the only answer I want to hear is that he's done what we've asked," Uncle said, displaying far more impatience than was normal.

"I'm on it, boss," Fong said.

Uncle was neither surprised nor discouraged by the change in the way customs clearances would now be handled. It seemed to him that the new China's concept of capitalism was going to be exercised most vigorously at the individual level. The state might open its own businesses and let them operate along capitalistic lines, and it might regulate and restrict the inflow of foreign capital, but on the ground, on an individual basis, it looked like it was going to be a free-for-all, a case of grab what you can as fast as you can — and that suited him just fine.

7

AT ELEVEN, UNCLE, FONG, AND XU LEFT THE OFFICE and made their way to the station to catch the train to Shenzhen. At two they were standing with more than a hundred people in front of Ming's factory. The majority of the people there were plant employees. The balance was a combination of Ming's friends and neighbours, Peng and a handful of other government officials, and Uncle's Hong Kong contingent, including two Mountain Masters, each with their White Paper Fan and Straw Sandal. As the mixed group mingled before the ceremony, Uncle saw Peng eyeing the Hong Kongers apprehensively.

"Our guests from Hong Kong will be customers for Ming's clothes," Uncle said, as he moved next to Peng. "They own and operate stores and markets. Many of them belong to the same fraternal organization, which is why you see some tattoos."

"I see," Peng said, sounding uncomfortable but letting it go without asking the name of the organization.

"You'll get a chance to talk to some of them if you're coming to our dinner," Uncle said. "But now we should start the ceremonies."

"Of course."

"Ming told me you're going to cut the ribbon to officially reopen the factory, and that your associate Lau is going to do it for the new plant."

"That is the plan," Peng said. "Lau, by the way, is now responsible for issuing all the building permits in the zone, so I thought it wise to include him and for you two to meet."

"He looks young to have that kind of responsibility," Uncle said.

"He's very smart, ambitious, and hard-working," Peng replied.

"I'm assuming he's diligent enough to have already issued all the permits we need."

"He has. Your investment in our Hong Kong venture helped make that possible, in case you were wondering."

"I wasn't, but I'm pleased to know, all the same."

"But remember, each of your projects will require its own helping hand and have its own cost attached to it."

"I haven't forgotten."

"Good. Then let's get started," Peng said. He walked towards the plant entrance, where a long red ribbon was stretched across the door.

Ming, Lau, and two workers from the factory joined them. One of the workers handed Peng a giant pair of scissors.

"I hope this is only the first of many plant openings I will attend with Mr. Ming. There's one more that I know for certain will be happening, because after I cut this ribbon, my colleague Mr. Lau is going to join Mr. Ming in turning the soil for a new factory, one that will be as productive as this," Peng said. He smiled and turned towards the entrance. After holding the scissors in the air for a few seconds while a photographer took pictures, he cut the ribbon with a flair that surprised Uncle.

"The plant isn't running today but will be in full operation tomorrow," Ming said. "Still, I'd like to invite you all inside so you can see the changes we've made. With our new equipment we will be the most modern garment factory in the entire region — until, of course, our new factory is completed."

Uncle knew that none of the triads had any idea about what they would see inside the factory, but he was pleased that they were polite enough to go in anyway. Fong and Xu — both of whom had been involved in the equipment purchase and had learned at least some rudimentary information about garment production — went in with their triad colleagues. Uncle lingered just inside the entrance, watching Fong point at equipment and try to explain to the triads how it operated.

After about fifteen minutes, the visitors left the plant and the group regathered in the yard. "It's only a short walk to the new site," Ming said.

When they reached the other building, Uncle saw another red ribbon strung across its main door. On the wall there was a banner that read FUTURE HOME OF MING NUMBER TWO GARMENT FACTORY.

As Lau and Ming approached the ribbon, Uncle moved close to Yin and Tse. "This isn't just the future home of a factory. It's the first step towards reclaiming our place in China," he said.

"I know you believe that, but I still have trouble accepting that it's possible," Tse said.

"We'll discuss it at the restaurant before dinner," Uncle said. "I have a plan I want to share with you."

"I wouldn't be here if I wasn't prepared to listen," Tse said.

Without any speeches, Lau cut the ribbon, and then he and Ming posed for some photos.

"Is that it?" Uncle said to Fong.

"I know it wasn't much, but it meant a lot to Ming," Fong said.

"When will the new plant be open?" Tse asked.

"We'll be up and running in a couple of months," Uncle said.

"It isn't like you to move so quickly on anything, let alone something that requires this size of investment," Tse said.

"Things have started to change on this side of the border, and we either run with it right now or lose an opportunity that may never present itself again," said Uncle.

8

IT WAS LATE AFTERNOON BEFORE UNCLE, XU, FONG, and the men from Kowloon and Happy Valley had gathered in a private room at the Emerald Dragon restaurant in Shenzhen. There were nine of them, but the room's single large round table could have accommodated twenty. Xu had pre-ordered tea and water, and as servers set glasses, cups, pots, and a jug on the table, Uncle asked, "Would anyone like beer or something stronger?"

"What time is dinner?" Tse asked.

"It will start at seven and go on for at least a few hours. There'll be lots to eat and drink. Our partner, Ming, has earned that kind of celebration."

"Then I'd better pace myself," Tse said. "I'll stick to tea for now."

"I'll have beer," Yin said.

"Me too," Uncle said, and then smiled as the other men ordered exactly what their respective bosses had.

"Did anyone have a problem getting across the border?" Fong asked.

"We didn't know what to expect, so we left early," Tse said.

"I'm glad we did, because it took us about two hours to get through. What a pain in the ass."

"We take the train. It's much faster and easier," Uncle said.

"You were born in China, weren't you?" Yin asked.

"I was, and so was Xu."

"That hasn't been an issue with the Chinese officials at the train station?"

"No, but then all we've ever shown them are our Hong Kong passports and ID cards, and we both make a point of speaking Cantonese."

"And how about the fact that you're a triad?" asked Yin.

"Why would it come up at the border?"

"I mean with your partner here, and with the government officials you've been dealing with. None of them have mentioned it?"

"It's never been raised, let alone discussed, by any of the government people or by Ming."

"No one is the least bit curious about how you earn your money?"

"Just a moment," Uncle said as the server returned with a tray loaded with beer. He waited until the bottles were placed on the table, the server had left, and the door had closed behind him before continuing. "Peng — the man who cut the ribbon at the plant — runs the Special Economic Zone Development Corporation, so he's the front man for Beijing in Shenzhen. He's also helping himself to a piece of every dollar that finds its way into the zone. I know that for certain, because I've paid my share. Having said that, I don't think he's keeping it all for himself. Some of it's being used to keep the other Communists here onside, and I'm convinced some of it is finding its way into the pockets of officials in Beijing."

"So this Peng doesn't care where the money originates?"

"He doesn't give a damn. In fact, he went out of his way to tell me how to get around the investment regulations he's supposed to be enforcing."

"That's a lot looser than the way things operate in Hong Kong these days," Tse said. "A man can't spit on the street or fart in a restaurant without getting the cops all over him."

"Which is why I invited you Mountain Masters to come here today, I want you to see and understand what's happening in China — at least, in parts of China."

"Some of the others were nervous about crossing the border, but that doesn't mean they're not interested," Tse said. "In fact, they asked me to tell them how I find things here."

"Since you drove, you must have seen all the construction that's going on," Uncle said.

"The whole area looks like one huge building site."

"Two years ago there were about thirty thousand people living here. Now there's close to a hundred thousand, and there's no end in sight to Shenzhen's projected growth," said Uncle. "They're coming here for jobs and our challenge is to help provide them. If we do, and if we continue to look after Peng and his cronies, I can scarcely begin to imagine the freedom we'll have to pursue business here."

"It can't be that easy," Yin said.

"Nothing worth doing is, but if you take the time to understand how things operate on this side of the border, it isn't that difficult either," Uncle said. "The key, I believe, is to establish a visible, legal presence that conforms to the objectives of the Chinese government. Once we're in place and they've accepted us, we can begin to expand our areas of operation. For example, I can envision a day when we'll be able to open betting shops."

"Do you need the betting shops to pay for this factory?"

"No," Uncle said, more bluntly than he intended. "The current factory is already profitable, and the new one will be as well, almost from the day we open it."

"Assuming that we help to provide you with a market," Yin said.

"Why wouldn't you if you're making money from our products," Uncle said. "And truthfully, if you decided not to support us, we'd find other markets. There's a very large demand for Ming's clothes."

"I'm just saying."

"Of course you are, and what I'm saying is that I want to keep what we have going here within the brotherhood, and I want to see the brotherhood take advantage of the opportunities that these special economic zones are offering."

The conversation had been so intense that neither Yin nor Uncle had touched their beer, and because they hadn't, neither had any of their men. Now Uncle picked up his bottle. "Good health and much wealth," he said and took a swig.

"The same to you and all of us here," Yin replied.

"Uncle, tell me, how do you make money here? Is it through manufacturing or is it through selling to us? And if it is selling to us, does your partner here share in the profits?" Tse asked.

"Those are some excellent questions," Uncle said, and then paused to take another swig. "Our partner makes money only from manufacturing. We have agreed to pay him twenty percent above his total costs — costs that we monitor. Of course, as a partner, we share in the profit. Any additional profits we make through selling those goods to an outside market accrue one hundred percent to us."

"There's another benefit," Xu said. "We pay tax in China only on the profit we make here."

"And that tax rate is only fifteen percent," Uncle said.

Tse glanced at Yin and then at Uncle. "Why are you telling us this? Aren't you afraid that we'll come into Shenzhen and try to do the same thing?"

Uncle smiled. "That's exactly why I'm telling you this. I want you to understand the potential I see here, but it's a potential that could go up in flames if any of our brothers decide to set up shop in Shenzhen and then go about trying to do business the way they conduct it in Hong Kong. Right now we're operating below the radar. We're building relationships and partnerships that in due time we're prepared to share, but for now we need all of you to stay out of Shenzhen and let us build the foundation."

"No one I know, including myself and Yin, has talked about operating in Shenzhen," Tse said.

"I know that's probably true, but once our factories are in full production and the brothers see the money that can be made here, they'll head for the border."

"You've got some nerve, Uncle, telling us how much money you think you can make here and then saying we should stay out," Yin said.

"I apologize if I've offended you," Uncle said. "My intention was to explain the potential I see, but also to make it clear that we have a clean slate here. If we build strong relationships, if we work with the Communists, if we help further the Beijing government's objectives, we have an opportunity to re-establish a triad presence in China.

But that's not something we're going to accomplish if we start running protection rackets or dealing drugs. All that would do is bring the local cops or — God forbid — the PLA crashing down on us, and we'd be thrown out of China again."

"Speaking of drugs, Wu has been saying some very unkind things about you," Yin said. "I hear from him every week, and so do many other Mountain Masters. He claims that when it comes to doing business with you, it's strictly a one-way street. You think you have the right to sell goods wherever you want but you won't let him sell into your market, and you've have been very unbrotherly to his men."

"You all know I won't allow drug-dealing in Fanling, and I warned him what would happen if he tried it."

"We know your stance, but he argues that you shouldn't impose that restriction on him. He says there's a big demand there, and all he wants to do is meet it."

"There will be no drug-dealing in Fanling, and sure as hell none in Shenzhen either," Uncle said.

"I'm not sure Wu will go along with that where Fanling is concerned. He's trying to build alliances, and if he feels he has the support of other Mountain Masters, he might get more aggressive."

"We can handle any aggression he decides to utilize."

"Do you have any flexibility at all? None of us wants to see another a war," Yin said.

"The last thing I want is a war, but I'm not prepared to change my position," Uncle said, and then turned to Tse. "Do you remember calling me after your son got into that bar brawl in Kowloon that resulted in the death of an American sailor?"

"How could I forget?"

"After talking to you, I made one phone call. Two days later your son was released and no charges were laid," Uncle said. "If I allowed drug dealing in Fanling, that kind of phone call would no longer be possible. Is supporting Wu worth the risk of losing that kind of influence?"

"I know that it's not, but not everyone thinks the way I do. I understand that we can't sacrifice the future for short-term greed," Tse said.

"But every gang needs income, so what do you expect us to do while you're making new friends and new money in China? Sit in Hong Kong and wait for you to give us approval to do business here?" Yin asked.

"No. I want you to do in other parts of China what I'm doing in Shenzhen."

"Where? How?" asked Tse.

"There are two other special economic zones designated, one in Guangdong province and the other in Xiamen, in Fujian province."

"Where in Guangdong?"

"In Zhuhai, next door to Macau, and in Shantou, which is only a few hundred kilometres from Hong Kong," Uncle said. "It seems obvious that the Chinese are trying to build economic bridges between the mainland and Macau and Hong Kong before the territories are scheduled to be returned."

"As you know, there is a gang in Macau," Yin said.

"A gang that knows only drug dealing, pimping, and extortion," Uncle said. "There's no way they could stay out of trouble in Zhuhai, even if they did have the sense to set up operations there. As it is, I'm sure they've never heard of a special economic zone and have zero interest in doing any kind of business in China."

"I don't know anyone in Zhuhai, Shantou, or Xiamen, and I've never been to any of them," Tse said.

"Me neither," said Yin.

"Before I came to meet Ming, the last time I was in Shenzhen was twenty years ago, and that was for two days. After we met, we chatted, one thing led to another, and he led me to Peng," Uncle said. "Now what I'm counting on is that all the other SEZs have someone like Peng at or near the top."

"What if they don't?" asked Yin.

"Then we won't be doing business there — but I'm willing to wager ten thousand HK dollars that they do," Uncle said.

"How do we confirm that without sticking our necks out?" Tse asked.

"I'm prepared to talk to Peng about it. He'll know," Uncle said.

Tse turned to Ma, his Straw Sandal. "What do you think?"

"I really like the idea of getting in on the ground floor. And if Uncle is right about the Chinese officials being willing to partner with us, it could be a tremendous opportunity."

"I agree, but I don't want to waste too much time or money finding out about the Chinese officials," Tse said.

"If you want, I'll talk to Peng tonight," Uncle said.

"What do you think?" Tse said to Yin.

"I'll be interested in what Peng has to say," Yin replied.

"Me too, and if it's encouraging, then I'd be prepared to look at Zhuhai," Tse said.

"Why should you get Zhuhai?" Yin asked.

"I'm closer to it than you are."

"By maybe ten kilometres."

Yin shrugged and looked across the table at Uncle. "If this works for us, what do you expect to get out of it?"

"Nothing directly from either of you, just goodwill," Uncle said. "But indirectly, I would like both of you to stay out of Shenzhen and to convince the other Mountain Masters to do the same until I've established a strong enough base."

"I can do that," Yin said.

"Me too," said Tse.

"And there's one more thing," Uncle said.

"There's always one more thing with you," Tse said.

"It isn't anything that will cost you," Uncle said, and then looked over at Xu. "My White Paper Fan was in Shanghai when Mao drove the triads out of China. He kept a house there and wants to go back. If you have no objections, my plan is to have him establish a presence in Xiamen. It isn't Shanghai, but it's almost halfway between there and Hong Kong. Who knows, one day he might make it all the way back."

9

THE EMERALD DRAGON WAS REPUTEDLY THE BEST RES-
taurant in Shenzhen, which in Uncle's view meant it might
have made the list of the top two hundred restaurants in
Hong Kong. Anxious to make a good impression and not
willing to let the restaurant go it alone, Uncle had instructed
Fong to hire some Hong Kong chefs to prepare the meal. To
his credit, the restaurant owner had been happy to go along
with the plan. As the first dishes were brought to the tables,
Uncle knew they were in good hands.

Shark-fin soup was almost mandatory for such an occa-
sion, and it was excellent. But even better was the cold sliced
abalone, served on a platter with jellyfish and slivers of
translucent raw lobster meat. It was imaginative, incredibly
tasty — and expensive. The cost, as always, was factored into
the appreciation shown by the diners.

"This is absolutely wonderful," Peng said. "I had no idea
the restaurant was capable of preparing food like this."

Peng sat to Uncle's right and Lau was on his left. Ming
was next to Peng, and Yin, Tse, Fong, and Xu completed the
table. Uncle had hoped that Liu, the new customs director,

would join them. Peng said he had invited him and there was a chance he'd show, but there was still no sign of him when dinner began.

"We enlisted the assistance of some chefs from Hong Kong, but they tell us that your local chefs are entirely capable," Uncle said.

There were four glasses in front of each of the diners, for beer, wine, Maotai, and cognac. Every glass was full, and it was kept that way by a circulating crew of servers. Uncle had experienced this kind of banquet many times before. Sooner or later someone would say *ganbei* and everyone at the table would feel obliged to empty the glass they were drinking. He sipped beer, preserving sobriety for as long as he could.

Uncle engaged both Peng and Lau in conversation, but they were continually being interrupted by the arrival of platters of food, which both men quickly dug into. Still, over deep-fried whole pomfret he managed to learn that Peng's grandfather had been on the Long March with Mao, and as a reward was named party secretary in Guangzhou, a position Peng's father had inherited.

Lau was a self-made man, or as much one as anyone could be in China. He came from Beijing. His parents were Party members but had never held senior positions at any level of government. Nonetheless, they had had enough influence to get their only child into the University of Science and Technology, and he had been smart enough to graduate with an engineering degree. He was still in his thirties, and his appointment in Shenzhen, he assured Uncle, was only a stepping stone to much grander positions.

As dishes of roast duck, fragrant fried rice laden with shrimp and scallops, sizzling sliced beef, and cold Sichuan noodles were being served and consumed, the servers kept pouring alcohol. Yin and Tse were both drinking Maotai, a much more potent beverage than beer or wine, and Uncle was beginning to worry that they might become indiscreetly verbose.

Then Peng said, "There's Liu. He made it after all."

Uncle looked towards the entrance and saw a trim young man of medium height. He had a thick head of jet-black hair combed straight back and a full moustache that extended down beside his mouth. He wore the official uniform of a senior customs officer, a blue jacket and pants. The jacket had gold buttons down the front and on each breast pocket. Above the pocket on the right breast was Liu's official number. On the shoulders were gold epaulettes that indicated what Uncle thought might be the rank of colonel. Under the jacket he had on a white shirt and a black tie, and tucked under one arm was a white cap with a black brim and gold braid.

Uncle watched as Liu glanced around the room in a manner that seemed serious, pensive, and maybe even questioning. *This is a man not to be taken lightly,* Uncle thought as he turned to Peng. "Tell me, is Liu aware that you know about his side business?"

"I don't think so."

"It might be wise to keep it that way," Uncle said. "He doesn't look like the kind of man who wants his secrets shared."

"I've met him only a few times, and always on business," Peng said. "He is indeed tight-lipped."

"You should go and meet him while we make room for him at the table," Uncle said. "Fong, could you ask one of the servers to reset your place, and then will you join Tse and Yin's men at their table, please?"

"Sure thing, boss."

As Fong and Peng got up, Uncle noticed Lau looking at him questioningly. It dawned on him that maybe he was the one who had just been indiscreet. Peng had told him that Lau had been paid for issuing the permit, but perhaps Lau didn't know that Peng had told Uncle. He made a mental note to ask Peng who knew what, and chided himself for not having done it already.

"It doesn't appear that Colonel Liu will be keeping us company," Lau said

"I beg your pardon?" Uncle said.

"Peng is motioning for you to join him at the door," said Lau, gesturing to the entrance.

Uncle looked over and saw Peng dong exactly that. "Excuse me," he said and stood up.

Peng and Liu were having a conversation that stopped abruptly as Uncle reached them. "Thank you for joining us," Uncle said to Liu.

"As I was explaining to Peng, I can't stay, but I wanted to meet you and thank you for your invitation," Liu said.

"It would have been an honour to have you as our guest," Uncle said.

"We'll have to make it some other time. Peng tells me you are a valued investor in the SEZ."

"We are impressed with what Premier Deng is trying to accomplish and we feel an obligation to do our part, however small that may be," Uncle said. "By the way, how should I address you, as Colonel Liu?"

"My name is Liu Leji. My friends call me by either name."

"I am Chow Tung. My friends call me Uncle."

"That's an unusual name for a man so young."

"It's a long story."

"Perhaps you can tell it to me when we have a chance to talk more fully," Liu said.

"How shall we arrange that?" asked Uncle.

"When do you plan to revisit Shenzhen?"

"I'll come back when the plant conversion is underway, perhaps in a month or so."

"Contact my office when you do and we'll set up an appointment."

"I'll be sure to do that."

Liu turned away as if he was getting ready to leave, but then he swivelled back. "You speak excellent Mandarin for a Hong Kong native," he said.

"I was born in China."

"Where?"

"In a village near Wuhan, in Hubei province."

"When did you leave?"

"In 1959."

Liu nodded. "The time of Mao Zedong's Great Leap Forward."

"Yes, exactly that time."

"My uncle stood alongside Deng Xiaoping during those years. He and Deng were removed from their positions at almost the same moment."

"Your uncle?" Uncle said, feigning ignorance.

"My uncle is Liu Huning. He's now the sixth-ranked member of the Politburo Standing Committee."

"That's very impressive. Did he and Premier Deng find their way back into power together?"

"They have always supported each other," Liu said, and then glanced at Peng and paused. "That's history best left for another day. Maybe when we meet we can revisit it, but for now I really must be going." With that, he put on his cap, nodded, and left.

Uncle waited until Liu was out of sight before saying to Peng, "Let's go outside for a smoke."

As part of the celebration, a pack of cigarettes and a silver-plated lighter engraved with the date and the Ming factory name had been left at every seat. Peng brandished his as he lit a Panda-brand cigarette. Uncle lit a Marlboro with his old Zippo.

"What are your impressions of Liu?" Peng asked.

"Like you, he's a man to be taken seriously," Uncle said, hoping the flattery wasn't too obvious.

"We're big fish here, but only minnows compared to a man like his uncle."

"Is the uncle close to Deng?"

"So I've been told."

"And Liu is obviously close to his uncle."

"He wouldn't have got this appointment otherwise."

Uncle took a deep drag, then raised his head to blow smoke into the night air. "As I remember, you told me that Liu's uncle's wife is a partner in the brokerage company."

"She and Liu's wife own a numbered company registered in Hong Kong. The company owns the brokerage."

"How did you manage to unearth that information?"

"I paid for it. Obviously we're not supposed to know. I suspect it could be dangerous if they knew we were aware of it."

"Thanks for that advice."

"I was speaking for myself as much as I was warning you."

"How about Lau?" Uncle asked. "I might have screwed up earlier by hinting that I know money has changed hands between the two of you."

"He knows where the money originated and he knows what it was intended to accomplish. I didn't tell him that you know he's taking it, but he would be an idiot to assume otherwise — and he's not an idiot."

"Still, I'll try to be less obvious in the future."

"I'd appreciate that," Peng said.

Uncle threw his butt on the ground, lit another cigarette, dragged on it, and said, "I've been thinking about the economic zones in Xiamen, Zhuhai, and Shantou. Is there any business to be done there?"

"You want to expand into those zones already?" Peng asked.

"Not me, but my friends Yin and Tse seem interested in the opportunities presented in those SEZs," Uncle said. "The question — the big question — is whether or not there are people in positions of power there who are as accommodating as you've been here."

"The short answer to that is yes."

"And what's the long answer?"

"I would have to contact each of my colleagues to confirm they're willing to co-operate, and I would need to make the introductions when the time came."

"I assume the introductions would come at a price."

"That's correct."

"But a one-time price?"

"Of course," Peng said.

"That seems reasonable enough. But tell me, how do you know your colleagues will be as helpful as you've been?"

"That isn't something I'm prepared to discuss. You need to take my word for it."

"I wouldn't want to place my friends in a compromising position," Uncle said.

"Have no worries about that."

"Okay, then I'd appreciate it if you'd make initial contact with your colleagues in Zhuhai and Shantou. If they agree to meet, you might also ask them to prepare a list of local companies they think could benefit from an inflow of foreign capital."

"I'll do that. But what about Xiamen?"

"I'm thinking it would be a good fit for my associate Xu, but I'd like to talk to him before making any commitment on his behalf."

"Uncle, you are a very thoughtful man," Peng said. "When Liu asked me to describe you, those were the first words that came to mind."

"People who think only about themselves eventually end up alone," Uncle said. "I value my friends and try to put their interests at the same level as my own."

"That is a rare quality here in China. All that matters is the Party and family, and seldom do the interests of the two match."

Peng had said that casually, but Uncle knew it would be foolish to get into a discussion about the Communist Party. "We're beginning to get philosophical. Perhaps that's a sign we've had a bit too much to drink," he said, then looked at his watch. "I have a train to catch in about an hour. I should try to clear my head before heading to the station."

THE OUTFITTING OF MING GARMENT FACTORY NUMBER Two went much more quickly than anyone had anticipated. By late October the interior had been refurbished and was ready for equipment installation. In mid-December nearly all the equipment was in place and Ming was ready to do some trial runs. He invited Uncle, Fong, and whomever else they wanted to bring with them to observe. If all went well, Ming would start hiring the staff he needed to put the plant into full production.

Uncle hadn't been back to Shenzhen since the ceremony in September. He trusted Ming to stick to the budget and the schedule they'd set, but he had still assigned Fong to supervise the project. To Uncle's satisfaction, Fong had taken the responsibility very seriously, making several trips a week to Shenzhen. From all indications he had established an excellent working relationship with Ming.

Under normal circumstances, Uncle would have asked Xu to be his eyes and ears in Shenzhen, but Xu was preoccupied with trying to establish a foothold in Xiamen.

Uncle didn't want him to spread either his energy or his attention too thin.

After the celebratory dinner at the Emerald Dragon, Peng hadn't wasted any time contacting his peers in Xiamen, Shantou, and Zhuhai. They all shared the same problem of not yet enough industrial investments and were eager to talk to anyone willing to put money into their SEZs — and, although it was left unsaid, into their pockets. Peng had set up separate meetings in each zone. He and Uncle attended them all to act as short-term intermediaries. Tse and the economic development director in Zhuhai hit it off, as did Xu with the official in Xiamen. It didn't go so well for Yin in Shantou, and he had decided to stay out for the time being. Uncle didn't pursue it any further, figuring that the results in Shenzhen, Zhuhai, and Xiamen would prove how realistic his hopes were.

Uncle checked his watch and saw that they'd be leaving for the train station in less than fifteen minutes. He opened the file that contained the production numbers from Ming Garment Factory Number One and smiled. The combination of the new equipment they had installed and better raw materials had indeed tripled the factory's output. What was particularly encouraging was that they had no problem selling the goods; in fact, demand had kept growing and far exceeded their current capacity. It was a trend that would need to continue once the second factory was fully operating. With that thought in mind, Uncle reached for the phone.

"Yes, boss," Fong answered. "Are you ready to leave for Shenzhen?"

"In a few minutes. Come by my office first."

Uncle continued to study the numbers in the file until Fong arrived and took a chair opposite him. Then he looked up and said, "I know we're selling everything we're producing, but I'm concerned that if we let Ming go full-out with the second plant we'll flood our markets. The last thing we need is falling prices or growing inventories."

"Do you want me to tell Ming to scale back his production plans?"

"Only if you think we won't sell the output."

Fong pressed his lips together, raised his eyebrows, and shrugged. Then, to Uncle's delight, he said, "We'll sell whatever Ming can produce. The markets in Kowloon, Hong Kong Central, Sha Tin, Fanling, and Tai Po are booming. Some of those guys have opened up secondary markets and are reshipping our clothes to places like Manila, Bangkok, and Jakarta. Some of them are even talking about sending shirts to the U.S. I don't see any end to it unless we start to get competition from other SEZs."

Uncle knew Fong wasn't pleased about his decision to invite other gangs to invest in the SEZs. He wasn't quite so sure how his Straw Sandal felt about Xu staking out a position — even with Fanling's help and affiliation — in Xiamen. But however Fong felt, Uncle wasn't about to offer any justification. "I'm not worried about Zhuhai and Xiamen because our brothers aren't going to invest in clothes manufacturing. Xu believes there's a lot of money to be made in leather — specifically in designer bags — and Tse has found a watch manufacturer with the right machinery to duplicate high-end brands like Rolex."

"What about other gangs, the less friendly gangs? You don't think they'll try to grab a piece of our action?"

"They won't be able to do that without establishing relationships. We're the first ones in, and as long as we keep our new friends close, we can make it difficult for anyone else to get a foothold."

Fong sighed. "Uncle, I have to tell you that what's going on in Shenzhen is kind of crazy. Even in the past few months I've seen a difference. Money is rushing in now. There are more restaurants and hotels being built than I can count. Ming has started going to a massage parlour every night after work, and he has a choice of parlours — and of massages. It wasn't like that a year ago, and massage parlours are the kind of business that brothers from other gangs understand."

"Are you telling me they're involved already?"

"No," Fong said quickly. "I think it's strictly locals running things, but once the word gets out it won't take long for our brothers to find their way across the border."

"And run smack into the PLA if they try to muscle in on local businesses. None of us wants that to happen."

"Is the PLA more efficient than the Hong Kong police?"

"I think 'more brutal' is a better description," Uncle said, closing the folder and rising from his chair. "We should get going now."

They left the office and caught a taxi to the station. Uncle was surprised by the traffic outside, and again by the number of people jostling on the platform. "It's busy here. Is something special going on?" he aked Fong.

"No. In the past few months, as construction has picked up in Shenzhen, so has the number of people heading there," said Fong. "This is normal now."

The train arrived a few minutes later and the crowd surged forward. Uncle hung back; it wasn't his nature to be part of any mob. He and Fong waited until the platform was almost clear, then walked towards the last car, where they knew seats would most likely still be available. They found two together.

"Have you given any more thought to expanding our interests in Shenzhen?" Fong asked as the train left the station.

Uncle smiled. The immediate success of the reinvigorated Ming Garment Factory Number One had been noticed by many other local businessmen, some of them friends of Ming, and they had inundated Fong with proposals to expand their own businesses that he had duly forwarded to Uncle. Thus far, Uncle hadn't acted on any of them. "I've never stopped thinking about expanding our interests, but you know how cautious I am," he said. "Once Ming's second factory is running smoothly and we know roughly what our income flow will be, we can turn our attention to adding new business. The worst thing we could do is be rash. Going forward, slow and certain has to be our operating mode in Shenzhen. I've told Tse and Xu the same thing about Zhuhai and Xiamen. We all need to keep a low profile, and we can't do that if we're running around aimlessly."

"What about Xu?" Fong asked, his tone hinting at tension. Although they were friends, Fong and Xu were both competitive by nature. Fong had never voiced any jealousy about the potential rise to prominence for Xu afforded by the Xiamen project. Their Fanling positions as Straw Sandal and White Paper Fan were equal within the executive structure, but it was obvious that if Xu made Xiamen a success and established his own organization there, he had a chance to become a Mountain Master.

"What about Xu?" Uncle answered.

Fong shook his head. "Sorry, I might be overstepping with a question like that."

"Nonsense. Speak your mind."

"Well, I've been wondering if you intend to leave him in Xiamen or if he'll be coming back to Fanling after he sets up there."

"His dream is to go back to Shanghai."

"I know, but Xiamen isn't Shanghai."

"But it is in China, and a year ago the idea of our being able to operate anywhere in China was unthinkable. If we can make Shenzhen, Xiamen, and Zhuhai work, who knows where we'll be a year from now. "

"I understand that, boss, but that doesn't really answer my question about Xu."

Uncle turned his head and looked out the window. "I think you can assume that if he is successful in Xiamen, he won't be coming back to Fanling for anything other than to collect his wife and son and say goodbye to us," he said, and paused. "He'll have my blessing and continued support if that's the case, but we've a very long way to go — maybe years — before a decision like that has to be made."

Fong fell silent, and Uncle knew he was calculating what it all might mean for him. He would have liked to tell him, but the truth was that Uncle had no idea what the future held for any of them. What he did have was hopes and expectations, and those becoming a reality was daunting to contemplate. So many things had to break their way, and his experience was that it was irresponsible — and often dangerous — to assume they would.

"Xu is a good man," Fong said finally. "He deserves whatever he gets."

Uncle nodded and thought about saying something, but an announcement over the loudspeaker that they were nearing Shenzhen interrupted him.

When the train came to a halt, neither Uncle nor Fong left their seat. Through the window they could see the horde that had descended on the train now pushing and shoving their way onto the platform and racing towards the immigration booths.

"I can't get over how many people there are," Uncle said.

"It shouldn't take too long. I know it looks chaotic, but they're efficient here," Fong said. "We should get in line now."

Ten minutes later the line hadn't shortened by much, and even Fong was starting to fret. "There'll be another train arriving in about twenty minutes, and if these lines haven't improved, it will get crazy here."

"Is something going on?" Uncle asked for the second time that morning.

"The immigration officers do seem to be taking a lot of time."

Ahead of them one of the lines had thinned, and Uncle was able to look past it and into the station's interior. "Over there on the left, on the other side of the booths, is that a cage I see?" he asked Fong.

"Yeah, it is," Fong said, his surprise evident.

To Uncle's eye the cage wasn't much different from one he'd seen at a circus that had visited Fanling the year before. That one had been big enough to accommodate eight lions sitting on stools and their tamer. There were no stools or lions in the cage at the station, only a large number of men sitting on the floor or standing and looking through the bars. Around the structure, several PLA soldiers stood with guns held across their chests.

Uncle felt a chill. "Why are those men in that cage? Why are they being guarded?" he asked Fong.

"I don't know. Maybe they were trying to sneak across the border into Hong Kong," Fong said. "Or maybe their papers weren't in order."

Almost subconsciously, Uncle's right hand reached for the inner breast pocket of his suit jacket, where he touched his home-visit booklet.

The line shuffled forward and Uncle saw several people in front of him whispering to each other. They looked concerned, and that only increased his feeling of disquiet. He thought about turning back and catching the next train to Fanling, and then just as quickly dismissed the idea. Ming and the others were expecting him. There was no real reason — other than paranoia — not to stay in line.

"Do you have any idea what's going on?" Fong asked a man wearing an expensive suit in the line next to him.

"Not really, though it was like this yesterday as well. All they did then was check my papers and wave me through. Maybe they're just getting more bureaucratic."

They were separated from the immigration booths by only a handful of people when Uncle heard a commotion behind him. He turned and saw that the next train had arrived and a swarm of people was running towards them. "What a mess this is," he said to Fong.

Fong stepped behind Uncle as if trying to shield him from the onrushing mob. "We'll be through in a few minutes," he said.

Finally Uncle was at the front of line, and a minute later he was waved forward by a middle-aged customs and immigration officer. As he approached the booth, the officer held out his hand without looking up. Uncle gave him the booklet.

The officer opened it. He took more time with that, reading it more intently than Uncle thought was merited. Then he raised his head and looked squarely at Uncle. "It says here that you were born in Hubei province."

"I was."

"So you are Chinese?"

"I am a citizen of Hong Kong now, as you can tell from the permit."

The officer nodded, turned away, and said something to another officer who was standing behind the booth. A few seconds later that officer stood beside Uncle. "You need to come with me," he said.

"Why?"

"You'll know soon enough," the man said. "Just come with me and don't make a fuss, or I'll be forced to involve one of the soldiers."

"What's going on?" Fong said from the adjacent booth.

"None of your business," the officer said, and then pointed at Fong. "Are his papers in order?" he asked the officer looking at Fong's visa.

"No problem here" was the reply.

"Let's keep it that way," the officer said to Fong, his hand now gripping Uncle's elbow.

"Am I going to be detained?" Uncle asked.

"You are."

"Why?"

"Just start moving towards that cage."

Uncle hesitated, felt the grip on his elbow tighten, and knew he wasn't in a position to argue. "Call Peng," he said to Fong. "Tell him to fix this, whatever this is."

"This is bullshit," Fong said angrily. "And there isn't a payphone inside the station. I'll have to go outside."

"Just do it from wherever you can."

"Let's go," the officer said.

"Your colleague still has my permit," said Uncle.

"You'll get it back later."

Again Uncle knew it was useless to protest. The officer tugged at his arm and Uncle followed him towards the cage. As they neared it, one of the soldiers in front of the door turned and inserted a key into a padlock. The door opened and Uncle was pushed through.

"When are we getting out of here?" someone in the cage shouted at the officer.

"There are trucks on the way to collect you. It shouldn't be long before they arrive."

"We were told that an hour ago. I've been in here for close to three hours and I'm going to piss myself if I don't get out of here soon," the same voice said.

"Suit yourself," the officer said.

There were only men in the cage. Uncle counted sixteen, excluding himself. It was a diverse group, but as he looked at them he saw they had one thing in common — they were all afraid.

11

UNCLE LEANED AGAINST THE BARS AND WATCHED FONG hurry out of the station with a worried look on his face. When he had disappeared through the exit doors, Uncle turned to the man next to him. "Do you have any idea what this is about?"

The clothes of most of the men in the cage — jeans, peasant pyjamas, T-shirts, sweaters — looked the worse for wear. Uncle imagined that the majority of them worked with their hands for a living. The man he spoke to was wearing jeans, but they weren't ripped or soiled, and he had on a neatly pressed blue shirt.

"They told me my papers aren't in order," the man said.

"How so?"

"They didn't tell me the details."

"Where are you from?"

"A town about fifty kilometres north of here. There's no work there, at least none that pays enough for a man to be able to look after his family. I was told there's lots of work in Shenzhen. That's why I came. Most of these other men will tell you the same kind of story," he said. He stared at Uncle's black suit and crisp white shirt. "If you don't mind me saying, you don't look like you belong in here with us."

"I don't think I belong in here either, but that has nothing to do with your company," Uncle said.

"Why are they holding you?"

"I don't know. They wouldn't say," Uncle said, and then paused. "The soldier told the guy who needs to pee that some trucks are on the way. What's that about?"

"Whatever the reason, it can't be good."

"Well, they can't leave us in this cage forever."

"Maybe not, but at least in here we're safe."

"What are you implying?" Uncle asked.

"I don't know about you, but where I'm from they don't bother with trials when you break the law. A bullet in the back of the head is quicker and cheaper," the man said. "Some of the other guys are scared that they're going to truck us to a field somewhere and get rid of us that way."

"I didn't break any law."

"Neither did I — at least none that I know about."

"I'm from Hong Kong and have a home-visit permit."

"Hong Kong? Why would you leave it?"

"I'm doing some business in Shenzhen."

"That's what we all want to do, and look where it's got us," the man said.

Uncle started to respond but stopped when he saw a group of soldiers approaching, led by a young officer. The soldiers were all armed and looked menacing. The officer halted at the cage door and motioned for one of the guards to unlock it. When the padlock was removed, he stared into the cage, his eyes focused above their heads.

"My name is Captain Tung," he said loudly. "We're going to be taking you from here to trucks that will take you to a processing centre. When we open the door, I want you to come out in single file and follow the soldiers. Keep your hands by your sides. Don't rush, push, or try to run off. We will shoot anyone who tries to escape. Is that clear?" He waited perhaps five seconds and then said to the guard, "Open the gate."

Uncle was working to stay calm. Common sense told him that his cage partner's comment about getting shot was a wild exaggeration, but it still created a flush of irrational fear. The captain's mention of a processing centre, and then his threat to shoot anyone who didn't cooperate, generated concerns that couldn't be so easily dismissed. Uncle decided he had to speak to Captain Tung, but not in the midst of this crowd and confusion. So he waited in the cage until everyone else had left and formed a line in the station, with armed guards ahead, on either side, and behind them.

"Why aren't you joining the others?" Tung asked.

"I think there's been a mistake," Uncle said.

"Of course you do. And so does everyone else."

"No, seriously. One phone call should clear this up."

"You can explain it all to the people at the processing centre."

"I'm a businessman from Hong Kong. Mr. Peng, the director of the Development Corporation, can vouch for me."

"Then he can vouch for you when you're at the processing centre," Tung said. "My orders are to pick up this group and transport you there. That's it, nothing more, and that's all I intend to do. Someone else can decide what to do with you when I get you there."

"This is silly — "

"Enough!" Tung interrupted. "Get in line with the others."

Uncle stepped out of the cage. A soldier stepped behind him and shoved him in the back until he was next to the man in front of him. Uncle looked towards the station entrance, anxious to see Fong or Peng or anyone he knew, but he was quite alone.

The line began to move in fits and starts through the station in the opposite direction from the main doors. Arriving and departing train passengers came to a halt and stared at them as they passed. He might be out of the cage, but that didn't stop Uncle from feeling like an animal.

When they reached a door with the CUSTOMS AND IMMIGRATION OFFICIALS ONLY stencilled on the lintel, Captain Tung went to the front of the line. "You will walk through here in an orderly manner and then exit on the other side of the office into a laneway," he said. "There is a truck parked there. Climb into the back and take a seat. If there is no disruption, we will be at the processing centre in less than an hour."

The men shuffled through the office, no one speaking but their apprehension apparent all the same. An open door awaited them at the other side, and through it Uncle could see an olive-green military truck with a green canvas roof. Two soldiers flanked the exit and two more stood near the rear of the truck. As the men left the office they were guided by gun barrels until they climbed into the truck. Uncle was the last civilian to clamber up. The truck had a steel floor, canvas walls, and wooden benches along each side. Two soldiers sat facing each other on the benches closest to the driver. Two more climbed into the truck after Uncle and took positions nearest the tailgate. The gate closed.

Uncle turned to the soldier sitting next to him. "You look like you've done this before," he said.

"This is the second time today, and yesterday we made three trips. You people are nuisances," he said.

"What do you mean by 'you people'?" Uncle asked.

The soldier dug the butt of his gun into Uncle's side. "I think you should keep quiet."

The truck started up and lurched forward, causing several of the men to slip from the benches and land on the floor. Four guns were aimed at them as they struggled to their feet and retook their seats. Uncle closed his eyes and took a deep breath. *Where the hell is Fong? Where is Peng?*

The truck groaned and creaked as it made its way through Shenzhen. Uncle could see a little through the opening between the tailgate and the roof. After about twenty minutes there were fewer buildings, and ten minutes later he saw glimpses of countryside. The roads deteriorated as they went along, and it became increasingly difficult to stay on the bench. Some of the men held onto their neighbours to help stabilize themselves.

After about half an hour of being tossed around, the road improved and the ride became smoother. Uncle looked out, but all he could see was trees and fields. The truck stuttered to a stop and then made a left turn along a paved road. A few minutes later Uncle saw a steel Quonset hut, then another, and then they were in the middle of an area that seemed full of them. The truck began to slow and finally came to a halt. No one inside moved. Uncle thought the soldiers looked bored and guessed this was part of a familiar routine. Then, without warning, the tailgate clattered down.

The two soldiers sitting closest to the gate stood, jumped out of the truck, and joined a cluster of six other soldiers standing ten metres away. A sergeant stepped towards the truck. "I want you to exit this vehicle one at a time," he said loudly. "After you do, you will move immediately to the right and stand there to await further instructions."

Uncle looked at the man seated directly across from him. "Do you want to go first or will I?" Uncle asked.

"You go," the man said, his voice trembling as if he expected something dreadful to happen.

"That's fine," Uncle said, rising and taking two steps to his left before jumping onto the ground.

"Over there," the sergeant said, pointing his rifle towards a Quonset hut.

The windowless half-cylinder building sat on a bed of gravel. Made of galvanized steel, it was perhaps five metres high in the middle, ten metres wide, and about thirty metres in length. On its double doors were painted the words IMMI-GRATION PROCESSING.

As the other men gradually joined him, Uncle tried to make sense of his situation. The sign on the Quonset hut at least provided a clue. It seemed that the fact he had been born in China could now be an issue, when it hadn't been on previous border crossings. But why hadn't his Hong Kong passport been enough to establish his credentials?

While Uncle was pondering these questions, the door opened and an immigration officer appeared. He looked at the group of men, shook his head, and said to the sergeant, "Is this the last load for today?"

"I hope so."

"Bring them in," the officer sighed.

The sergeant nodded. "Go through the door in single file," he said to the men. "Once you're inside, take a seat on a bench."

"Why do I have to do this again? I did it at the train station. Besides, they took my papers there and didn't give them
back," one of the men said.

"Shut up about your papers. You're here to answer questions, not ask them. Get moving," the sergeant said.

Uncle walked towards the door, which was flanked by two
soldiers. He entered the hut and blinked. It was badly lit and
he could barely see to the far end. He took several tentative
steps and felt gravel under his feet.

"Take the seats on the left," the immigration officer yelled.

Uncle's eyes began to adjust, and as he looked in that
direction he saw two rows of benches. There were two other
rows on the right, and one of them was occupied by seven
men. Straight ahead were four desks occupied by immigration officers. Men stood in front of the desks, and behind
every desk was an armed soldier. Behind the benches on
both sides were other rows of soldiers. Uncle walked to the
bench and sat. A few moments later, he was joined by the
other men from the truck.

He could hear some of the immigration officers asking
questions of the men who stood in front of them. Their
answers were muffled, but Uncle could tell from their lowered heads and slumped shoulders that it wasn't going well
for them. The officer farthest from Uncle said something
sharply and then slammed a stamp onto a piece of paper.
The legs of the man in front of him buckled and he fell to his
knees. The officer turned and spoke to the soldiers behind
him. They moved quickly to the man's side, grabbed him
under the arms, and hoisted him to his feet.

"This is a mistake," the man howled.

"Don't make us drag you out of here," the soldier said to him.

The eyes of every man who had been on Uncle's truck were fixed on the terrified man as the soldiers half-walked and half-dragged him from the hut.

"This doesn't look good," said the man seated next to Uncle.

When the soldiers and the man had left the hut, the immigration officer shouted, "Woo Jun." A large man rose from the bench across from Uncle and lumbered towards the desk.

On it went for another fifteen minutes, until that bench was empty. There weren't any more scenes involving men being dragged from the hut, but there weren't any happy faces either. When the opposite bench was clear, the captain who had accompanied them from the station entered the hut, carrying a file folder. He approached the immigration officers and gave the folder to the first in line.

"Those must be our documents," Uncle said.

The immigration officer glanced quickly through the folder's contents, took out a small pile of paper, and passed the folder to the officer sitting next to him. He repeated the process, as did the next man.

Uncle drew a deep breath, wondering which officer had his permit and how long he would have to wait before his name was called. He tried not to feel anxious, but his lack of control over the situation gnawed at him. In the past twenty years since he'd left China, he couldn't remember feeling as helpless. Where the hell was Peng?

"Yao Ban," an immigration officer yelled.

As a man three seats down from Uncle got to his feet, sharp noises rang out. They came from outside the hut, and although they didn't seem close, they were loud enough to be distinct. The man whose name had been called froze. "Were those gunshots?" he asked Uncle.

"I don't know," Uncle said, although he was sure enough that they were.

"Yao Ban, don't keep me waiting," the immigration officer said. But then something caught his eye and he jumped to his feet and immediately stood at attention. The other officers followed his example. Uncle turned to look towards the entrance. Colonel Liu Leji was standing there.

Liu strode towards the desks. "I want the papers for Chow Tung. He's coming with me."

12

UNCLE LEFT THE HUT WITH LIU, NEITHER MAN SAYING a word until they were outside.

"Get into my jeep. We'll ride together back to Shenzhen," Liu said.

"Thank you for this," Uncle said. "Though I have to say I expected to see Peng and not you."

"Peng phoned me. Luckily we connected, because he wouldn't have been any use to you here."

"I see," Uncle said, and then stopped and looked at the rows of huts stretching in all directions. "What is this here? Why so many huts?"

"The PLA needs accommodation, and the immigration department, and some of my customs people. This camp is a temporary solution. We're building more permanent quarters."

Uncle climbed into the jeep, surprised not to see someone behind the wheel. "I thought a man in your position would have a driver," Uncle said.

"I do, but not today — at least, not for this trip."

Uncle glanced at Liu. In the daylight he looked even younger than he had at the restaurant after the garment factory ceremony. He was in his mid-thirties, Uncle guessed, and carried himself with the easy confidence of a man who hadn't encountered much resistance or hardship in his life. He also wondered if Liu's long, thick moustache was an attempt to add gravitas to his otherwise youthful appearance. "Again, I need to stress how much I appreciate your intervention," Uncle said. "Although I have to say it's a bit surprising. I wouldn't have thought you'd remember who I am, let alone take time out of your day to help."

"I remember you well enough. You have a distinctive air about you," Liu said. "But there's no need to go on about that. Coming here wasn't particularly difficult for me to do, nor was getting you released. You shouldn't have been detained in the first place."

"Which leads me to ask why I was."

The jeep lurched forward along a gravel road. Liu changed gears rather awkwardly, and he didn't answer Uncle until the vehicle was in fourth gear and moving smoothly. "We've had an enormous influx of people trying to get into Shenzhen over the past few weeks," Liu said. "There are jobs here that are steadier and better paying than those for hundreds of kilometres around. Word has spread. But the thing is, we can't allow everyone to come here. We can't let things get out of control, so my colleague who runs the immigration division decided to put his foot down."

"But surely you need labour. Those new factories, apartment buildings, office towers won't build themselves, and who's going to work and live in them when they're built?"

"Of course we need workers, but if we let everyone into the zone who wants to come, we'll be overrun. So we've put restrictions into place. Anyone who wants to work in the zone needs a special permit that they have to get in their hometown. That's been the case for a while, but we weren't enforcing it as stringently as we should have been. Now we are, and nearly all the men you got caught up with today don't have the proper permits. The fact that you were born in China was a red flag for the immigration officer at the train station," Liu said, and then paused. "Those officers are dedicated and do their best to apply the regulations, but many of them lack subtlety when it comes to exercising judgement. And truthfully, we'd rather they apply the regulations as bluntly as possible than try to interpret them too finely."

"But I have a home-visit permit —"

"Which says you were born in China, so you'll have to forgive us for laying claim to you — however briefly — as a Chinese citizen," Liu said. "Although in ten years or so, when Hong Kong is returned to us, you can be a Chinese citizen again."

Uncle thought about disputing that but knew this wasn't the best time to get into a political discussion. "Tell me, what's going to happen to those other men?" he asked instead.

"They'll be shipped back to where they came from and told not to try it again or they'll face prison time."

"All of them will be returned?"

Liu turned to him. "What are you trying to say?"

"When I was in the hut, I saw a man being dragged out by two members of the PLA. A short while later I heard gunshots."

"Not everyone trying to get into Shenzhen has the sole objective of finding work."

"Meaning?"

"Some people have a past that they're trying to escape, and Shenzhen is still a favourite departure point."

"To get to Hong Kong?"

"Yes."

"And when they don't make it and the past catches up to them, they're shot?"

"It's cheaper and more efficient than sending them back to get shot in their hometown," Liu said. He shook his head as if aware how raw that sounded. "At least, that's what the PLA officers tell me. The decision about what to do with those men rests completely with them."

"It doesn't sound to me as if you disagree."

"Whether I do or don't doesn't matter," Liu said. "I have enough on my plate managing customs. And besides, the PLA has no interest in my opinions about how they conduct their business."

Uncle turned and looked out the jeep's window. The huts were now well behind them and the countryside seemed more familiar. Just as he was thinking that, he saw a cluster of buildings ahead and realized it was Ming's garment factories. He had never driven past them before, so he'd had no idea what existed beyond them. He wondered if Fong or Ming knew that such a large military installation was in their backyard. "Are you going to drop me off at the factory?" he asked Liu.

"If you wish, but I was thinking maybe it's time that you and I had a chat," Liu said. "After meeting you at the restaurant with Peng, I had expected to see you again before now."

Is this a setup? Uncle thought immediately. *Did he arrange to have me stopped at the train station?* "I haven't been back to Shenzhen since then," he said.

"That explains it, but now that you're here we shouldn't waste the opportunity," Liu said. "There's a restaurant close to my office that I frequent. You must be hungry after your ordeal."

"That sounds just fine," Uncle said, sensing that the invitation was more of an order than a request. "But if you don't mind, I'd like to stop at the factory for a few minutes to let my people know I'm okay."

"Sure, we can do that," Liu said.

A few minutes later, Liu made a right turn onto the Ming Garment property. He parked in front of the entrance to Factory Number One. "I'll be right back," Uncle said as he exited the jeep.

Fong and Ming weren't in the old factory but Uncle found them at the new one, watching a production line spit out T-shirts bearing the Ferrari logo. He approached them from behind and tapped Fong on the shoulder. Fong turned, grinned, and threw his arms around Uncle.

"Take it easy. I'm all right," Uncle said, uncomfortable with the display of emotion.

"Did Peng come to get you?" Fong asked as he disentangled himself.

"No, it was Liu, the customs director. He's outside waiting for me in his jeep. We're going to have a meeting in town."

Fong's smile disappeared. "He has a reputation for being a hard case. What does he want?"

"Nothing I can't handle."

"Of course not. I wasn't suggesting otherwise; I've just been worried."

Uncle looked at his watch. "It is almost four o'clock. Meet me at the train station at seven. If I'm not there, wait for me at the ticket counter."

"Okay, boss."

Uncle nodded and said to Ming, "I like the look of those T-shirts. We should have a good market for them."

"This is just basic stuff. We'll really show you something when we've worked out all the kinks in this machinery," said Ming.

"I'm looking forward to that," Uncle said. "Now I really need to get going. I can't keep the customs director waiting."

Liu was smoking by the side of the jeep when Uncle left the factory. Uncle reached into his jacket pocket for a pack of Marlboros and his black crackle lighter. He lit a cigarette and took some deep drags as he walked over to Liu.

"We can go now. I told my man Fong to meet me at the train station at seven. Will that give us enough time to talk?"

"That will be more than sufficient."

Uncle climbed back into the jeep, and after some noisy gear changes they made their way back to the road in the direction of Shenzhen. Both men continued to smoke rather than talk, which suited Uncle because he was still trying to figure out what Liu wanted from him.

As they reached the outskirts of the city, Liu broke the silence. "When was it you left China?"

"Nineteen fifty-nine."

"Yes, now I remember, you told me that at the restaurant. That was during the Great Leap Forward."

"Or, as they called it in my village, the Years of Slow Death."

"I detect anger in your voice."

Uncle shrugged and thought, *What's the worst that can come from being honest?* "My father's family had farmed the same small plot of land for over two hundred years. No one became wealthy, but he and his ancestors could feed their families. That changed in 1958, when my father was forced to hand over his farm to a village commune run by the local party secretary. A year later my grandmother died of starvation, quickly followed by my father, mother, and sister. I lost my entire family to the famine created by Mao's policies."

"The policies weren't inherently bad," Liu said carefully. "It could be argued that they were badly implemented."

"Bad policies or policies badly implemented, it doesn't make any difference. I still lost my entire family because of them."

"It was a challenging time."

"Not having anything to eat and watching your family die is more than a challenge."

Liu flicked a hand in the air as if shooing away a fly. "There's no point in talking about things that happened long ago and can't be undone," he said. "Besides, you left it behind. You made it to Hong Kong. You survived, and obviously you have thrived."

"I swam across Shenzhen Bay," Uncle said, figuring that would be Liu's next question. "There were twelve of us when we got in the water. Only nine of us made it out."

"How did you lose the three?"

"The PLA didn't shoot them in the water, if that's what you're thinking," Uncle said. "The bay was dirty and dangerous enough to take lives without any assistance."

Liu took out his pack of Zhonghua cigarettes — Mao's favourite brand — and offered Uncle one. Uncle shook his head. "I only smoke Marlboros," he said, reaching for his pack. They both lit up.

"I have to say I appreciate your candour," Liu said. "Although I do have to tell you that leaving China the way you did is illegal. I would advise against sharing that story with less understanding officials."

Uncle shrugged. "What I'm trying to figure out is why *you* are being so understanding."

"There's no mystery to it," Liu said, and then glanced at Uncle to see if there was a reaction. When there wasn't, he continued, "I know you're paying Peng,"

What kind of game is this? What does he want? Is he trying to bring Peng down? "I don't know what you're talking about," Uncle said softly.

"I'm glad you said that, and I appreciate your reticence. A man can't be too careful when it comes to discussing matters like this," Liu said. "But surely you can't believe I'm trying to entrap you or cause harm to Peng. If I had wanted either of those things, I could simply have left you in the hut with the others. You would have been interrogated about Peng until we had the truth, and then you would have been sent back to Wuhan or taken into the field behind the hut and shot. Instead I came to get you, and now I'm driving you to Shenzhen to have what I hope will be a pleasant conversation over a beer and a plate of barbecued pork."

"Why?"

"Why what?"

"Why are you doing this? What have I done to justify this kind of treatment?"

"I like the way you do business."

"There isn't that much to like. The only business I've done here is with Ming, and it's still early days," Uncle said.

"I'm talking about the businesses you have in Fanling, and the way you conduct them," Liu said, smiling. "Let's not be secretive. If this is going to be work, we both need to be candid."

"If what is going to work?"

"If you don't mind, I'd like to save the details until we're at the restaurant."

"Okay, but tell me, what do you actually know about my businesses in Fanling?"

"More than I think you'd like me to know."

Uncle took a deep drag of his cigarette. "I need to think about this conversation," he said finally.

"I wouldn't expect anything less," Liu said as he looked at his watch. "We'll be at the restaurant in about fifteen minutes. That should give you enough time."

13

THE RESTAURANT WAS IN A SECTION OF SHENZHEN THAT Uncle hadn't visited before. From its name — Johnny's Noodles — Uncle assumed the owner was from Hong Kong. It was on the ground floor of a ten-storey building that, like every other building nearby, was new, and the air around it had the lingering odour of wet cement. Liu parked directly in front of the restaurant in a spot designated for SEZ officials.

"My department has leased the top three floors of this building, but we don't move in for another two weeks," Liu said. "This restaurant has been open for about a month and I've eaten here every time I've come to inspect the progress on our office. So that's at least eight times."

"Is Johnny from Hong Kong?"

"There is no Johnny; the owner's name is Han. He's from Guangzhou, but he thought an English name would give the place a Hong Kong feel. Hong Kong cuisine does have a great reputation in this town."

"I'm impressed that you took the trouble to find out about Johnny, or Han."

Liu shrugged. "I'm curious by nature, and since we're neighbours and I'm going to be a regular customer, it made sense. I always like to know who I'm doing business with."

Johnny's Noodles had a large plate-glass window through which Uncle could see three rows of tables running in a straight line from front to back. Most of them were occupied. "The place looks busy," he said.

"I asked Han to hold a table for us."

"You were that confident that I'd come with you?"

"It would have been ill-advised not to, and from everything I've heard, the last thing you are is rash," Liu said, opening the front door.

Uncle followed him inside and the odour of wet cement was replaced by the delicious aromas of garlic and ginger. Almost instantly, his appetite returned.

"Mr. Director, welcome back," a lean, short woman said as she left the hostess stand and hurried towards them with her head lowered deferentially.

"Is my table available?" Liu asked.

"Of course. I'll take you to it."

The restaurant was nearly full and almost every head turned in their direction as they passed on the way to their table. Liu wasn't wearing an easily recognizable uniform, but it was official looking enough to catch and hold a lot of nervous attention.

The hostess led them to a table tucked into a corner at the back of the restaurant. "The same as usual to drink?" she asked Liu.

"Please," he said, and turned to Uncle. "I'm going to have Tsingtao beer. Will you join me?"

"Gladly," Uncle said.

"Another of my traits is that I'm a creature of habit," Liu said. "When I find something I like, I tend to stick to it."

"I'm much the same."

"Are you hungry, or has this afternoon ruined your appetite?" Liu asked.

"I'll stick to beer for now," Uncle said, anxious to get on with whatever business Liu wanted to discuss.

Liu sat back and surveyed the restaurant. "It didn't take long for this place to earn a good reputation. When you conduct business properly, a good reputation almost naturally develops. Ming is another example of that."

"Ming knows what he's doing," Uncle agreed.

"And you knew enough to invest in him."

"Yes, but we didn't simply throw money at him or give him free rein. We were already buying from him, so we had a firm idea of his potential," said Uncle. "Also, my partner Fong looks after most of the marketing and keeps an eye on Ming's operations."

The hostess brought two Tsingtaos to the table. When she had left, Liu raised his bottle. "Here's to us," he said.

Uncle nodded, took a swig, and said, "I hope you don't mind if I ask you a few questions."

"No, not at all. I'm sure you must have a few."

"Thank you. To start, what did you mean when you said, 'If this is going to work,' and when you said you know more about my business affairs in Fanling than you thought I'd like?"

"Which subject would you like me to deal with first?"

"My business in Fanling."

Liu smiled. "When I met you at the restaurant and saw some of your colleagues, I didn't think you looked like our typical Hong Kong investors, so I asked Peng about you. He was evasive, which heightened my interest enough for me to review your investment application file. I found that you had cobbled together an interesting array of small companies to get around the investment guidelines. At that point I called an old friend of mine who lives in Fanling and asked him about you," Liu said, his smile broadening. "To my surprise, he knows you. In fact, he told me he knows you very well."

Where is he going with this? Uncle thought. "Fanling isn't that large a town. Most businesspeople have crossed paths at least once."

"My friend isn't in business," Liu said.

"Mr. Director," Uncle said softly, "I'm not good at guessing games, so it's unlikely I'll come up with the name of your friend without your help."

"I'll give you a clue," Liu said. "This friend told me you are the head of a very successful triad gang in Fanling. Could that be true?"

"Triads are outlawed and banished from China and prosecuted and sometimes persecuted in Hong Kong. I am a businessman conducting legal business in Shenzhen and Fanling, nothing more than that," Uncle said, more calmly than he felt.

"Please, there's no need to play games with me. My source is impeccable, and I wholly believe him. But frankly, I couldn't care less about your triad involvement. I'm more concerned about what kind of businessman you are and whether I can trust you," Liu said. "My source told me that you're a very capable businessman, and that he would trust you with his life. That's why you and I are having this conversation."

"Who is this source?"

"I don't think he would appreciate it if I shared that information with you. Is it enough to tell you that he is knowledgeable about both you and your business operations?"

"No, it isn't enough," Uncle said. "Earlier you said we shouldn't be secretive. I can be open, but that can't cut one way."

"A point well made and taken," Liu said, the middle finger of his right hand lightly stroking his moustache. "I spoke to Zhang Delun."

"Superintendent Zhang Delun, of the Hong Kong Police Force?" Uncle asked, hardly believing his ears. Zhang was his long-standing connection to the Hong Kong police, the man he went to when he needed help, the man to whom he'd promised there would be no drug dealing in Fanling. He and Uncle had been brought together as young men by Tian Longwei, and Tian was the only person who knew about their relationship.

"Yes. He told me that you and he have been acquaintances for many years. He implied, but didn't say directly, that the two of you have a mutually beneficial working relationship," Liu said. "He has tremendous respect for you, Uncle. He said you are trustworthy, reliable, and know how to keep confidences — all characteristics that I'm looking for in a business partner."

"Zhang and I do know each other. He's a fine man," Uncle said, noting but letting pass Liu's use of the word *partner*. "How did you come to know him?"

"I attended university in Hong Kong for two years. He was a classmate. We became friends and have remained so."

Uncle drained his beer, lit a cigarette, and took a deep drag while he thought about Zhang and Liu. If the two men were friends, Liu couldn't have a better recommendation. If

they weren't, why would Liu lie about it when it was something that could be so easily proven false? "I am triad," Uncle
said finally. "But the reason Zhang and I can co-operate is
that he knows we don't exploit people in Fanling. We don't
sell drugs. We don't deal in extortion. We don't operate
brothels. We never embarrass him or the police."

"But you do manufacture and import illegal counterfeit
clothing," Liu said matter-of-factly.

"Yes, and we sell the clothing at a night market we operate, to people who can't afford the real thing," Uncle said.
"We also have off-track betting sites, some small casinos, a
couple of restaurants, and several massage parlours. Not all
of them are exactly legal, but Zhang has accepted that we're
providing services the public wants, and has left us alone."

"Do you pay him?"

"No. He's never asked and I've never offered. If either of
us had, I think our relationship would have ended instantly.
It's based on trust, and the moment you put a price on trust,
it disappears."

"I would like our partnership to operate in a similar manner," Liu said. "Tell me, did you know that my wife and aunt
started a brokerage business?"

"No," Uncle lied, baffled by the question.

"Well, they did, but then I found out that their involvement wasn't a secret. Peng knew, for example. I'm not sure
how he found out, but he did, and he told enough people that
it eventually got back to me. The instant it did, I had my wife
and aunt quietly sell the business and remove themselves
completely from any contact with it. You see, given my position, I need secrecy, and I need a partner whom I can trust
completely — someone like you."

"I don't understand what you mean when you refer to me as a partner."

"It is true that we haven't ironed out the details yet."

"What details are you talking about? Why don't you start with those and see where they lead," Uncle said.

"They aren't complicated. The special economic zone affords us the opportunity to build businesses and provide security for our families. My position precludes my direct involvement and any overt involvement of my family, including my wife and aunt. We need a partner to help us get off the ground. The initial requirement is money."

"Money to do what?"

"The initial thrust will be to build warehouses. There aren't enough of them for the business that's going to be done in Shenzhen," Liu said. "There'll be a huge need for warehouses for raw materials, for finished goods, and for anything in between. You build them and I'll make sure they're full."

Uncle didn't have to ask how Liu would fill the warehouses. "My partners and I know nothing about building or managing warehouses."

"You don't have to know anything. We'll build them and manage them from behind the scenes. My wife and aunt are both competent businesspeople, but this time — with your help — we'll make sure they remain invisible."

"So why do you need us?"

"Besides the money, someone has to establish a business and apply for the appropriate permits."

"And assuming this had any interest for us, what would we get in return?"

"Half the profits."

"When you say you'd manage from behind the scenes,

does that include controlling the money?" Uncle asked softly.

"We would want to have our fair share of input into how the money is spent and allocated, but we would have open books and we would expect you to provide banking support. Our names — directly or indirectly — would never appear anywhere on the bank documents, and I can also tell you that we would be extremely cautious in terms of withdrawing funds. Does that satisfy you?"

"It sounds fine, but I still don't fully understand why you've chosen us to partner with you."

"Uncle, you keep referring to *us*," Liu said. "I know nothing of your colleagues. Do I need to be concerned about them?"

"We are a brotherhood, so any decision I make has an impact on them and is judged by them. I don't take my brothers for granted," Uncle said. "But, that aside, you don't need to know them or be concerned. They follow my lead."

Liu drained his beer and held the empty bottle in the air. Less than a moment later the hostess arrived at the table with two new bottles. Liu drank from his and then leaned towards Uncle. "Returning to your question about why I've chosen you to be our partner, we need to do business with someone who is reliable. As I mentioned earlier, Zhang made it clear that that's one of your strengths."

"It was kind of him to say that."

"We also need a partner who has enough money to finance the construction of a large number of warehouses and whatever comes after," Liu said. "Am I correct in assuming you have that capacity?"

"We can finance — within reason — any project that makes sense to us."

"I thought that would be the case. So that leaves us with perhaps the most important quality we need in our partners: the ability to keep their mouths shut about our involvement. We need someone we can trust never to divulge our involvement. From what I know about the relationship between you and Zhang, I think you meet that criterion."

Uncle ran his index finger down the side of the beer bottle as he digested Liu's words. "Do you expect me to respond to that comment? It seems to me that we wouldn't be having this conversation if you hadn't already decided that we can be trusted."

Liu nodded. "You are correct. So, all that being acceptable, does this give you sufficient understanding?"

"I have another question," Uncle said abruptly.

"I'm listening."

"I am inclined to pursue this conversation about a partnership, but I'd like to know what would happen if, after all our talk, I decided that the partnership wasn't for us?"

"There would be no animosity on my part, but you could forget about doing more business in the SEZ. And the business you have with Ming would be — how can I say it? — in peril."

"Ah," Uncle said.

"That outcome is simply a matter of practicality; it isn't personal," Liu said. "I can't have someone who knows as much about me as you do operating in an ad hoc manner inside my territory. Regardless of what Zhang said about your trustworthiness, I wouldn't sleep well. I'm sure you can understand that."

"Actually, I can."

"Excellent. So where does that leave us?"

"It leaves me interested but in need of more detail," Uncle said.

Liu reached into his coat pocket and extracted several sheets of paper, which he passed to Uncle. "This details the cost of building one medium-sized warehouse and projects the income it can generate if it is fully utilized," he said. "As you can see, it isn't particularly expensive to build what is basically an empty structure. And another positive note is that it can be built quickly. We could be generating income in a matter of months."

Uncle scanned the pages quickly. "There's no land cost mentioned."

"That's because we don't have to buy the land. The powers that run the zone have decided that creating the infrastructure necessary to support industrial expansion is of the highest priority. We'll be given fifty-year leases on any vacant land we choose at rates we can build into our operating costs."

"Who do you mean when you say *powers*? Are you talking about Peng?"

"He's certainly part of the structure, but there are decisions that he isn't consulted about or even informed about until long after the fact — if at all," Liu said.

"And who is making these decisions?"

"Ah. That is something I can't disclose. Not yet, anyway."

"Wheels within wheels?"

"Exactly. Is your organization any different?"

Uncle hesitated and then said carefully, "Truthfully it isn't, but when I give you my word, no one in my organization will ever overturn it or contradict it."

"Let me assure you that my word is equally as binding."

"Then in that case, I'll tell you that I like your business plan."

Liu leaned towards him. "One more thing I need to mention is that it will be my wife — and, from time to time, my aunt — who you will have to deal with on this project. Is that a problem?"

"Not at all, and I trust it won't be a problem for them to deal with whoever I designate to represent our side on a day-to-day basis."

"No. In fact, I wouldn't have expected anything else," Liu said, and smiled. "Does this mean we have an understanding?"

"It does."

"Does that mean we have you as a partner?"

"I want to go over the numbers again, but if they make sense, I think you can assume you have a partner," Uncle said.

(14)
September 1983
Shenzhen, Special Economic Zone, People's Republic
  of China

EVERY TIME UNCLE WALKED OUT OF THE TRAIN STATION
into Shenzhen he noticed something new. It didn't matter
if he hadn't visited for several months or just a week; there
was always something old being torn down or something
new being built. Change was the constant in Shenzhen, a
sleepy country town no longer, with a population pushing
200,000 and no end to its growth in sight. Liu Leji had told
Uncle that the city would reach a million inhabitants before
the end of the decade.

As usual, Fong was waiting for Uncle when he emerged
from the station. Crossing the border wasn't as arduous a trip
as it had been before, since Uncle now had, in addition to his
permit, a special pass issued by the Department of Customs
and Immigration that gave him no-questions-asked rapid
entry. Another customs department permit allowed Fong to
park his car directly outside the station, in an area otherwise
reserved for buses and taxis.

It was just after eleven a.m. and Uncle had already been up for more than five hours, after less than four hours' sleep. The night before he'd gone to Happy Valley for the horse meeting and returned home just before midnight. The gang's income from gambling had continued to decrease, but the revenue from Ming's factories and their new warehouse operations made that no longer a serious concern. *Thank god for Shenzhen*, he thought as he waved at Fong, who was standing beside his car.

One of the downsides to the gang's involvement in the SEZ was that Fong spent most of his time in Shenzhen, performing an on-site management role. Before their expansion into China, Fong and Uncle had seen each other virtually every day. Now, although they talked daily on the phone, they often didn't get together for weeks at a time. Uncle missed the camaraderie. It was a loss he felt even more acutely with Xu, because his closest friend was now spending much of his time in Xiamen.

The Xiamen project had been harder to get off the ground than Shenzhen, but Xu's efforts were starting to pay off. As positive as that was, it brought with it several problems that Uncle had put off resolving. Xu was still officially Fanling's White Paper Fan, but because of his absences, nearly all of the job was being done by an assistant. The time was quickly approaching when Uncle would have to make a decision. Should he leave Xu in Xiamen and appoint a new White Paper Fan in Fanling, or should he bring back Xu and replace him in Xiamen? Xu had never voiced his preference, which made Uncle's decision that much harder. He knew they would eventually have to talk, and it wasn't an idea he relished. He didn't want to lose Xu, but neither did he want to hold him back.

And then there was an even larger issue to consider. Xu had quietly established the first triad foothold in more than twenty years in a part of mainland China not attached to any foreign territory. For the sake of the broader triad society, Uncle believed the foothold had to be preserved and slowly expanded, and Xu was intelligent, thoughtful, and careful enough to do that. Xu's dream of returning to Shanghai was still out of reach, however. There was a large difference between operating within the framework of the special economic zones and establishing a base in a city that didn't offer any cover, but Xiamen was a start.

"Is everything okay, boss?" Fong asked as Uncle reached the car. "You look worried."

"Our racing receipts were down again last night. Not by a lot, but the trend continues."

"That goddamn Hong Kong Jockey Club."

"You can't blame them for running their business so efficiently. If we were in their position, we'd be operating the same way," Uncle said as he got into the car.

"Do you think it might be time to open some betting shops in Shenzhen? The Jockey Club can't compete with us here, can it."

"No, it can't, and that is something to consider, but we'd have to talk to our partners here before making a move like that."

"Which partners, Peng or the Liu family?"

"Who do you think is best positioned to keep the police and the army off our backs?"

"The Lius."

"I agree."

"Do you want to raise the subject today?" Fong asked.

"No, it's too soon. We need to think this through more carefully before bringing it up with the Lius," Uncle said. "And, if we do decide to discuss it, I'll go to Liu Leji first for a one-on-one chat."

"Speaking of Liu Leji, did he tell you if he'd be joining us for lunch?"

"We spoke last night and he plans to be there."

"It's been a while since I've seen him."

"He prefers to keep a low profile. And besides, he trusts his aunt and wife to conduct their side of the business."

"They are capable, Ms. Gao — the aunt — especially. She's all about facts and figures," Fong said. "She keeps me on my toes."

"That's a good thing, yes?"

Fong nodded and glanced at his watch. "We should get going. I don't want to be late. Being on time is another thing she's fanatical about."

A moment later Fong eased away from the curb and began to drive across the city to its northern outskirts. While the Liu family insisted on regular meetings, they were careful about where they met. The Pearl Boat restaurant was their most recent preference. Located on the ground floor of a new shopping mall far distant from Liu's office, it afforded them privacy and served excellent dim sum.

"When did Ms. Gao arrive from Beijing?" Uncle asked.

"Yesterday morning. She and Meilin visited all the warehouses in the afternoon and early evening. I don't know why she bothers doing that. I mean, we're not going to tear one down while she's not looking," Fong said. Chen Meilin was Liu Leji's wife.

"I imagine she just wants to make sure they're being fully utilized."

"Her nephew makes sure of that. We're so busy at times that we have to turn customers away."

"We'll be building more warehouses soon."

"How many?" Fong asked.

"That's what we'll decide at lunch. It all depends on how much money we want to take out of the business and how much we want to reinvest," Uncle said. "Liu hinted last night that his aunt has her eye on a house in Hong Kong. It's on Victoria Peak, so it won't be cheap. If she wants to buy it with cash — which I would expect — and we take an equivalent amount, we might have enough left to put up two new warehouses."

"Some of our customers have been asking about cold storage. Is there any chance we can build a warehouse with refrigeration?"

"It would be at least double what a standard warehouse costs."

Fong left the city streets and turned onto a new highway that led north. They drove for about a kilometre before coming to a stop in heavy traffic. "So many goddamn trucks, and more and more cars every day," Fong complained. "What's crazy is that a lot of the people driving here don't have a licence. They don't think they need one or they just don't care. Either way, they're all over the road like drunken maniacs."

They crawled forward for about ten minutes until they reached a police cruiser parked behind two badly damaged cars on the side of the highway. One of the cars seemed to have turned into the other. "See what I mean?" Fong said. "They don't have a clue how to drive."

"Relax. We don't have to be at the restaurant until noon," Uncle said.

A few minutes later the pace of traffic improved and Fong's mood lightened. "Hey, boss, I was thinking of taking the weekend off. Do you think that would be okay? I could leave Ban in charge. He's very responsible."

"It should be fine. What will you do?"

"I'll go to Macau. I haven't been in a while."

"Do me a favour. Don't leave all your money with Stanley Ho," Uncle said. Ho was the only person legally permitted to operate casinos in Macau.

"He has enough of it already. I thought I'd spread it around a bit this time. There are some new restaurants I want to try, and there's a mama-san who enjoys my company and has been asking me to come stay with her."

"Have you thought of paying a visit to Zhuhai? It's right next to Macau."

"Why would I go there?"

"I'm curious to hear first-hand what you think of Tse's watch factory."

"Those goddamn watches are making Tse's gang a fortune. He can't even come close to meeting demand."

"I know that, but what I don't know is why he hasn't expanded production. Is it that the manufacturing process is too complicated, or is he having trouble getting permission from officials in the SEZ? Or does he simply not want to saturate the market?"

Fong pressed on the horn as he passed a truck that was weaving in and out of its lane. "I swear, even the truck drivers don't have licences," he muttered, and then turned to Uncle. "I'll try to take a trip there. Maybe the mama-san will come with me. If she does, I'll buy her a watch."

"She'd want a fake Rolex?"

"Why not? Who's to know its fake?"

"She will."

"She'll appreciate the thought," Fong said.

"Enjoy your weekend in Macau." Uncle laughed. "And don't bother bringing me back any gifts."

Fifteen minutes later, at ten to twelve, they reached the Pearl Boat. Fong parked directly in front. Uncle got out of the car and stood on the sidewalk, examining the neighbourhood. The restaurant was to the far right of a set of revolving doors that led into a two-storey mall. To its right was a line of shops, some of which weren't occupied and had FOR LEASE OR PURCHASE signs in their windows. Across the street were four apartment buildings, identical in design and each about thirty storeys high. The buildings were mainly concrete and brick and looked dull and institutional. Uncle saw that cranes were still in place around them and trucks were parked beside them. "Those buildings don't look occupied," he said to Fong.

"That's the way they do things here. They build them first and then worry about filling them. Eventually — in fact, probably sooner rather than later — they'll all be filled and this mall and the stores will be doing a booming business."

"How can they be sure about that?"

"I don't know, but so far no one in Shenzhen has lost money by putting up an apartment block or building a mall on spec. Businesses and people just keep coming here. There seems to be an unlimited supply of both."

"How did Ms. Gao find this place?" Uncle asked, pointing to the restaurant.

"I don't know for certain, but I suspect she's invested in it or the mall. So make sure you like the food."

Fong opened a plate-glass door and stood to one side. Uncle walked past him into a restaurant that looked big enough to accommodate several hundred customers. But only a handful of its fifty or so tables were occupied, and those by what looked like construction workers on lunch break.

Fong approached a hostess. "We're joining Ms. Gao. I believe she has reserved a private room," he said.

The hostess, dressed in a tight-fitting blue cheongsam, nodded and said, "Yes. Ms. Gao has already arrived."

Fong looked at his watch. "We're early, but we still couldn't get here before her."

"I'll take you to the room," the hostess said.

Uncle had met Ms. Gao and Chen Meilin several times with Fong, always in Shenzhen, and the meetings had always focused on business. He had met Meilin more often, as she often accompanied her husband when he came to Hong Kong — trips that typically ended with Uncle buying them dinner in an expensive restaurant in Central. Despite his extra interactions with Meilin, Uncle couldn't say that he knew either of the women very well.

Ms. Gao lived in Beijing with her husband, and she made no bones about how important he was — and, by extension, how special she was. Uncle wasn't good at gauging a woman's age, and Ms. Gao's was particularly hard to pinpoint. Given that her husband was in his seventies, he thought she could be in her sixties, but she looked nowhere that old. She dressed as fashionably as any Hong Kong matron, was always impeccably groomed and made-up, and her skin seemed taut and unmarked by anything more than a few crow's feet around her eyes and some lines at the sides of her mouth.

Fong was intimidated by Ms. Gao, partly because of her Beijing connections, but in truth, mainly by the way she treated him. Legally they were partners, but Ms. Gao spoke to Fong as if he were an employee, and a lowly employee at that. After the first time he experienced this attitude, Uncle pulled Fong aside and told him he didn't have to put up with it. Fong just shrugged. "She's married to Liu Huning and she's old enough to be my mother. But even if I didn't care about her connections or being respectful to my elders, she's smart, she's tough, and she knows more about doing business than I'll ever know. She can be as rude to me as she wants, as long we keep making money."

Uncle didn't find Chen Meilin any more convivial. She was a tiny woman and quite reserved, but Uncle quickly learned that her physical size and apparent timidity weren't any indication of her character. When she spoke, it was with an authority and conviction that only the most self-assured can muster. Her husband rarely argued with her when she made her pronouncements, and Uncle himself learned that disputing them would result in frosty silence.

But, their characters aside, the two women had good business minds and Uncle respected them. He didn't know where their expertise came from and he had never bothered to ask. It was enough for him that they were competent and reliable partners — and, of course, married to two of the most powerful men in China and Shenzhen. In effect, the two women had created a protective shield over Uncle's businesses that he could never have generated on his own. For that he was grateful. For that he was willing to smile and bow in their direction as he entered the private dining room in the rear of the Pearl Boat.

"Uncle, how are you? It's always such a pleasure when you join us," Ms. Gao said when she saw him.

He didn't know why, but she seemed to like him. It wasn't something he took for granted. "I promise you, the pleasure is as much mine," he said.

The two women sat together facing the door. Uncle and Fong took chairs directly across from them. A pitcher of water and two teapots were in the middle of the round table, and five places had been set for lunch.

"Leji didn't come with you?" Uncle asked.

"He had some last-minute business to take care of at the department," Meilin said. "He should be here soon."

"If you're hungry we can start lunch now. I'm sure he won't mind," Ms. Gao said.

"No, I would prefer to wait for him, although we could discuss some business in the interim."

Ms. Gao patted the file folder that lay in front of her. "Have you seen the final numbers from our last quarter?"

"I saw only some preliminary ones, and I have to say they were impressive. Has there been any dramatic change over the past two weeks?"

"Look for yourself," Ms. Gao said as she passed stapled sets to Uncle, Fong, and Meilin.

Uncle read the first page, his index finger moving down the columns of numbers. Smiling, he turned to the next sheet. When he had finished all six pages, the smile had turned into a grin. "Record revenues and profits — this is even better than I expected."

"And those numbers were achieved without opening a new warehouse," she said.

"Did we raise our rates?" Uncle asked.

"No, although that is something we're considering for the next quarter," Ms. Gao said. "I think we have to attribute these outstanding numbers to good management."

"Was there increased demand?"

"Yes, but the demand had to be accommodated. I thought we were operating at maximum capacity, but evidently we weren't," Ms. Gao said, and then lifted a teacup. "I believe thanks are in order for a job well done, to both Meilin and Fong."

Uncle reached for the pitcher and poured water into his and Fong's glasses. "Here's to Meilin and Fong," he said, raising his glass.

Meilin began to lift her teacup but then froze as her attention moved to someone entering the room. Uncle turned and saw Liu Leji standing in the doorway.

"What's happened? You look like you've seen a ghost," Meilin said to her husband.

Liu shook his head and pressed a hand against the door jamb as if he needed support. "Lau is dead and Peng has been arrested," he said.

15

LIU WALKED AWKWARDLY TOWARDS THE TABLE, WHERE everyone sat in stunned silence. He sat down in a chair between his wife and Uncle, poured a glass of water, and said, "What I really need is a beer."

"Fong, get a waiter," Ms. Gao said.

Fong rose from his chair. "I'll have a beer as well. In fact, bring enough for everyone," Uncle said.

No one spoke until Fong had left the room, and then Ms. Gao turned to her nephew. "How did you hear about Peng and Lau?"

Liu furrowed his brow. "Peng's secretary told me about him when I called there a couple of hours ago," he said finally.

"How did she know?" Uncle asked.

"She was in the office this morning when a PLA officer arrived with a full contingent of soldiers. She heard the officer tell Peng he was under arrest, and then they dragged him out of the building."

"And how do you know about Lau?"

"I called a friend who's a captain in the PLA to ask about Peng. He confirmed that Peng was picked up as part of a campaign against corruption in the SEZ," Liu said. "Then I asked him how many other people had been arrested. He was reluctant to talk but I pressed him, and eventually he told me that Lau was the other main target. Lau evidently knew the PLA were coming to get him. He tried to sneak out through the back door of his office building to avoid them. They caught up to him in the back alley, and some supposedly undisciplined soldiers shot him."

"*Supposedly* undisciplined?" Uncle asked.

"My contact used the word *undisciplined*. But where the PLA is concerned, I don't believe in accidents or happenstance. Things happen for a reason, and there's usually an order attached to that reason."

"Was it just Peng and Lau who were targeted?" Ms. Gao asked calmly.

"Peng and Lau were the priorities, but I'm told there's a list of other officials and businessmen whose lives might get turned upside down," Liu said.

"How did Peng and Lau get to the head of the list?" Ms. Gao asked.

"They've been fools, splashing money all over the city and drawing attention to themselves. The final straw was side-by-side mansions they're building outside the city, near Wutong Mountain."

"That is so damn stupid it makes me angry," Ms. Gao said.

"Do you know who else might be on the list?" Meilin asked.

"No, and I didn't think it was wise to ask."

"Is it possible some of us could be on it?" she asked.

"There's no chance anyone from the family has been named. Your uncle would have been told if that was the case.

Besides, we've had absolutely nothing to do with either of those men," Ms. Gao said.

"That's not true for Uncle and Fong," Meilin said. "They've often interacted with both of them."

"That is a fact, and even if the PLA doesn't know that now, we have to assume they will after they've finished interrogating Peng," said Ms. Gao.

"And we have to assume he'll talk," Liu said.

"Does Peng know anything about our business arrangement?" Ms. Gao asked Uncle.

"Only three people on my side know about our partnership: me, Fong, and my administrator. No one else knows anything. Who have you told?"

"No one."

"What about your husband?" Uncle asked.

"We have quite deliberately told him nothing about the specifics," Ms. Gao said. "He knows we're doing business here, but he has no detailed knowledge about the nature of the business or our partners."

"If that's the case, then it seems to me the only people at risk are those who have dealt directly with Peng, and that's Fong and myself," Uncle said.

Ms. Ko's eyes were focused on Uncle, as if she was weighing the ramifications of what he'd just said.

Liu took a swig of beer and glanced sideways at his aunt, whose attention was still fixed on Uncle. "What was your arrangement with Peng?" he asked abruptly. "I know you were paying him, but how was it done?"

"We made only cash payments and never anything of an ongoing nature," Uncle said. "He set a price for approving whatever project we brought to him, we'd haggle, we'd settle, and then I put money for him into a Hong Kong bank account."

"The account was in his name?"

"No, it was a corporate account. I never bothered to actually check its official company registration to see if his name was attached to it."

"Are you saying you paid him money to get his approval for our warehouses?" Liu asked.

"Of course, and I'm surprised you would have thought otherwise," Uncle said. "But we were careful. The payments were always in cash, in odd amounts, and the money was accounted for as part of our construction costs."

"I apologize. My question was for confirmation and not meant as a criticism," Liu said. "From what you're saying, there's nothing to connect Peng to the warehouses other than that he approved their construction and your business plan, and that was his responsibility anyway."

"I'm not aware that he did anything exceptional or even slightly out of the ordinary in terms of evaluating and approving our proposals. We made sure our submissions met all the investment criteria, and all Peng did was process the paper."

"But is there anything to connect him directly to your organization?" Ms. Gao pressed.

"No. As I said, we were careful. There's no paper trail."

"Even if that is the case, there's nothing to stop Peng attaching your name to his problem," she said.

"I can't control what Peng tells the PLA or the Department of Justice, but I don't know why we would be of any more interest to them than the other businessmen whose investments he's approved. I imagine many of them have paid him far more than we did," said Uncle.

"Uncle is right," Liu said. "Over the past few years Peng must have approved a hundred or more applications that he's been paid for, so unless the PLA decides to round up every businessman in Shenzhen, it seems to me that we don't have that much to worry about."

"I still can't help feeling uncomfortable. I've lived through several government purges, and one thing I've learned is that it's hard to predict who will get caught up in them," Ms. Gao said. She turned to Uncle. "My husband was sent to a re-education camp during the Cultural Revolution. He spent six months there and another two years working as a farm labourer."

"I don't see a similarity between the Cultural Revolution and the PLA going after a couple of corrupt officials in Shenzhen," Uncle said.

"All I'm saying is that when the PLA gets the bit between its teeth, sometimes it doesn't want to let go of it. We need to be very careful," she said, and paused. "I know we have capable people managing the warehouses, but can they maintain the status quo without Fong or Meilin being physically present?"

"What are you suggesting?" Uncle asked.

"I think Meilin should come back to Beijing with me and Fong should stay on the Hong Kong side of the border for the next week or two, until things settle down or become clearer," Ms. Gao said. "Leji can keep his ear to the ground here and I'll ask my husband to make some discreet enquiries in Beijing. We can stay in touch by phone."

"I have to say I agree with keeping a low profile," Liu said.

Uncle finished his beer and reached for a second. "I have a question along those same lines, and I want to apologize in advance if it gives offence," he said.

"Go ahead," said Ms. Gao.

"My understanding is that you've been thinking of buying a house in Hong Kong. We're certainly holding enough cash on your behalf to make that happen, but I'm wondering if that would be a wise thing to do right now."

"It wouldn't be wise and I won't be doing it," she said. "But I am nervous about leaving all our money in your bank accounts."

"They're company bank accounts, not my accounts."

"You know what I mean," she said with an impatient, almost dismissive wave of her hand. "My point is that if your luck runs out and the PLA target you, they could find the money and convince the banks to freeze the accounts, or even seize the money."

"These are Hong Kong banks we're talking about."

"They're banks that are becoming friendly with China. And with the handover looming, I can't imagine many of them are prepared to anger the Chinese government."

"I can't argue with you there. I'll do whatever you want me to do with the money. After all, it is yours," Uncle said.

"I'll need to make some phone calls, but I should have things sorted out in a day or two as to what I want you to do."

"That's fine. Let me know when you've made your arrangements."

"I'll talk to Leji. He can pass on the information to you," Mrs. Gao said.

"Will you want all your money or will you leave enough to fund your portion of our expansion plans?"

"I think we should put the expansion plans on hold," she said, and then added quickly, "But for now, leave the money we've budgeted in the accounts. There's no point in moving funds back and forth between banks and incurring fees."

"I'll wait for your instructions," Uncle said, and then smiled wryly. "Well, this meeting didn't turn out the way we'd expected, but it's undoubtedly a good thing that we were all here in Shenzhen when Peng took the fall. At least we had the opportunity to talk it out face to face."

"Hell, who knows, he might survive," Liu said.

"I don't think that's likely. It seems to me the only question that remains is whether he'll take other people down with him," Uncle said. "And with that front of mind, I hope no one objects if Fong and I leave now. I believe the sooner we're across the border and back in Hong Kong, the sooner all of us can start to relax."

"That's very sensible," Ms. Gao said.

Uncle pushed back from the table and stood up. Fong and Liu did the same, but the two women remained seated. "Stay in touch. We need you to keep on top of what's happening with Peng," Uncle said to Liu.

"I'll do everything I can, but I can't be too intrusive."

"The moment you hear anything, I want you to call me."

"I will."

Uncle nodded and then said, "Ladies, have a safe journey back to Beijing."

Uncle and Fong didn't speak until they had left the restaurant and were in the car. Then it was Fong who said, "Holy shit, what a mess this could be."

"Where did you plan to leave the car?" asked Uncle, ignoring Fong's comment.

"How long do you think I'll be leaving it?"

"We'd better count on a few weeks."

"Then Ming should have it."

"In that case, drive to Ming's factory. He can take us to the train station," Uncle said.

"Okay, boss."

"And Fong, do me a favour and don't ask me any questions for a while. I need to think through what just happened to us."

"What did happen?"

"That is a question."

16

UNCLE AND FONG WERE ON THE TRAIN AND HALFWAY to Fanling before Uncle spoke again. "What did you think of Ms. Gao's reaction to the news about Peng?" he asked.

Fong turned away from the window and gathered his thoughts. "She didn't seem especially rattled, but then neither did Meilin. Liu was the only one who displayed any sign of emotion."

"Maybe because he's the one stuck in Shenzhen. He can't just packs his bags and fly to Beijing."

"I can't imagine the PLA laying a hand on any of them."

Uncle shrugged. "Ms. Gao said one thing that was absolutely correct: the PLA is hard to control. Once they start down a path, there's no telling when or where they'll stop. One positive thing is that both they and the Chinese legal system normally move quickly. Liu should know soon enough what will happen to Peng and should be able to give us some idea about what else could be in store."

"What's the best-case scenario?" Fong asked.

"We want the speediest possible resolution."

"How fast can it go?"

"I've heard of people who were charged, tried, made an appeal, and were executed all within a week."

Fong stared at Uncle. "Do you really think they'd execute him?"

"I have no idea, but it is possible — maybe even likely. In China, sentences sometimes have less to do with punishing the crime than helping the state send a message," Uncle said. "The government has a lot invested, politically and otherwise, in Shenzhen and the other special economic zones. If they're serious about ending corruption, then killing Peng would be a clear message. Lau is dead already, and that could have been deliberate."

"Then why didn't they kill Peng?"

"I've always suspected that the money flowed through Peng and that Lau was dependent on him. If that's true, then they've kept Peng alive to get as much information out of him as they can. When they've finished milking him, they'll get rid of him."

"That won't be good for us," Fong said.

"That isn't necessarily the case," Uncle said. "Liu was correct when he said Peng extracted money from hundreds of investors in Shenzhen. We're simply one of many. If the prosecutors or the army goes after every investor who paid a bribe, they might as well shut down Shenzhen, because there'll be no one left doing business there."

"Does Peng know we're triads?"

The question surprised Uncle, but then he realized he'd never actually discussed with Fong how much their various partners knew. "I'm sure he has suspicions, especially after meeting Tse, but they were never voiced. I certainly never talked to him about our Fanling roots," Uncle said. "The Liu family knows, and in a strange way I think that's one reason why they chose us as their business partners."

"Why is that?"

"I think they believe it gives them leverage if ever there's a falling out between us."

"Well, it's a good thing Peng doesn't know about us, because for sure he'll blab."

"Yes, he will, but I'm hoping the PLA has no interest in pursuing investors and will focus their questioning on which officials are taking bribes."

"Do you really believe they will?" Fong asked. The train was starting to slow as it neared Fanling.

"If the government wants to keep investment money flowing into the SEZs, it's the only approach that makes sense. Punishing investors whose only crime was to play according to the system would be stupid. As I said, it would drive investors out and discourage any new ones. The zones are too important to Beijing and the long-term economic health of the country to allow that to happen."

"You've convinced me," Fong said. "Let's just hope the powers that run Shenzhen think the way you do."

"I suspect we'll know soon enough," Uncle said as the train stopped at Fanling station. "If, in a week from now, Peng has been executed, I'll be taking that as a positive — if gruesome — sign."

The two men left the train. It was late afternoon, but Uncle felt as if the day had gone on much longer. Normally he would have dropped into the office, but despite his conversation with Fong, his head was still full of questions about Shenzhen, and he knew he wouldn't be able to concentrate. "I'm going to walk to my apartment from here," he said to his Straw Sandal.

"Do you want to grab something to eat?" Fong asked.

"No, I'll get something later from the restaurant down-stairs. Besides, you can go to Macau tonight if you want — you don't have to wait for the weekend. If you leave now, you can catch a jetfoil and be there in time for a late dinner."

"Okay, I think I'll do that — but I want you to stay in touch. I'll be staying at the Lisboa. The mama-san always takes a suite there when I visit. Her name is Jessie Ng."

"If anything happens, you'll hear from me."

"Uncle, are you going to give Xu and Tse a heads-up about what happened in Shenzhen?" Fong asked.

Uncle smiled. Fong's breezy nature sometimes made it easy to overlook the fact that he had a fine mind. "Phone calls to both of them are the first thing on my list of things to do when I get home," he said. "If everything is quiet in their zones, it's going to make me suspect that Shenzhen is an isolated event, one that has more to do with Peng and Lau flaunting their wealth than it does with some broader government anti-corruption campaign."

"Let's hope you're right," Fong said, and then checked his watch. "I'm going to take a taxi back to my place so I can pack. Do you want me to drop you off at your apartment?"

"No, I'm going to walk. The exercise might help clear my head," Uncle said.

September in Hong Kong was still hot and muggy, with the late afternoons particularly vulnerable to sudden cloud-bursts, but on this day the sky was cloudless and the humid ity was low. Uncle's route from the station to his apartment took him past a newsstand where he often bought the racing form, and a bakery that sold fresh buns stuffed with barbe-cued pork. On most days he would have stopped, but even the aroma wafting from the bakery wasn't tempting enough to draw him inside. His mind was locked onto the events of that day in Shenzhen, and there was no room for distraction.

His apartment was above a Cantonese restaurant that hadn't changed much in twenty years. It still had the same owner and basically the same menu, and Uncle either ate there or bought takeout three or four nights a week. Thoughts of food did cross his mind as he walked past its front door to the stairs up to his apartment, but he decided to wait. What he needed first was a cold beer and an hour or so in his chair to do some thinking.

He entered the apartment and went directly to the fridge, opened a bottle of San Miguel, and carried it to the living area. He took a deep swig and then put the bottle on the table to his right while he reached for his cigarettes. He lit a smoke, placed the pack and his lighter next to the ashtray on his left, and then reclined the chair until his feet were waist high.

Was that a message Ms. Gao was sending me today, or am I simply being paranoid? he thought. It was in his nature to worry. As a young triad he had learned quickly that nothing could be taken for granted, and as he rose through the ranks that belief became an irrefutable tenet. If it wasn't the Hong Kong police looking for ways to infiltrate and bring down the gang, it was other gangs prodding and poking as they looked for weaknesses they could exploit. He had cut a deal with the police — with Zhang Delun, the man Liu Leji had spoken to — that provided them with some protection, but he knew that was good only for as long as Zhang was in place, or until some unforeseen event cratered the agreement and forced Zhang to move against them. He had also worked hard at creating alliances with other gangs. Fanling hadn't come under serious threat for many years, but he knew all it would take to pull things apart was a new Mountain Master like Wu in Tai Wai New Village, someone with ambitions that went beyond his own borders, or a gang whose circumstances forced them to attack other gangs in order to survive.

Then there were the economic realities. He had virtually emptied the reserve fund and tapped out their lines of credit at the bank to make the investments in Shenzhen. Now the income the gang was generating in Shenzhen and Xiamen was quickly rebuilding those resources, but he was facing a dilemma that had the possibility of becoming a crisis. If the PLA, if any part of the Chinese government decided to bring down the hammer on the Ming garment factories and their warehouse operations, the gang would lose nearly all its capital, its access to credit, and a huge portion of its cash flow. If that happened, there would be only one person to blame, and that was him.

Uncle had known he was taking a risk when he put so much money into the factories and warehouses, but when he weighed the risks against the rewards, he thought the potential returns justified the investment. So far he had been proven correct, but if those businesses were closed or taken over by the Chinese government, the cash flow they generated would go up in smoke.

What was odd was that he hadn't envisioned so much risk when it came to putting up the money to build the warehouses; all of the initial money had come from the gang, not the Liu family. He had assumed that the Liu family would make sure the warehouses were full and that profits were as good as guaranteed. It had been an accurate judgement, but he had also assumed that the Liu family was untouchable and that by proxy it would provide protection for the gang. It was those assumptions that Uncle was beginning to doubt. After learning about Peng and Lau, it hadn't taken very long for Ms. Gao to decide to return to Beijing with Meilin and to move their share of the cash on hand out of the company bank accounts. She had agreed to leave the portion they'd decided to reinvest, but Uncle wouldn't be surprised if, when the transfer request came through, it would be for all the money.

We are their only weakness, he thought as he finished the last few drops of his beer. *No one else knows about our business relationship. Ms. Gao is afraid that the PLA will pursue our connection to Peng and get their hands on Fong or me, and that we'll squeal. So she wants as much distance between us as fast as she can get it, and of course she wants to get her hands on the money.*

Uncle lowered the chair, slid to the floor, and walked to the kitchen with the empty bottle. He placed it on the counter, opened the fridge, and took out another beer. When the cap was removed, he opened a small drawer and took out a black notebook. He turned to the back page, walked over to the phone, and called Xu's office in Xiamen. The woman who answered told him Xu was on the factory floor with the owner.

"Get him, please. Tell him Uncle is calling and it's urgent," he said.

As he waited, his thoughts returned to the Liu family. Ms. Gao had disappointed him — he hadn't expected her to panic at the first sign of trouble. While she had seemed outwardly calmer than her nephew, her actions seemed a truer indication of her feelings. That thought irked and frustrated him in almost equal measure. If she had been another Mountain Master he wouldn't have hesitated to share his feelings. But this was different, and now something he'd always sub-consciously known was glaringly obvious: he was far more dependent on the Liu family than they were on him. They could disown him at the drop of a hat and there wasn't much he could do if they did. Hell, he might not be allowed to cross the border again, let alone find a way to retaliate. The only leverage he had was his ability to make money for them and the fact that they trusted him.

"Uncle, what's going on? The secretary was quite alarmed," Xu said.

"We have a problem in Shenzhen. Peng has been arrested and Lau was shot trying to escape the PLA. They're on an anti-corruption crusade, but so far Peng and Lau are the only casualties," Uncle said. "It happened this morning, so it's too soon to know who else might get caught up in the mess. My hope is that the PLA will concentrate on the people taking bribes and not on those giving them."

"Are Fong and Ming alright?"

"Ming has nothing to fear. He knows absolutely nothing about our deal with Peng," Uncle said. "Fong returned to Hong Kong with me a few hours ago. He'll be on his way to Macau by now to spend the weekend. Neither he nor I will be crossing the border again until we know for certain what's going on."

"What about the Liu family?"

"As long as Liu Huning is a member of the Standing Politburo, I can't imagine the PLA will go near them, but the way Ms. Gao acted, you'd think they were facing immi-nent arrest."

"You don't sound pleased with her," Xu said.

"I'm not, but there's nothing I can do about that situation right now. All we can hope is that she's never put in a situation where she has to choose between us and her own interests. I suspect she'd throw us over without a second thought."

"That's not good."

"I know, but it isn't something we're facing yet. And truthfully I think Leji is made of sterner stuff. Hopefully she'll spend more time in Beijing and leave Shenzhen to him and us," said Uncle.

"What will happen to Peng?" Xu asked.

"He'll be charged, tried, convicted, and then either shot or jailed."

"He's not a bad guy," Xu said. "I mean, when you bribed him, he stayed bribed; he never came back for seconds and he always delivered."

"Is your guy in Xiamen as reliable?"

"He is."

"Is he safe? That's one of the reasons I'm calling. It would be useful to know if this anti-corruption thing is limited to Shenzhen or if every zone is getting the same treatment."

"He was fine when I talked to him an hour ago," Xu said.

"That's good to hear. I'm hoping that Peng and Lau were targeted for being overtly extravagant, which we're told they were."

"My guy here lives a simple life. I don't know what he's doing with the money he's raking in, but for sure he's not flaunting it."

"Still, you should give him a heads-up about Peng."

"I will. Have you spoken to Tse yet?"

"He's my next call."

"I'll handle it if you want," Xu said. "We're scheduled to talk in an hour. We're trading watches for bags."

"I'd appreciate that," Uncle said.

Xu was quiet for a moment, then said, "Things have been going so well that we should have expected a bump in the road."

"As long as it's just a bump and not a landmine that blows up in our faces," Uncle said. He put down the phone. He'd been swigging beer while he talked to Xu and had distractedly finished the bottle. When he went back to the fridge for another, he discovered there were none. "Shit," he muttered.

A few minutes later he walked into the restaurant downstairs, placed an order, and then, while his meal was being made, went to the newsstand to get a racing form. When he returned to the restaurant, he bought four beers to take upstairs with his food. Going directly into the kitchen, he put three beers in the fridge and then stood at the kitchen counter to eat, the mound of glimmering slivers of wok-fried beef and soft egg noodles quickly disappearing. When he was finished, he opened another beer and retreated to his chair with the racing form and a pen.

He lit a cigarette, took a deep, satisfying puff, and opened the form. Horse racing, or more specifically betting on horse racing, was his sole hobby, and one of the few things that allowed his mind to focus on something other than business. Before the Sha Tin racetrack opened in 1978 that had entailed making the trip from Fanling to the Happy Valley Racecourse on Hong Kong Island twice a week, on Wednesday nights and Sunday afternoons. Now the horses ran at Happy Valley only on Wednesdays and at Sha Tin on Sundays. Sha Tin was in the New Territories and much closer to Fanling, but that convenience hadn't changed Uncle's track preference. While Sha Tin was newer, could hold close to 90,000 people as opposed to Happy Valley's 55,000, had two track surfaces that were longer, wider, and able to accommodate a greater variety of races than the tight turf course at Happy Valley, Uncle didn't have quite the same affinity for it. Happy Valley had been built in 1845, and even though it been modernized many times, it had a historic aura, a sense of timelessness that appealed to Uncle's romantic attraction to the spectacle of horse racing.

The opening of Sha Tin had presented another challenge for him. Now, in addition to the myriad variables he normally considered, he had to factor in the differences between the two tracks in terms of surface and configuration. Races of the same distance, even if both were run on turf, were marginally quicker at Sha Tin. As he began to analyze the Sunday card, his pen marked the pages with question marks, exclamation points, and numbers. It was a process that would continue until he was physically at the track and almost right up to post time. It amazed him that, no matter how often he read a race's form, he always found a new nuance to consider.

It had been Fong who introduced Uncle to horse racing. For Fong it was just another form of gambling, but to Uncle each race was a mathematical puzzle that had to be dissected and understood. It was his judgement against the oddsmakers, against the betting public, and there was nothing more satisfying than handicapping a race correctly.

As was his habit, he took a preliminary look at all the races and made his initial assessment. Unusually, though, his mind wandered several times and he found himself staring

blankly out the window onto the street below. The events
of the day in Shenzhen had shaken him. Not so much the
loss of Peng and Lau; he hardly knew Lau, Peng had never
been a friend, but the two men must have been aware that
their behaviour carried risks. What bothered him most and
what kept creeping into his mind was the reaction of the Liu
family. There had been a touch of panic in Leji's voice when
he asked about the arrangement Uncle had with Peng. And
what about Ms. Gao? Uncle tried to remember her manner
when she asked him to transfer the cash the gang was holding for the family. She had seemed calm enough, but there
had almost been a sense of finality in her request. It was as
if she were closing the door on their partnership.

"Shit," Uncle said and sat up in his chair. He picked up
the phone and called Xu.

"Hey, Uncle," Xu answered.

"Have you spoken to your man in Xiamen?"

"I spoke to him and Tse twice," Xu said. "All is well in both
zones as far as we can tell. No one has been arrested and no
one seems particularly concerned or surprised about what's
going on in Shenzhen. According to our zone contacts, Peng
has been out of control for quite a while, spending money
right, left, and centre. It was bound to draw attention and
they're not shocked that it has."

"None of them are worried about Peng implicating them?"

"Implicating them in what? They operate completely independently of each other. Peng has no idea about our business
arrangements here and, as you know, they're different than
they are in Shenzhen."

Uncle nodded. Rather than paying for project approval
in Xiamen, the gang was putting cash into a numbered

company's Hong Kong bank account every month. "So no worries on your end?" he repeated.

"We aren't taking anything for granted and we'll be alert, but so far, so good," Xu said.

"And Tse feels the same way?"

"Nothing he's heard from his people in Zhuhai is giving him any concern."

"I should call him."

"He thought you might, but he told me he'll be out for most of the night."

"Then I'll call him in the morning," Uncle said, and hesitated.

"Are you okay, boss?" Xu asked, always sensitive to Uncle's moods.

"I'm not pleased with the Liu family's reaction to what happened today. I can't stop thinking about it," Uncle said. "They've made a point of stressing how much our relationship depends on trust, but I sense that our definitions of trust are quite different. We value trust because in tough times it can offer protection. I can't shake the feeling that the family has a more pragmatic attitude."

"What do you mean by that?"

"Maybe I'm reading too much into it, but I can't help thinking that their form of trust is somewhat less binding. I can imagine it changing depending on the circumstances," Uncle said. "Bluntly, I have my doubts that these are people we can count on in a difficult situation."

"What does this mean for our business with them?"

"Right now it means nothing until the dust settles and we know where we are with the PLA," Uncle said. "But once things calm down, we need to talk about how we move with the Lius. We have too much capital tied up in projects with them to become hostages to their whims."

Xu was the one person within the gang structure whom Uncle felt comfortable sharing his concerns with. Xu never overreacted; he understood that just because Uncle was talking about something didn't mean change was imminent. "We are making a lot of money with them, though, and the only people listed as owners of those warehouses are us."

"Both things to be considered when the time is right," Uncle said. "Now listen to me, if you get wind of a problem emerging in Xiamen, I want you on the first plane for Hong Kong out of there."

"You can count on that."

"Good. Let's stay in touch even more than usual," said Uncle, and then put down the phone.

He looked at his bottle of beer. It was empty. *Three down and three to go,* he thought. Even with the racing form to distract him, it was going to be a long night. As he got up to walk to the fridge, the phone rang. He turned back and picked up the phone, expecting it to be Xu. Instead he heard Wang's worried voice.

"Boss, we have a problem. That fucker Wu has been at it again," Wang said.

"What's he doing?" Uncle asked.

"Tai Wai has been selling drugs out of a massage parlour in Fanling about a kilometre from our offices. One of our forty-niners heard a rumour about it this morning and went to check. He called me an hour ago to confirm it was there and that it had been dealt with. He and a Blue Lantern shut it down."

"How long had it been open?"

"The woman who owns the parlour said they've been using her place on and off for a couple of weeks."

"You said you knew this an hour ago. Why didn't you call me then?"

"I wanted to wait until our men got back from the hospital."

"Our men were hurt?"

"No, the opposite. Ho — the forty-niner — and the Blue Lantern laid a beating on the two guys from Tai Wai who were working in the parlour. Ho swears they were provoked and acting in self-defence. The bad news is that the Blue Lantern has quite a temper and appears to have lost control. The guy he was hitting is in rough shape, which is why they took him to the hospital."

"How rough?"

"They were afraid he was going to die before they got him there. He didn't, but he's in intensive care and the doctors don't sound positive about his recovery."

"What about the other man?"

"He was put in a taxi and told to get his ass back to Tai Wai."

"So Wu will already know what happened."

"I think we can take that for granted," Wang said. "Do you think he'll retaliate right away?"

Uncle shook his head. "Give me a minute. I'll be right back."

Not more than a minute later he put a fresh bottle of beer on his table and slid into the red leather chair. "I didn't need this tonight," Uncle said.

"We don't need it anytime, but we weren't the ones sneaking into someone else's territory to peddle drugs."

"Knowing Wu, he'll be on the phone telling the other Mountain Masters that two of his men were in Fanling visiting a sick aunt when they were ambushed by our men and beaten almost to death," Uncle said. "He'll twist and turn it so that however he decides to respond will appear to be justified."

"So you think he'll retaliate?"

"I don't know, but to be safe you should keep as many men on the street tonight as you can," Uncle said. "In the meantime, I'll start calling Mountain Masters to give them our side of the story. They all know my position on drugs, and most of them are aware that I've been saying no to Wu's requests to sell in our territory."

"Let's just hope that guy doesn't die," Wang said.

"Indeed, that would complicate things," Uncle said. "By the way, what's the name of this Blue Lantern who lost his head?"

"Kwok, Sonny Kwok."

"Should we keep him?"

"He's been with us for only three months, and until today he was making a sound impression," Wang said. "He's big, tough, follows orders well, and is intensely loyal. I think he'll make a great forty-niner as long as he can learn to keep his temper under control."

"Talk to him about it, see how he reacts, and then decide if you want to keep him or not."

17

UNCLE WOKE UP TO SEE LIGHT POURING THROUGH HIS bedroom window. He sat up, surprised, looked at his watch, and saw it was ten past seven. He couldn't remember the last time he'd slept so late. He was normally awake before six and greeting the sunrise as he made his way to Jia's Congee Restaurant. His mouth felt like he'd been eating mud and his head was thick. *You idiot! Six beers was too many,* he thought.

He couldn't remember when he'd gone to bed. After talking to Wang he had made phone call after phone call to Mountain Masters, some of whom had already heard from Wu. On balance he thought it had gone well and that they believed his version of the events. That didn't mean they all agreed with him or that Wu didn't have some sympathizers, but his intent had been to blunt any excuse Wu might have to retaliate, and he thought he had accomplished that — with one caveat. If the triad in hospital died, he knew some of the Mountain Masters would turn a blind eye to whatever Wu chose to do.

After the last phone call his mind had still been churning. Knowing he wouldn't sleep, he opened the racing form and started to burrow into its numbers. He had left the chair three times — once to get a fresh beer, the second time to pee, and the third to get his last beer and a fresh pack of cigarettes. He had dozed off at one point but roused himself and did at least another hour of work on the form before making his way to the bedroom. When he put his head on the pillow, he had fallen asleep almost at once, the combination of beer and factoring countless numbers in his head having driven the Liu family and Wu from his thoughts.

Uncle went into the kitchen. The light on his answering machine wasn't on, but he checked for messages anyway and was pleased there were none. He phoned Wang. "Is the Tai Wai guy still alive?" he asked when Wang answered.

"He was an hour ago."

"Good. And it was a quiet night in the town?"

"Nothing out of the ordinary happened."

"I spoke to just about every Mountain Master, so they know our side of the story. That might be enough to inhibit Wu."

"Our men will stay on alert."

"At some point I'll have to call Wu, but not until we're sure the guy is going to live."

"What will you tell him?" Wang asked.

"Exactly what I have been telling him. Hopefully what happened at the massage parlour will demonstrate how serious we are."

"Are you going to the office this morning?" Wang asked.

"I'll go after breakfast."

"I'll see you there."

Uncle put down the phone, took a jar of Nescafé instant coffee from the cupboard, put a heaping teaspoonful into a mug, and poured hot water into it from the Thermos that sat on the counter. As he sipped, he made a mental list of things that needed to be done that day. Because of Xu and Fong's frequent absences from the office, he had been doing more administrative work than was typical for a Mountain Master, but he didn't mind, since it kept him in touch with the nuts and bolts of the business. Speaking of which, he thought, one of the people he had better talk to was John Tin, president of the Kowloon Light Industrial Bank. The gang did nearly all its banking there and had multiple accounts, including those for the warehouse operations.

Uncle finished his coffee, made his way to the bathroom, and half an hour later left the apartment freshly showered and shaved, wearing a freshly cleaned suit over a crisp white shirt, and holding the racing form in his hand. About halfway to Jia's he stopped at a newsstand and bought the *Oriental Daily News* and *Sing Tao*. He quickly scanned the front pages; when he saw no mention of Peng or Lau, he tucked the papers under his arm.

"You are late this morning. Are you feeling well?" Jia asked when he reached the restaurant.

"I drank too much last night."

"You aren't as young as you used to be," she said.

Uncle smiled. Jia always said that the only two men she cared about were him and her husband. "Did you keep my table?" he asked.

"Of course. I'd never let anyone else sit there until you've had your breakfast."

He followed her to the booth farthest from the front door. "I need something substantial this morning that isn't too spicy," he said as he slid into it. "I'll have Chinese sausage and diced pork belly, a hundred-year-old egg, and scallions, and bring me a double order of youtiao."

"There isn't anything better for a hangover than youtiao dipped in congee," she said.

He opened the *Oriental Daily News*, then moved it to one side as Jia brought a pot of jasmine tea to the table and poured him a cup. He picked up the cup and sipped repeatedly as he read the paper more carefully; still he couldn't find a word about Peng, Lau, or Shenzhen. *Sing Tao* was equally lacking in news about any of them. Uncle wasn't sure if that was good or bad but, his curiosity satisfied, he turned to the racing pages in the *Daily News*. The newspaper's handicapper was very good, but because his recommendations were closely followed and backed, they rarely generated decent payouts. As a result, Uncle was more interested in what the handicapper had to say about Uncle's preliminary picks. To his chagrin, he and the *News* handicapper agreed on three races. This didn't mean Uncle would abandon his selections, but he would consider other choices if the odds were too short.

Jia's arrival at the table with the congee and its add-ons interrupted Uncle before he could see what the *Sing Tao* selector had written. He put aside the papers and focused on his food. "The youtiao was freshly made for you," Jia said, putting a plate with three pieces on the table.

He smiled as he picked up a stick of golden-brown fried bread and found it warm to the touch. He added the scallions and white pepper to the congee, dipped the bread into it, and took a large bite. The bread was so soft he hardly had to chew. He finished the entire stick before turning to his meats and egg.

By the time he had finished eating, Uncle felt almost normal and his head was clear. When Jia came to take away the congee remnants, he asked for a second pot of tea and then lingered for ten minutes reviewing what the *Sing Tao* horse-racing expert thought of Sunday's card. He had picked only one of Uncle's horses to win. It was with his mood much improved that Uncle left Jia's for the walk to his office.

Fridays were typically hectic as the gang prepared for a pickup in business at the massage parlours, mini-casinos, and street markets, so Uncle wasn't surprised to arrive at the office and find it humming. He greeted the staff and asked them if there was anything urgent he had to attend to. When there wasn't, he told them he needed privacy until they heard otherwise. With that he went into his office and closed the door behind him.

He sat at his desk and looked at the income reports from the day before. Normally, reviewing them was how he began his day, but this wasn't a normal day. He reached for the phone and dialled Shenzhen.

"Director Liu's office," a woman's voice answered.

"This is Mr. Chow from Fanling. Could I speak with Director Liu, please?"

"Just one moment," she said.

"Uncle, how are you?" Liu said seconds later.

"That depends partly on how you are."

"Considering the circumstances, I'm okay."

"Did Meilin and Ms. Gao go back to Beijing last night?"

"They're leaving this morning."

"Has Ms. Gao decided where she wants me to send her money?" Uncle asked.

"Not yet. I imagine she'll talk it over with my uncle when she gets back to Beijing."

"That makes sense," Uncle said, surprised that Liu had

mentioned his uncle. It was the first time Liu had acknowl-
edged his direct involvement.

"Did you speak to your colleagues in Zhuhai and Xiamen?"
Liu asked.

"Yes, and everything was calm there."

"I was told the same by my contacts, so it appears that this
anti-corruption campaign is limited to Shenzhen."

"Has anyone been arrested beyond Peng and Lau?"

"Not that I've heard, but the contacts in the PLA I spoke to
were reluctant to discuss the matter in any detail," Liu said.
"One of them did tell me that the orders to pick up Peng and
Lau came from the top, but other than knowing that, he said
information is being tightly contained."

"Is that normal?"

"With the PLA one is never sure what's normal."

"Maybe things are simply on hold until they finish questioning Peng."

"That is a possibility," Liu said. "I have no doubt they'll get
everything out of him he has to give. But as to where that
will lead or how vigorously they'll pursue his information,
I have no idea."

"It sounds like this could drag on for some time."

"For days most certainly, and maybe even weeks, though
I can't imagine Peng will resist answering their questions
for any length of time — if at all."

"I agree, but what matters is if their interest in him ends
when he incriminates himself or if they decide to take it
further," Uncle said.

"Well, regardless of how that plays out, in the meantime
all we can do is run our businesses the same as usual."

"So you'll still be directing shipments to the warehouses?"

"Of course. They're necessary to the economic well-being of the zone. There's no reason not to keep them busy."

Uncle hesitated, not sure he should raise the concerns that had nagged at him the night before. Then he thought, *What the hell.* "I have to say, Leji, that Ms. Gao didn't seem quite so positive about maintaining the status quo."

"My aunt is very cautious. She's also highly suspicious."

"Suspicious? Have we done anything that would cause her to doubt our commitment and trustworthiness?"

"It has nothing to do with you," Liu said quickly.

"Then what does it have to do with?"

"It isn't something she would like me discussing."

"Hey, we're partners or we aren't. And our necks are on the line far more visibly than yours. If there's a chance someone wants to chop our heads off, I expect some kind of warning," Uncle said. "Leji, you don't let partners get blindsided."

"Believe me, if there was something definite I could tell you, I would, but there isn't," Liu said. "My aunt has survived — and helped my uncle survive — their ups and downs within the Party by anticipating trouble. It's true that she often imagines threats where there are none, but in the past, when the threats turned into reality, at least she and he were prepared."

"Who would threaten a member of the Politburo Standing Committee, or his wife?"

"You could have asked that same question thirty years ago, when he was Deng's assistant and they were running the Chinese economy. Their positions didn't protect them them from being demoted to nothing jobs that were meant to humiliate them," Liu said. "You could also have asked that question twelve years ago, when they were running the economy again, only to find themselves exiled to labour camps for years and their immediate families being subjected to abuse by the Red Guard."

"But Deng is premier now."

"Yes, but he's only one member of the Politburo. There's no more Mao, no more chairman with almost total power."

"Are you saying that Deng is being challenged?"

"No," Liu said loudly. "I'm simply trying to explain that there are twenty-five members on the Committee, and not all of them are aligned with the premier and not all of them agree with opening up our economy the way he's done. But even if they do disagree with him, it's highly unlikely that any of them would dare to take him on."

"But your aunt is afraid they might go after him indirectly, by targeting your uncle. A man who's been joined at the hip with Deng for fifty years."

"It was her first thought," Liu said with an uncomfortable laugh. "She can't see a shadow without imagining something terrifying lurking behind it. Both Meilin and I have told her she's being too dramatic; trying to connect the downfall of a couple of minor party officials to a broader conspiracy is completely far-fetched."

"Still, it's her past experiences, not just paranoia, that are behind the way she feels," Uncle said.

"That's true. And although times have changed, her need to be cautious hasn't."

"Which helps explain why she wants me to move your money out of our bank accounts."

"Only some of our money."

"Whatever the amount, I think I understand her better now. I'm grateful to you for sharing that information with me."

"Information that perhaps I shouldn't have shared, and which I never want you to repeat, not even to your closest colleagues."

"You have my word on that."

"Good. Now I need to get back to my work here," Liu said. "Once I have her banking instructions or if I hear anything else of interest, I'll call. And I'll expect the same from you. But other than that, I suggest you stay in Hong Kong and go about your normal activities until the situation is absolutely resolved."

"That is my plan." Uncle put down the phone and sat back in his chair.

Liu's forthrightness about his aunt had surprised him, but as he thought about what Liu had said, it started to explain why Ms. Gao had reacted so suspiciously. She knew first-hand how fickle and brutal the Chinese Communist Party could be. Being on top or in a position of power didn't mean you were immune to swings in mood or policy. She had seen her husband's career and fortunes collapse twice before. It was only natural for her to be wary, and Uncle silently chided himself for not being perceptive enough to grasp that.

With that in mind, he called John Tin at the Kowloon Light Industrial Bank and was immediately put through to him.

"Uncle, how nice to hear from my favourite customer," Tin said.

"Except you may not like what your favourite customer will be wanting you to do," Uncle said.

"I can accept anything other than your closing all your accounts and moving to a new bank."

"Well, I'm not going to do that, but I will need you to move a substantial amount into what I expect will be a foreign bank account," Uncle said. "I don't know how much yet or where it's going, but I wanted to give you fair warning."

"Do you have any idea how much?"

"Just a second," Uncle said as he opened a desk drawer and took out the latest bank summaries. "The money will be coming from our five warehouse accounts. According to my quick calculation, it will total about ten million HK dollars."

"If you're sending the money overseas, do you want it sent in HK dollars or converted to American dollars?"

"What makes the most sense?"

"I'd be surprised if the overseas bank didn't prefer American dollars, and if that's the case you're better off converting them here, because I can give you our preferred rate."

"Okay, I'll let you know what we decide," Uncle said. "Now, one more thing, since I'm moving the money from five accounts, should we send it in five separate transactions or can we combine the funds and send them in one shot?"

"The five accounts represent five different registered companies. I would maintain that integrity. It's much cleaner from an accounting and tax viewpoint. You don't want to raise any red flags at Internal Revenue."

"That was my thinking as well."

"When do you expect to make this transfer request?"

"Sometime in the next few days, maybe even later today. Is that a problem?"

"No, we can handle it."

"Thanks, John."

"Uncle, I have a few questions that you might think are none of my business, but we've known each other a very long time."

"Ask away."

"Are you starting to wind down these companies?"

"No."

"Do I have any reason to worry about the loans we've made to you?"

"No."

"Is this kind of transfer going to be a regular occurrence?"

"I don't think so."

"Good, because those companies and the Ming factories have been making you more money in the past year than during the very best years of doing business the old way."

"I know, and they're nice clean businesses that are of no interest to the police."

"I didn't want to say that," Tin said.

"But you've been thinking it."

"I have."

"Me too. Now let's just hope we can keep things going in the same direction," Uncle said.

He was sitting back in his chair feeling satisfied with the way the morning had gone when Wang suddenly appeared in his doorway.

"I just spoke to the hospital. The guy is hanging in there."

"That isn't particularly encouraging."

"My experience is that if they're going to die, they usually do it quickly," Wang said. "Every hour this guy survives adds to his chances of making it."

18

THE NEXT THREE DAYS PASSED SO SLOWLY THAT UNCLE wondered if time was playing tricks on him. The businesses in Fanling almost ran themselves and didn't need his involvement. He touched base with Ming and a couple of their warehouse managers in Shenzhen and was told that everything was operating normally. He phoned Xu and Tse every day, but they had nothing new to report. He did not hear from Liu or Ms. Gao, but given how calm things were in SEZs, he saw no reason to reach out to them. Once he called the Lisboa Hotel in Macau to talk to Fong, but there was no answer in the mama-san's suite and he didn't phone again.

The one piece of definitive news had come from the hospital. Wu's man had been taken off the critical list and was on the mend. That said, Uncle still wasn't ready to call Wu, and Wang was keeping their men on alert.

On Sunday he went to the races in Sha Tin, and even those four hours seemed to drag. He felt engaged during each race, but he spent most of the time between events thinking about what was going on in Shenzhen. He couldn't get rid of the feeling that things weren't quite right there. He had nothing specific to pin his unease on; it just worried him that it was so calm. He sensed danger but was frustrated that he couldn't say exactly why. During his years as a triad, Uncle had always trusted his instincts. Now they were screaming that trouble was brewing. *Stop being paranoid. You're over-thinking this. Concentrate on the racing form,* he told himself several times, but after a few minutes his mind would drift back to Shenzhen.

He stayed at Sha Tin until the last race and left the track with a profit of eleven thousand HK dollars stuffed into his suit pockets. A win like that usually lifted his spirits, but he remained in a sombre mood as the taxi took him back to Fanling. The thought of going home to his apartment held no appeal, so he told the driver to take him to Dong's Kitchen.

Dong's was on San Wan Road, near the centre of Fanling. It specialized in Cantonese cuisine and served all-day dim sum. The house specialty was chicken feet marinated in a secret sauce that combined sweet, sour, and the sharp heat of some unknown chili. But as good as the food was, that wasn't Uncle's main reason for going there. On Wednesdays and Sundays Dong's became one of the gang's betting shops, and despite the competition from the Royal Hong Kong Jockey Club's new outlet, it was managing to hold its own. Uncle attributed that to the talents of Tian Longwei, who had been running the operation for more than a decade. Uncle's trip to Dong's was motivated by a desire to talk to Tian, a man he trusted as much as Xu.

Tian had been Uncle's triad mentor and sponsor. He was the uncle of Tam, one of Uncle's friends who had made the swim from China with him in 1959. Tam had planned to join the triads as well, but he didn't have the stomach for the life and quit after a few months. Luckily for Uncle, that was time enough for Tam to introduce Uncle to Tian and for the two men to become friends and, later, confidants. Tian was now semi-retired and worked only on race days. He was in his sixties, but if anything he looked older. His hair was completely white, his face was etched with deep lines, his cheeks were sunken, he bent over when he walked, and he had trouble getting to his feet from sitting. His arthritis gave him constant pain, though he claimed that a new medicine was making his life more bearable. Uncle had suggested more than once that Tian retire fully and come to Dong's only when he wanted the company of colleagues. Tian always refused, saying that while his body was failing him, managing Dong's betting operations kept his mind sharp, and he wasn't about to give that up.

Dong's was still crowded when Uncle arrived. Some horse players were watching race replays on the televisions, either reliving wins or dissecting losses, while others had stayed to eat. Uncle saw Tian at his usual table near the back of the restaurant, a stack of betting slips, an adding machine, and a notepad in front of him. Uncle knew the day's cash returns were already stashed in the safe they'd installed in the restaurant owner's office. As he walked towards Tian, a forty-niner standing next to him nudged him and said something.

Tian looked up and smiled. "Hey, boss, we haven't seen you in here for a while," he said.

"I was at Sha Tin, and on the way home I had this sudden urge for Dong's chicken feet."

"How did you do today?"

"I won about ten thousand."

"Then I'm glad you gave them your business and not us," Tian said.

"How did we do today?"

"We're up about a hundred thousand."

"How large was the handle?"

"We're down a little bit from the same week last year, but it isn't too bad."

"That's good to hear," Uncle said. "You know I'm worried about the Jockey Club eating into our business."

"We have a few advantages. I think our location is better, we've built trust with our players over the years, and, of course, you can't get Dong's food at the Jockey Club."

Uncle pointed to the betting slips. "Are you almost finished with the day's accounts?"

"Five minutes more should do it."

"Can you join me for a beer and some dinner when you're done?" asked Uncle.

"Of course. Grab a table."

Uncle sat at a table off to one side, set against the wall.

Dong, the owner, ran over as soon as he saw him. He put down a pot of tea. "Uncle, it's an honour to have you back," he said. "Are you staying for dinner?"

"I'll order something to eat when Tian joins me. For now I'll have a San Miguel."

Uncle's first beer turned into a second as Tian's five minutes turned into fifteen. Uncle didn't mind waiting. There was something warm and welcoming about Dong's, and he always felt relaxed when he was there. The air was aromatic, the servers were polite, pleasant, and attentive without being pushy or rushing a customer through a meal — traits not easily found in many Fanling restaurants — and then of course there was the food.

"Sorry, I had to recheck some numbers. I have a boss who gets pissed off when they don't add up properly," Tian said with a smile as he finally joined Uncle.

"Having numbers that add up properly sounds to me like a perfectly reasonable request for a boss to make, but that's just my opinion," Uncle said, returning the smile. "Do you want a beer?"

"No, I'd better stick to tea. I'm on medication that doesn't react well with beer."

"You seem to be moving a little more easily."

"Not really, but it doesn't hurt so much when I do move."

"Can your medication handle Dong's chicken feet?"

"If it couldn't, I'd stop taking it," Tian said. "I don't have many pleasures left, and that's one I value."

Uncle held his arm in the air, which brought a server to the table. "A large portion of chicken feet with the secret sauce, an order of har gow, and some fried noodles with shrimp and scallops," Uncle said.

Tian poured tea and raised his cup towards Uncle. "Good health and good luck," he said.

"The same to you, my old friend."

Tian sipped at his tea and then eyed Uncle. "So tell me, what is it that's bothering you?"

"How do you know something is bothering me?"

"When you came through the door, you looked like the weight of the world was resting on those skinny shoulders of yours. I've seen that look too many times not to recognize it. In fact, the very first time we met, when Tam introduced us, you had it. I obviously knew what you'd gone through and didn't need to ask why," Tian said, "but today I don't know. So tell me, what's bothering my Mountain Master?"

"You know that I've put a lot of the gang's resources into Shenzhen and to support Xu in Xiamen?"

"I do, although I know absolutely nothing about the details. I will say it caused a lot of talk at first, but all I hear now is how much money we're making there."

"It has been profitable, and the assets we have there are worth many times more than the money we put into them."

"Then why are you concerned?"

"I'm afraid that the assets and the cash flow they provide could be at serious risk."

"How? From whom?"

Uncle took a swig of beer and slowly shook his head. "That's the problem. I don't know, or maybe I should say I'm not sure."

"You must have some idea or you wouldn't have mentioned it in the first place."

Uncle paused and pursed his lips, then shrugged. "Let me explain to you who we're doing business with and what's happened, and then you tell me if you think I should be worried."

"You flatter me with your trust, but go ahead. I'll listen as well as I can."

"It started with the clothing factory Fong was doing business with," Uncle began. Twenty minutes later he had finished. Meanwhile their food had arrived, but it remained untouched.

"That is a complicated situation," Tian said. "Have you spoken to Zhang Delun about this Liu Leji?"

"I did around the time Leji approached me. Zhang confirmed that he had spoken to him about me and said some very complimentary things about him. He said Liu is a man to keep an eye on because he's going to go far, and that I would be smart to associate myself with him."

Tian nodded. He was the person who had introduced Uncle to Zhang and had mentored them both during the initial stages of their establishing a working relationship. "I'm impressed if Zhang thinks that much of him."

"It isn't Liu who's my main concern, it's his aunt."

"So you've explained," Tian said, plucking a har gow from its basket. He ate the shrimp dumpling slowly and then took a chicken foot.

Uncle followed suit, his mood starting to improve as he saw how unperturbed Tian was by the recitation.

Both men ate until the chicken feet and har gow were gone and only a small cluster of noodles was left. Tian poured more tea, offered Uncle a Marlboro, and then lit both of their cigarettes. "Returning to your problem," Tian said, "it seems to me that at this very moment you really don't have one. All our businesses are operating as usual. None of our people or your partners have been detained or even spoken to. It sounds like this guy Peng and his friend Lau were out of control. You can't do what they did and then flaunt it so blatantly not to have the system slam you — especially a system that's supposedly opposed to anyone getting too far out in front of the pack."

"I know that's logical, and it's how Liu feels," Uncle said. "I also haven't heard much from him or Xu, or anyone else on the mainland, since Peng was arrested. If there was trouble, I know someone would have contacted me."

"Then why are you so worried?"

"I'm actually feeling less worried now."

"Ah, the power of Dong's chicken feet."

"No, the power of your ability to listen and provide perspective," Uncle said.

"If you don't mind me saying, you've always had a tendency to overthink things instead of trusting your instincts, and you have very good instincts. What are your instincts telling you about Liu?"

"He'll stay the course with us."

"How about his aunt? Has she cut and run?"

"She's nervous, and after everything she and her husband have gone through, who can blame her? But now that I think about it, she's been back in Beijing for three days now and hasn't followed up with a request to transfer their money out of our accounts."

"That's a good sign."

"That's a very good sign," Uncle said, finishing his beer. "I know I overthink things, but sometimes I get an idea in my head and I can't get rid of it. I'm like a dog chasing its tail, just running in circles. That's why I came here. Ideas that seem sensible in my head seem different when I talk about them out loud. You know, you and Xu are the only two people I feel I can say anything to. I don't know what I'm going to do if he ends up in Shanghai or if you ever retire."

"Do you want to know when I will retire?"

"You have a date in mind?"

"Yes. The day I die," Tian said with a laugh.

The two friends left the restaurant together, Tian's arm looped through Uncle's for support. They caught a taxi, and ten minutes later Uncle dropped off Tian at his apartment and continued on to his own. He went immediately upstairs, walked directly over to his chair, and picked up the phone. Despite — or maybe because of — telling Tian that not hearing from Liu, Xu, and Tse indicated all was well, it had sparked a need for confirmation. In rapid succession, he phoned them. Tse was in Kowloon but had spoken to his manager in Zhuhai, and the factory was operating as usual. Xu had just finished dinner in Xiamen with two of their partners in the leather business and reported that there had been no disruptions. Finally he called Liu.

"Uncle, do we have a problem?" Liu asked abruptly after he'd answered.

"No, and I know we agreed we wouldn't communicate unless there was one, but curiosity got the better of me about what's going on in Shenzhen."

"As far as I know, nothing has changed since the last time we spoke, but I have been keeping my ear to the ground. In fact, I spoke to a contact in the justice department this morning and got an update. If I'm interpreting what he said properly, this corruption sweep will start and end with Peng and Lau."

"What will happen to Peng?"

"He's been formally charged with corruption against the state. He's scheduled to be tried this Wednesday evening."

"How long will the trial last?"

"If he pleads guilty — which he would be smart to do — it will last less than an hour. If he disputes the charges, it could on for a few hours more. Either way, it will be over by Wednesday."

"That's a real rush to judgement," Uncle said.

"Why prolong things when the outcome is so obvious? And as far as I'm concerned, the faster it's done, the better it is for us."

"I'm not disputing that," Uncle said. "What kind of sentence will he get?"

"If he pleads guilty, he can expect a fifteen- to twenty-year jail term. If he doesn't, he could end up on his knees with a gun pointing at the back of his head."

"So as far as we're concerned, it's business as usual?"

"I see no reason to think otherwise," Liu said.

"What does your aunt have to say?"

"I was actually going to call you tomorrow to talk about her," Liu said. "She, Meilin, and I spent an hour on the phone this morning going over the warehouse expansion plans."

"You still want to move ahead with those plans?"

"We do, and no one is keener than my aunt."

"That is most reassuring to hear."

"Uncle, I know you weren't pleased when she told you she wanted to move our money out of the business accounts."

"I wasn't displeased," Uncle said. "It is your money, and you can do what you want with it."

"It was a knee-jerk reaction on her part. She's had three days to think about what happened here, she's spoken to my uncle, and she's decided to maintain the status quo."

"So now she doesn't want me to transfer the money?"

"Perhaps a modest amount, and there's no urgency about doing it immediately. She'll talk to you about it when she comes back to Shenzhen."

"When will that be?"

"She doesn't know yet. She wants to be absolutely certain that no further repercussions come out of the Peng affair."

"And Meilin?"

"She'll come when my aunt does."

"What do you think I should do about Fong?" Uncle asked.

"Do you absolutely need him to be in Shenzhen right now?"

"No, he can stay in touch by phone for at least a couple of weeks."

"That would be prudent. Let things settle. We can coordinate his return with my aunt's."

"I agree. I'll talk to him tomorrow," Uncle said. "And Liu, the next time you speak to your aunt, please pass along to her my appreciation for the trust she's showing in our partnership."

"Was it ever in doubt?" Liu asked.

"No, of course not," Uncle said.

Uncle put down the phone and drew a deep breath. The stress he'd felt at the Sha Tin Racecourse had started to ebb while he was at Dong's. Now it was almost entirely gone and he felt his body sag in reaction. He reached into the fridge for a San Miguel. *All that worrying for no reason. I'll sleep well tonight,* he thought.

19

UNCLE SLEPT WELL, ROSE AT HIS USUAL HOUR, HAD CON-
gee at Jia's, and was at his desk by seven-thirty, going over
the weekend accounts. The night street markets — now
selling fake designer bags and Rolex watches as well as
a wide variety of Ming Garment Factory clothes — had
increased sales and profits. On a year-to-year basis, business at their restaurants and massage parlours was flat. The
mini-casinos — typically one roulette wheel, a couple of
baccarat tables, and a large room for mah-jong — had had
a strong weekend, but wagers on the Sha Tin races at the
betting shops were well behind those from the year before.
Tian had been right that the Dong's takings had slipped by
only a bit, but the other shops were down almost twenty-
five percent.

At ten o'clock Uncle left the office and walked to a bakery across the street, where he bought a coconut bun and a
bottle of mango juice. When he returned, he found Fong in
conversation with his deputy Straw Sandal.

"You're back early," Uncle said to Fong.

"I took the midnight jetfoil."

."The mama-san didn't object to your skipping out?"

"I looked after her before I left. Besides, we've never spent three whole days together before, and I think we were getting tired of each other."

"How did you do at the tables?"

"I'd rather not talk about it."

Uncle smiled and shrugged. "Do you want to share my bun and juice?"

"I'll have some bun, thanks. Let me get a tea and then I'll join you in your office."

Uncle settled in his chair, tore the bun in half, and put Fong's piece on the far side of the desk. Fong appeared a minute later with a mug of tea. He sat down, put the mug on the desk, and devoured the bun in three bites. "Thanks, I needed that," he said and then pointed to the stack of papers in front of Uncle. "How was business this weekend?"

"Not bad, but the Jockey Club betting shops keep cutting into ours."

"It's got to the point where I expect that now," Fong said. "How are things in Shenzhen?"

"You haven't been keeping in touch with Ming and the warehouse managers?"

Fong looked momentarily pained, as if Uncle had reprimanded him. "This was my first weekend off in months, and you said you'd let me know if there was a problem."

"I wasn't being critical. I simply asked a question."

"I'm sorry if I sounded defensive," Fong said.

"Let's start over," Uncle said with a smile.

"Okay, how are things in Shenzhen?"

"Things are quiet in Shenzhen."

"You make that sound like they're too quiet."

"I didn't mean to," Uncle said. "It is also quiet in Xiamen and Zhuhai, so it doesn't look like this corruption eruption has gone beyond Peng and Lau. Peng is scheduled to be tried and probably sentenced on Wednesday. Our hope is that it brings closure."

"When do you think I can go back to Shenzhen?"

"There's no rush," Uncle said. "We should let the legal proceedings end and then give the situation more breathing room. I told Liu we'd go back when Ms. Gao or Meilin returns, which he thinks will be in a week or two. There's no reason to be the first to test those waters."

"But there's no reason I shouldn't be communicating with Ming and our warehouse managers?"

"Of course not. I just don't want you to cross the border until I think it's safe."

"That's fine; I've got lots I can do around here anyway. I haven't visited any of the street markets in ages. It will give me a chance to find out what else they want us to make."

"Before you start making those arrangements, do me a favour and call Ming and the others in Shenzhen," Uncle said. "Don't say anything about Peng and Lau unless they bring up their names. I'm curious to know if they've heard anything on their own."

"Okay, boss," Fong said. He started to stand up, only to sit down again and lean towards Uncle. "There's one thing, though, that was bothering me all the time I was in Macau."

"What's that?" Uncle asked.

"Ms. Gao," Fong said. "The more I thought about it, the more pissed off I got about her asking us to move their money out of the warehouse accounts. It was like she had already written us off."

"You wasted your energy getting pissed off," said Uncle. "She's changed her mind about the money. It's staying where it is."

"Good. Now that's the way I want a partner to act."

"Things are more complicated in China than they are here," Uncle said carefully. "Not everything is as it appears to be, and many things are done for reasons that aren't readily apparent. The deeper we get involved, the more time we need to spend trying to understand what's really going on around us. Taking things for granted or paying attention only to what's on the surface is an invitation to be blindsided."

20

ON WEDNESDAY AFTERNOON UNCLE MET FONG AT Dong's restaurant for dim sum. Fong was in good spirits. He had spent the previous two nights visiting street markets in Mong Kok, Tsim Sha Tsui, and Wanchai. He found business booming and Ming's clothes in great demand.

"We have six big-volume vendors in Mong Kok alone, and two of them are reselling our goods into Guangzhou and Macau. I spoke to Ming last night and told him we need to increase production. He also needs to add a couple of new lines, and when he's done that, we'll increase sales yet again."

"Can he increase production?"

"He's going to initiate a Sunday shift and, if he has to, he'll hire a night crew," Fong said. "Truthfully, Uncle, maybe it's time we started thinking about building another factory. We have the land we need, right next to the existing operations."

"Have you discussed the new plant idea with Ming?"

"He raised the subject with me."

"I don't see any harm in talking to him about what he has in mind, but we're not in a position to make any kind of commitment until this mess with Peng is behind us."

"There is no mess as far as Ming is concerned, or, for that matter, for any of our warehouse managers. For all of them it's business as usual. None of them said a word about Peng or Lau."

"That's good to hear," Uncle said, and then stopped speaking as the waitress reached their table. She brought them two bottles of San Miguel and a serving each of pork *siu mai* and Dong's special steamed chicken feet.

They tapped their bottles together and each took a sip. Then Fong said, "And nothing has happened in Xiamen or Zhuhai?"

"Nothing at all. According to Xu and Tse, the guys in those zones who are Peng's equivalents couldn't be less worried."

Fong took a *siu mai* from the basket, dipped it in chili sauce, and bit into it. "These are so damn good," he said a few seconds later. "I know you come here for the phoenix claws, but these and the steamed pork ribs are my favourites."

The two men ate quietly for a while, working their way through the first two dishes and then sticky rice stuffed with sausage, the pork ribs, and pan-fried turnip cake. They ordered another round of beer and sat back, contented.

"Did you see many of Xu's designer bags in the markets?" Uncle asked.

"They're everywhere, and they're popular as hell."

"Besides Hong Kong, Macau, and Guangzhou, he's now shipping them to Manila, Jakarta, and Bangkok," Uncle said. "He's working with two plants and negotiating to take production from a third."

"Have you given any more thought to taking an ownership position in them?"

"As long as we can maintain control of the plants' output, and unless the plant owners are in desperate need of a cash infusion, I prefer to keep our arrangements as they are," Uncle said, and then looked at his watch.

"Do you have a meeting?" Fong asked.

"No. Wang called me to say that Wu's man in the hospital is now officially out of danger. It's time for me to talk to Wu, and I've heard he starts drinking in the late afternoon, so I want to do it before he's too drunk."

"The men have been talking about Wu. They're really pissed that he won't back off."

"Maybe he'll get the message this time."

"Will you call him from here?"

"No, I'll go back to the office for the afternoon and then head to Happy Valley," said Uncle. "I'll also be talking to Liu today. Peng was scheduled to be in court this morning. It could be over by now."

"Will Liu know the result?"

"Oh yes, Liu will know. I'm quite sure he had someone in court this morning to observe," Uncle said, rising from his chair. "And now that I'm thinking about it, I don't want to wait until I get back to the office. Him I'll phone from here."

Uncle walked towards the rear of the restaurant, opened the door to the kitchen, and motioned to a man wielding a spatula over a wok. The man hurried over. "Mr. Dong, I need to make a phone call. Can I use your office?" Uncle asked.

"Sure, no problem. The door should be open," Dong said.

Uncle left the kitchen and in four steps was at the office door. He stepped inside a room that just had space for a desk, chair, filing cabinet, and the gang's safe. He sat at the desk, picked up the phone, and dialled the number of the customs headquarters in Shenzhen. A moment later he was connected to Liu's office, but his secretary said the director was out and she didn't know when he would be returning. "Shit," Uncle murmured.

"What's the news?" Fong asked when Uncle came back to the table.

"I couldn't reach Liu. I'll try again later. Let's head back to the office," Uncle said.

Fong stood up. "Hey, I was wondering, would you mind if I joined you at Happy Valley tonight?"

"No, that would be great. I can't remember the last time you did."

"Truthfully I find the action slow, which is why I prefer casino play," Fong said. "But after the beating I took last weekend in Macau, I'm thinking that maybe I need to give slow a chance."

"I've never found it slow. And let me remind you that it was you who introduced me to horse racing."

"I know. I spent ten minutes explaining how to read the racing form, and two weeks later you were a better handicapper than me," Fong said. "I hope you'll give me some of your picks for tonight."

The two men took a taxi back to the office. When they entered, Tan, the assistant White Paper Fan, ran over to Uncle. "I'm glad you're back. Someone from the customs department in Shenzhen has been calling."

"Who?"

"He said you'd know."

"Thanks," Uncle said. He walked straight to his office and dialled Liu's number.

"Uncle, I just missed you when you called earlier," Liu said.

"Thanks for getting back to me so promptly. I was wondering if you'd heard what happened with Peng."

"Yes, I had one of my people at the court. Peng pleaded guilty."

"What kind of sentence did he get?"

"As of today there's been no sentencing. The prosecutor asked the judge to postpone until Friday."

"Is that usual?"

"No. In fact it's quite odd."

"What could be the reason?" asked Uncle, sensing discomfort in Liu's voice.

"Maybe they're still trying to verify whatever information he gave them. They might want to hold off on a sentence until they're sure he was being truthful," Liu said.

"Is that a guess on your part or have you been told that's a possibility?"

"It's a guess."

"If that's the case, it worries me."

"Why?"

"They could be digging into his associates."

"Or they could just be trying to locate his money."

"Well, whatever the reason, it makes the outcome unpredictable," Uncle said.

"Not necessarily. According to my uncle, Peng and Lau's behaviour caught the attention of Beijing. He tells me Beijing doesn't want it to turn into a full-blown scandal. The SEZs are too important to let the corruption of some minor officials put them at risk. So, while they want to use Peng and Lau to send a message, they want it contained."

"Peng is no minor official. He ran the investment department in the zone."

"He's a senior administrator and that's all. On the scale of things in the government, he's insignificant. He wasn't even close to being on par with the party secretary or the PLA commander in Shenzhen."

"Or the customs director?"

"Yes, I am senior to him."

"So where does this leave us?"

"I could say it leaves us waiting until Friday, but I'm not prepared to do that. I'm as anxious as you are to get a firmer idea of the reason for the delay," Liu said. "And, I assure you, my aunt will be quite blunt about what she expects me to do. So when I hang up from you, I'll start making some calls and, if I can, I'll arrange to meet with someone in the prosecutor's office."

"Thank you. I appreciate the effort."

"Will you be reachable all day?"

"I'll be here in the office until about six and then in my apartment after eleven. In between I'll be at Happy Valley Racecourse."

"I'll try to get back to you before six."

Uncle put down the phone with a lot less enthusiasm than when he'd picked it up. *When the hell is this going to end?* he thought. He turned his chair so he could look down on the street. He wasn't sure how long he remained in that position. At some point the view of the street disappeared from his consciousness as his mind conjured up and factored the possible impact of events in Shenzhen. He was trying to remain positive, but when he thought about the delay in sentencing, all he could imagine were negative outcomes.

"Boss," Fong said loudly.

Uncle swung his chair away from the window and saw Fong in the doorway. "How long have you been standing there?"

"Not long, but I didn't want to disturb you. You looked preoccupied."

"Peng has pleaded guilty but they've put off his sentencing until Friday," Uncle said. "I've been trying to figure out if there's a hidden message in that."

"What did Liu say?"

"He thought it was odd but not necessarily a concern. He's making some calls this afternoon."

"Well, if there is a problem, it hasn't affected any of our businesses."

"That is comforting."

Fong stepped into the office. "You know, despite all the money we've made, there are days when I wish we hadn't gone into China. Things were simpler when all we had to worry about was Fanling."

Uncle shook his head. "In our life you either adapt to changing circumstances or you get run over. Sitting still and doing nothing is not an option. Going into China has had its challenges, but where would we be financially if we hadn't done it?"

"I know, and I'm not complaining that we did, but I just can't help worrying. When you were picked up at the train station and thrown into that cage, I worried whether I'd ever see you again," Fong said. "Fighting other gangs in Hong Kong is one thing, but trying to take on the Chinese government and the PLA is another."

"We're not taking on the Chinese government or the PLA. We're doing perfectly legal business there and nothing more,"

Uncle said, and tapped a stack of files that sat on his desk. "Now, Fong, you'll have to excuse me. I need to call Wu."

He had two phone numbers for Wu. No one answered the first. The woman who answered the second said he wasn't there and didn't know when he'd be back. Uncle did not leave a message.

Tan had left the files on the desk for Uncle to review. He opened the first and forced himself to concentrate on its contents. Two of the gang's massage parlours wanted to upgrade their facilities. They were operated by Yu, Uncle's deputy Mountain Master; although the request came from him, Tan had done a separate analysis and made a recommendation. To Uncle's relief, the two men's numbers matched almost exactly and Tan supported Yu's proposal.

Yu had been a member of the executive for more than twenty years and was now well into his sixties. He had been one of the first and most important of Uncle's supporters when he ran for Mountain Master, and Uncle had rewarded him by making him his deputy. But now Yu rarely attended executive meetings and was basically inactive — aside from his visits to the massage parlours — in the gang's day-to-day business. Uncle knew he should replace him as deputy, but he still valued his counsel and saw no pressing need to have a younger man in the job.

At the bottom of his analysis, the thorough Tan had typed in three possible places for Uncle's signature. One read "Approved," the next "Not Approved," and the third "More Information Required." Uncle signed under "Approved," closed the folder, and opened another. For the next three hours he worked steadily on the files, his mind focused on the minutiae involved in managing the gang and its operations. Some of the work should have been done by the White Paper Fan, and it would have been done by Xu if he had been in Fanling. Tan was a capable assistant, but Uncle wasn't ready to cede him the full authority of the position. And he actually enjoyed the work, if for no other reason than it reminded him of the more carefree days when he held the position.

At five-thirty he closed the last folder, bundled the files under his arm, and carried them to Tan's office. "Very nice work," he said as he handed them to the assistant. "Make sure you phone Yu tonight to tell him that his proposal has been approved."

He turned and was heading for Fong's office when he heard his phone. He hurried to answer it. "Yes," he said, before the sixth ring.

"This is Liu. I have news."

Uncle sat down in his chair. "I'm listening."

"I've just returned from the office of the procuratorate for the People's Court, where the friend of a very good friend gave me twenty minutes of his time," Liu said. "The bottom line is that the Peng affair is not as complicated as I feared."

"So he will be sentenced on Friday?"

"Yes, he will — sentenced to death."

"What?" Uncle said, stunned. "You told me he'd get no more than twenty."

"And I believed that, but Peng seems to have greatly offended people both here and in Beijing. They want him dead, so dead he will be," Liu said. "And I have to say, from our practical viewpoint it isn't a bad outcome, though even I will admit that the way they're going about this is particularly cold-blooded."

"What do you mean?"

"The reason for the delay is that the military procuratorate wants to take a crack at him to find out if any PLA officers were involved and if any bribes were attached to local military contracts," Liu said. "Given that he'd already agreed to plead guilty and was in the process of cutting what he thought was a deal with the People's Court procuratorate, Peng wasn't too keen on the idea. I can't say I blame him for that. The military prosecutors have a well-deserved reputation for being rather forceful in their questioning."

"Forceful?"

"Physical."

"Violent?"

"Not always, but sometimes."

"But you make it sound like he agreed to co-operate," Uncle said.

"Whether he agreed or not, they were going to talk to him. The guy I spoke to said they conned him into it," Liu said. "Even though they knew he was going to get the death penalty, the People's Court prosecutors told Peng they would recommend a prison term. They told him they were thinking of between ten and fifteen years, but if he co-operated with the military, they'd recommend ten."

"That is cold-blooded."

"As I said, a lot of people want him out of the way. And not all for the same reason, which I suspect has made his survival all the more tenuous."

"How much time will the military have with him?"

"He left the courtroom in military custody and they'll return him on Friday. Believe me, that's time enough for those guys to get everything out of him."

"And if he is sentenced on Friday, how soon will it be carried out?" Uncle asked, still processing the cruelty of it all.

"He'll be allowed to appeal, but that's a formality. I'd guess he won't be with us by two weeks from now."

"He doesn't deserve that type of punishment."

"Then he shouldn't have made a spectacle of his corruption when so much depends on the reputation and success of the special economic zones."

"I can't argue that he wasn't foolish," Uncle said.

"Anyway, soon enough we can stop worrying about Peng and get on with building our business," Liu said. "I'll stay in touch, and if anything happens that impacts us, you'll be the first to know."

"You mean I'll know before your aunt?"

Liu paused. "Perhaps not, but I'm sure you'll understand if that's the case."

"I will," Uncle said, and hung up the phone.

He closed his eyes and took several deep breaths. As tough as triads could be, they were at least bound by the Thirty-Six Oaths, which gave them a common code of behaviour. The PLA didn't seem to have any code at all. *How is this going to end?* he thought, just as his phone rang again. He picked it up. "Wei?"

"This is Wu. My housekeeper said you called."

"I did, but I didn't give her my name," Uncle said, his surprise evident.

"She worked for Lo before me. She recognized your voice."

"Then thank her for remembering me," Uncle said. "I was calling to tell you that your man in hospital is out of danger."

"That's supposed to make me happy?"

"If it was my man it would."

"Fuck you, Uncle."

Uncle sighed as he realized this was going to be a difficult conversation. "I don't understand why you have that attitude."

"Your people put him there."

"Only because you refused to respect our boundaries," said Uncle. "I told you how we would react if you tried to do business in Fanling. As I think you know, I'm a man of my word."

"I'm a man of my word as well," Wu said. "And let me tell you, this isn't over."

"Threatening us isn't going to — " Uncle began, and then stopped short as the line went dead.

21

PENG WAS EXECUTED TWO WEEKS LATER.

Uncle was leaving his apartment to go to Jia's for breakfast when his phone rang. He rarely got calls that early, and when he did, they invariably brought bad news, so it was with a slight hesitation that he said, "*Wei.*"

"This is Liu. I apologize for calling so early, but I thought you'd like to know that they shot Peng this morning at sunrise."

"How did you find out?"

"My contact in the prosecutor's office phoned me with the news."

"So finally it's done," Uncle said.

"Yes. It has been a difficult wait, but now it's over."

"And there's no indication that an investigation is still ongoing, that they're looking at other people who might have been implicated by Peng?" Uncle asked.

"My contact said — quite forcibly and without any prompting on my part — that the book is completely closed."

"That's very good to hear," said Uncle. "I'm meeting Fong for breakfast. He'll want to know when it will be safe for him to travel to Shenzhen."

"As far as I'm concerned, it's safe now. The passes I arranged for him and you are still valid?"

"I believe so."

"Then he should have no concerns, and I don't think you should either."

"I'll let you know when we decide to come over," said Uncle.

"That's fine. When I spoke to my aunt, she hinted that she might be going to Shenzhen in a few days. If she does, it makes sense to co-ordinate schedules."

"She'd come back that soon?" Uncle asked, making a mental note that Liu's aunt had indeed been the first person he called.

"Why not? There's no reason for her not to come," Liu said. "I know she feels our expansion plans have been on hold long enough. She's anxious to get started again."

"So are we. I'll talk to Fong about when he thinks he can get there."

"Are you implying that you'll just send him, that you won't be with him?"

"Our plan was always that he be the first to test those waters."

"Even though I'm telling you I don't think you have any reason to be worried?"

"I don't doubt you, Leji, but I am a cautious man, and I still have memories of being put in that cage at the station."

There was a pause. Uncle sensed that Liu thought he was being difficult.

"But Uncle, if my aunt does come to Shenzhen, she'll expect to meet with both of you. And of course Meilin and I would be there as well. In a sense we'd be restarting our last meeting, but this time on a better footing."

"I realize that's logical — "

"And there's one more thing," Liu interrupted. "My aunt wants to meet with you privately. She does want to move money from the warehouse bank accounts, but she prefers that the discussion take place with you alone. As cautious as you are, she is at least your match."

Uncle shook his head. He had no proof that anything Liu had said was untrue, and he couldn't argue that for all of them to meet together didn't make sense. To continue resisting would make it appear that Uncle was either cowardly or didn't trust Liu. Neither was an outcome Uncle wanted. "Okay," he said finally. "Finalize your aunt's schedule for her trip to Shenzhen. When that's done, set up a meeting. Fong and I will be there."

"I'll be in touch," Liu said.

Uncle put down the phone. The past two weeks had been excruciatingly full of worry. The worrying had begun when Peng did not make an appearance in court on the Friday after his plea. Liu had reported that he was still being held by the PLA, and he made the same report for the next five days. Every day added to Uncle's unease. What were the military interrogators asking Peng about? What was Peng telling them? Those two questions grew in intensity with each passing day. He tried to follow his normal routine and to hide from Fong and his executive team any anxiety he felt, but he had snapped at Liu on a couple of occasions, demanding to know why Liu couldn't get more accurate information.

Liu had someone observing in court when Peng finally made his return. "They broke him," he said. "My man said he could barely lift his head, and when he spoke, it was in a whisper. Even when they sentenced him to death, there was barely any reaction from him."

"Do we have any idea what he might have told them?"

"It couldn't have been much, because they didn't amend the charges against him. He was convicted of betraying his civilian office for personal gain, taking bribes in exchange for favours, and corrupting other public officials, but there wasn't a word about any involvement with military officers or contracts. That's a very positive sign."

"Unless you're Peng, because, positive or not, it isn't going to make any difference to him."

"I find your concern for Peng to be misplaced."

"He was reliable, honest with me, and not a bad man at heart. I admit that he got carried away with having a lot of money for the first time in his life, but in Hong Kong that's so commonplace it isn't worth mentioning."

"This isn't Hong Kong," Liu said. "And I don't think Peng is a subject worth addressing anymore."

"I agree, but he still has an appeal left, does he not?"

"It will be held early next week, but he has no chance of getting the sentence changed," Liu said.

That turned out to be true, and it had come down to waiting for the sentence to be carried out. It wasn't something Uncle thought about constantly, but every now and then an image of Peng would pop into his head, of him sitting in a cell. What was going through his mind? How did a man prepare himself for a death that was preordained? Did the seconds race by like hours? Did any part of the life he'd already lived have a single shred of meaning? Now it was over, and despite Liu's attitude that it was time to get back to business as usual, Uncle knew that a little piece of

Peng would continue to reside somewhere in his memory.

He left the apartment to walk to Jia's. The summer humidity had given way to more moderate heat and drier days, and he was taking advantage of them to walk as much as possible. He stopped at the newsstand to buy the *Oriental Daily News* before continuing on his way. As he neared the restaurant, he saw Fong approaching from the opposite direction. He waved, but Fong didn't notice him. Uncle smiled. It was perverse of him to schedule early morning meetings with the night owl Fong, but being Mountain Master gave him certain prerogatives, and deciding when and where to hold meetings was one of them.

"Hey, boss," Fong mumbled as they met at the entrance to Jia's.

"Sorry to drag you out so early, but as it turns out, the timing is perfect," Uncle said. "I just finished talking to Liu. Peng was executed this morning, and the family wants to get back to work in Shenzhen. Ms. Gao intends to go there in the next few days, and we're expected to join her."

"Poor Peng," Fong said.

"I know. I feel much the same way, but as far as Liu Leji is concerned, it's good riddance, and I'm not about to argue with him."

They entered the restaurant and walked towards Uncle's regular booth in the back. As soon as they sat down, Jia appeared with a pot of tea and another of hot water. She poured their first cups. "Same as usual, Uncle?" she asked.

"Yes, thank you."

"And I'll have whatever Uncle is having," Fong said.

When Jia had left, Fong leaned towards Uncle. "Are you serious about crossing the border so soon? I thought we were going to wait. I thought we'd see how it goes with me first."

"If we want to maintain a strong relationship with the Liu family, I don't think we have much choice. I don't want to offend Ms. Gao."

Fong nodded. "Then let's at least change it up a bit. Let's take a taxi to the border this time. We can clear Customs and Immigration and walk across."

"That isn't a bad idea."

"I'll get Ming to meet us on the other side. Do you want to schedule some time with him? He's really eager to talk about building another factory."

"We can talk to him in the car. You can tell him to come prepared to do that, but let's not plan anything else until we know when and where the Lius want to meet," Uncle said. "I may be ready to go to Shenzhen, but I'm not prepared to spend more than a day there. We go back and forth on the same day or I'm staying in Fanling."

22

UNCLE AND FONG LEFT FANLING JUST AFTER EIGHT FOR the trip to the Chinese border. They were in a green New Territories taxi, a common sight at the border, and the driver was an old friend of Fong's.

It was three days since Liu had told Uncle about Peng's death and about Ms. Ko's desire to quickly re-immerse herself in the business. He hadn't been exaggerating about his aunt. She and Meilin had flown into Shenzhen the night before and, along with Liu, would be meeting Uncle and Fong at the Pearl Boat at noon. Uncle wasn't sure that going back to the restaurant where they had first learned about Peng and Lau was good luck, but he hadn't raised the subject.

Though it was only a half-hour drive to the border, Fong had insisted they leave early. Traffic was heavy and slightly chaotic; cars coming from China, where they drove on the right-hand side of the road, had to move across several lanes to get to the left-hand side, which was the standard for Hong Kong. They hit heavy traffic about a kilometre from the border and then inched forward for about half that distance before coming to a full stop.

"We'll walk from here," Fong said to the driver, and then pointed over to the right. "There's a taxi stand on the other side. Be there by six and have your occupied light on. Don't leave, even if we're a couple of hours late."

Uncle and Fong got out of the taxi and saw they weren't the only people who intended to walk across the border. Uncle reached into his suit jacket pocket and fingered his permit and the pass that Liu had given him. It was the third time he'd checked that morning.

"This isn't too bad," Fong said. "They move pedestrians through quickly."

They got into a long line that fed into six booths, and shuffled forward. In less than ten minutes Uncle found himself in front of an immigration officer. Rather self-consciously he handed the agent his permit and the pass Liu had issued. The agent stared at the pass, then opened the booklet.

"How long do you expect to stay in Shenzhen?" the agent asked.

"Just today. I'll be returning to Hong Kong tonight."

"Enjoy your day," the agent said, passing the documents back to Uncle.

Fong was ahead of Uncle and his processing had been as speedy. He was waiting with Ming next to Ming's new Mercedes-Benz. He raised an eyebrow at Uncle. "That seemed easy enough," he said.

"Liu's pass hasn't lost its effect," Uncle said, and then smiled at Ming. If Uncle hadn't known about his transformation, he would never have recognized the factory owner. Ming had a proper haircut, his teeth had been repaired, and he wore only designer clothing — some of it knock-off, of course, but not all. He had also put on about ten kilos.

"I was telling Fong that it's so good to see you two again," Ming said. "I was beginning to worry that you'd forgotten about me. I mean, Fong phoned me quite often, but it isn't the same as being with old friends."

"Certain matters kept us on the Hong Kong side," Uncle said.

"Did it have anything to do with Peng?"

"You know about him?" asked Uncle.

"We just found out, and that's the only thing many of us have been talking about today. It was a shock to learn he'd been arrested, and almost unbelievable to hear that he'd already been tried, convicted, and shot."

"Chinese justice is swift," Uncle said.

Ming waved a hand in the air. "Chinese justice is shit. Once a man is arrested for anything he's as good as convicted. The police and the army never make a mistake, according to the way judges make decisions."

"Since I've had no experience with Chinese justice, I'm not in a position to comment," Uncle said. "But tell me, how did you find out about his arrest and execution?"

"Some officials attached to the People's Court called various businessmen to tell them."

"Why would they do that?"

"They were sending a message."

"What kind of message?"

'Uncle, I've never asked you directly if you cut a deal with Peng or what kind of deal it might be, and I'm not asking now. It's enough for me that the officials told us the next time they find corruption on this scale, they'll punish the bribe givers as much as the bribe takers."

"We've never bribed anyone, Ming, so you should have no concerns on that account," Uncle said.

"We have a few hours before we have to be at the Pearl Boat. How would you like to spend the time, Uncle?" Fong interrupted, none too subtly changing the subject.

"What do you suggest?"

"We have time to visit the factories, get up to date, and perhaps look at Ming's proposal for expansion."

"Let's do that, and on the way maybe Ming can start explaining what he has in mind."

"I'd be pleased to," Ming said.

The Mercedes smelled of new leather. "How long have you had the car?" Uncle asked as he slid into the rear seat.

"I picked it up last week, and this is its first real outing. You'll have to excuse me if I drive a bit slowly. The drivers around here don't care if they hit someone. In fact, most of them just keep going, if they can."

"Drive at any speed you want. I'm more concerned about arriving safely than quickly," Uncle said.

Ming eased into traffic and headed for the city. As the traffic around them thinned, he turned his head briefly towards Uncle and said, "I've prepared a written plan for the new factory for you to review. I'd build it next to our existing ones, and we can use the same basic construction. I figure it will pay for itself in less than a year."

"You aren't concerned about flooding the shirt market?"

"I don't want to make shirts there. A while ago Fong mentioned that designer jeans are a hot item and are selling for big prices. Since then I've been researching them. I believe we can copy just about any brand you can name — and make them for a twentieth of what some of them are selling for in Hong Kong stores."

"You haven't discussed this with Fong?"

"Not in any detail until now. I wanted to get my facts in order."

"Ming is right about the jeans market," Fong said. "It is hot, the volumes are large, and the profit margins are huge. Our customers would be climbing over each other to buy them."

"Would you make the denim at the factory?" Uncle asked.

"No, that's quite a specialized job. We don't have the expertise, and even if we did we'd need equipment that I'm not sure we could get our hands on," Ming said. "Where we are lucky is that most of the good denim is made in Japan. I've found three manufacturers who are prepared to sell to us as long as we pay in American dollars. Initially, of course, it would be cash up front."

"So we'd be running a cutting and sewing operation?" Fong asked.

"Primarily."

"Which means our equipment costs will be minimal," said Fong.

"That's right."

"I'm looking forward to seeing your numbers. If they're good, agreeing to build Ming Garment Factory Number Three doesn't sound like a hard decision to make," Uncle said.

"They're very good," Ming said.

Uncle smiled at his enthusiasm. "Who would have thought when we started that you'd end up with an empire."

"And who would have thought a few years ago that Shenzhen would look like this now," Ming said, gesturing out the window.

Uncle glanced right and left at the factories and apartment buildings standing on land that had been farms when he made his first trip to meet Ming. Now only about a kilometre of farmland remained between the outer edge of the city and Ming's factories, and Uncle assumed the speed and scale of development would soon swallow that up.

Two hours later they were on the road again, heading north to the Pearl Boat restaurant. The mood in the car was almost celebratory. After reviewing Ming's plans and budget, Uncle gave his go-ahead for Ming Garment Factory Number Three. The quick decision had surprised Fong, who was accustomed to a more deliberate Uncle.

It had all boiled down to two questions. "Are you confident that you can sell the volume of jeans that Ming says he can produce?" Uncle had asked Fong.

"If he can produce them at the costs he's projecting, I'll sell them all."

"And Ming, are those finished goods costs realistic?"

"I swear to you, Uncle, if anything, I've inflated them. I think I can actually come in lower."

"Then start construction as soon as you can," Uncle had said.

Uncle sat quietly during the ride, his mind focused on the meeting ahead. Fong and Ming chatted the entire time, which suited him perfectly. They reached the restaurant at ten to twelve and saw that Liu's government car was already parked outside.

"Do you want me to wait for you?" Ming asked.

"No, we'll catch a taxi back to the border," Uncle said.

"When will I see you again?"

"I'll be here tomorrow," Fong said. "I want to get started working on the new factory with you."

"And I'm not sure, but it won't be as long an absence as last time," Uncle said as he climbed out of the car.

Uncle and Fong walked to the restaurant entrance. "Business has picked up," Uncle said as he looked inside and saw that many of the tables were occupied.

"They've finished building the apartments," Fong said, pointing across the street.

They were met by a hostess who was coolly business-like until Uncle mentioned the name Gao. "I'll take you directly to their private dining room," she said, suddenly more welcoming.

The door to the dining room was closed when they reached it. The hostess knocked and waited. Seconds later Liu opened the door and greeted Uncle and Fong with a huge smile on his face. "Welcome, my friends," he said.

Ms. Gao and Meilin sat next to each other on the further side of the round table. They nodded at Uncle but didn't get up. He walked around the table and shook their hands gently. Ms. Gao had a pile of papers in front of her. Uncle pointed at them. "I assume we're going to continue the discussion we were having before we were so rudely inter-rupted," he said.

Ms. Gao laughed in a light, almost girlish way, and its tenor caught Uncle off guard. "It's so good to see you again, Uncle. I've been worrying about you," she said.

"I was sitting safely in Fanling, but I have to admit I was doing some worrying myself. I don't like uncertainty."

"That's a trait we share," she said.

"We've taken the liberty of ordering food to be brought in at one o'clock," Liu said. "We thought that would give us enough time to review the new warehouse proposals."

Uncle had thought that Peng might be the first topic, but seeing how relaxed the attitude in the room seemed, he guessed that Peng had already been scrubbed from memory. For the next hour they reviewed the plans for the coming year. Their cash flow was strong enough to enable them to build two new warehouses, and maybe even three.

"What do you think, two or three?" Ms. Gao asked Uncle.

"I don't like to put too much stress on our capital. I would be more comfortable if we maintained a healthy reserve."

"I agree, so let's go with two. Are you okay with that, Leji?"

"That's fine. Now we need to decide where to build them. We have seven possible sites," Liu said, spreading a map across the table.

Ms. Gao stood up. "If you don't mind, Leji, I'll let you start with Meilin and Fong. I need a few private moments with Uncle."

Even though Liu had mentioned she wanted to meet with him alone, the timing somewhat surprised Uncle.

"We can work on this without you," Liu said.

Ms. Gao smiled at Uncle. "You and I will find a quiet spot in the restaurant."

He followed her from the room. She made a quick right turn and walked directly to a table in the corner. As soon as she sat down, a server hurried towards them with a pot of tea and two cups. *This was preplanned,* Uncle thought.

"I hope you don't mind doing this," she said. "I have something I want to discuss with you that is quite personal."

"It isn't a problem, Ms. Gao."

"Please call me Lan. 'Ms. Gao' makes me feel old. I've been meaning to tell you that for ages."

"I've never thought of you as old," Uncle said. "And I'll be pleased to call you Lan."

"I have to say, you've never been what I expected," she said. She sipped tea, her eyes never leaving Uncle's. "When Leji suggested that we get into business with you, I was very reluctant. But he insisted that I meet you and that I'd find you look and act nothing like my idea of a triad. He was correct, of course, but I still had reservations that took more time to resolve. Now they finally are, and I have to compliment my nephew on his initial judgement that you are worthy of our trust."

"That's kind of you to say."

"You won't find many people who think I'm the least bit kind," she said. "I have a reputation as a hard, unfeeling woman. The truth is, I very often am that kind of woman, but if I wasn't, I wouldn't have survived the trials and tribulations of being my husband's wife."

"I've read about Premier Deng's life, and from what Leji told me about your husband, his seems to have run parallel."

"Xiaoping and Huning met during the Long March. Zhou Enlai brought them together. They remained loyal to him and to each other, which means they enjoyed success and failure in almost equal measure."

"Surely what matters most is that this recent chapter has the makings of a grand success."

"It's too soon to tell, but the early signs are certainly positive," she said, and then waved her hand in that dismissive way now familiar to Uncle. "But enough about my husband. He's not the reason I want to talk to you."

"What is?"

"Money."

"You want to move some out of our accounts?"

"Yes. Not a huge amount, but this business with Peng has made me nervous about accessing it. We have a bank in Hong Kong that we could have used as a conduit, but I heard through a confidential source that Peng used the same bank for some of his activities. That disqualifies it in my mind."

"I think that's a wise decision."

"That may be true, but it leaves me without a bank. I'm hoping that you might be able to help me in that regard," she said.

"What is it you want the bank to do, other than to be a depository for your money?"

"I still want to buy a house in Hong Kong, but I can't be identified as the owner. I need a bank that can help me work around the system."

Uncle nodded but said nothing as he calculated how close he wanted to get to this woman. *What the hell, we're in this deep,* he finally thought. "I think my bank might suit your needs."

It was her turn to hesitate, and he imagined she was going through the same thought process. "Your bank can accommodate the kind of privacy I'd need?"

"We own the bank. It's Kowloon Light Industrial, where we hold the company accounts," he said.

"You own that bank?"

"Not me personally, but my organization owns a piece of it and other triad organizations have shares. Together we own enough to control it," Uncle said. "But I have to stress that we've always allowed it to operate independently, as a proper bank. No one knows anyone else's business. The president, John Tin, is a man of the highest integrity who knows how to keep his mouth shut and protect his customers."

"Integrity is fine, but as I said, I need someone to help me work around the system."

"John is a creative banker. His integrity is rooted in his devotion to his customers, not to the banking rules of Hong Kong or anywhere else. If you want to buy a house anonymously, I can't think of anyone better to help you. He's also very adept at moving money offshore if you ever have that need."

"Will you make the introductions?"

"Of course. Just let me know when you want to meet him."

"Could you set up something for tomorrow?"

"If he's in Kowloon, I'm sure I can. I'll call him later. Do you want me to go with you?"

"I'd appreciate that."

"How will you get to the Hong Kong side? Will you drive or take the train?"

"The train."

"Then get off in Fanling. I'll meet you there and we'll drive the rest of the way together."

"Assuming that your banker is in Kowloon tomorrow, I think we have a date."

23

IT WAS ALMOST FIVE O'CLOCK BEFORE FONG AND Uncle made their way back to the border crossing. Lunch had been a long, drawn-out affair, with course after course served at a leisurely pace.

"This is more like a banquet than a lunch," Uncle had said at one point.

"Well, there are things to celebrate," Liu said. "After that unscheduled hiatus, our business is moving forward again, and in six months we'll have two new warehouses up and running."

Several times during lunch Uncle referred to Ms. Gao as Lan, and every time it drew curious stares from the others. "I told Uncle that from now on I want him to call me Lan," she finally said, and then turned to Fong. "But that doesn't apply to you."

"I never imagined that it would, Ms. Gao," Fong said.

At three Uncle excused himself and used the restaurant phone to call John Tin. He was in Kowloon, and an appointment was set up for Ms. Gao for the next day at one. He passed her a note with that information when he returned. She nodded and smiled.

When lunch ended, the five of them made their way to the street. Liu's driver brought his car over to the curb. Before she got in, Ms. Gao touched Uncle lightly on the arm. "Where can I reach you in the morning?"

"I'll be in my office by eight o'clock."

"I'll call before I head to the train station."

"Talk to you then," Uncle said.

"What was that about?" Fong asked as the car drove off.

"Ms. Gao — Lan — has decided that she and I are going to be friends."

"Better you than me," Fong said.

Uncle smiled and checked his watch. "I should call Wang to let him know we're on our way back. He was worried about us coming here."

"They don't have pay phones here," Fong said.

"I'll go inside. It won't take long. See if you can flag down a cab."

It took longer than he'd thought to persuade the restaurant manager to let him use the phone again, but eventually two hundred Hong Kong dollars did the trick. Uncle dialled Wang's number, half expecting to reach his answering machine, but on the second ring the Red Pole picked up. "*Wei*," he said.

"This is Uncle. Fong and I are getting ready to leave Shenzhen. We should be home in a couple of hours."

"Please get here as fast as you can, and come directly to the office," Wang said, his voice rising.

"What's happened?"

"Wu took one of our men off the street, cut his throat, and threw his body from a car in front of our office," Wang said. "Luckily we got the body inside before anyone called the police."

"How do you know Wu did this?"

"Our man had a note pinned to his shirt."

"What did it say?"

"*No one tells Tai Wai New Village how or where to do business.*"

"Wu is a stupid asshole," Uncle said, and then paused before asking, "How have you responded so far?"

"I contacted the rest of the executive committee to tell them what had happened and told them all to be on standby for a meeting when you get back."

"Good. That was exactly the right thing to do. We don't want to overreact. This is a time to think first and act later."

"But, Uncle, we can't take this lying down. They have to pay for this."

"And they will, but we have to be clever about how we do it," said Uncle. "Our response needs to be geared to bringing an end to the conflict, not escalating it."

"What do you have in mind?"

"Nothing yet, but I have a couple of hours to mull it over, and I'll see what Fong thinks," he said. "We should be in Fanling by seven. Call the executive and tell them to meet us at the office at eight."

"Okay."

"One last thing. Who did they kill?"

"Lam."

"If I remember correctly, he was initiated a year ago."

"That's him."

"Was he married?"

"No."

"And no children?"

"No."

"I was about to say that's a blessing, but he was so young, the fact that those things are denied him now actually makes it more tragic."

"Uncle, we need to get those fuckers," Wang said, his rage becoming more evident.

"I know we do," Uncle said. He paused again. "Fong and I will see you at eight."

Uncle left the restaurant to find Fong standing by a taxi. "There's a problem in Fanling," Uncle said quickly. "Wu killed one of our men, Lam. Wang is scheduling an executive meeting for eight o'clock."

"What the fuck!" Fong said.

"I know, Wu just won't back off. We're going to have to send him a message that will stick," Uncle said. "Now let's get to the border as fast as we can."

They climbed into the back seat of the taxi. "We're in a hurry," Fong said to the driver. "Take every shortcut you know, and don't be afraid to speed or cut corners. I'll give you a big tip when we get to the border."

Uncle turned to stare out the car window. Fong looked at him, noted the clenched jaw and rigid body, and knew he was seething. He had seen Uncle like this three or four times before, watching as he converted his anger into a calculated plan of action. Nothing seemed to scare him, nothing intimidated him, and no one person or gang could push him around. Fong sat back. This wasn't a time for him to speak. When Uncle had something to say, he'd say it. Until then, Fong knew he should be quiet.

The taxi driver took Fong's instructions to heart and raced through Shenzhen. Somehow he avoided an accident, didn't attract police attention, and came to a stop at the border crossing only twenty minutes after leaving the restaurant. Fong paid the fare and tipped him two hundred HK dollars.

When Uncle and Fong got out of the cab, they found the border quieter than it had been in the morning. In a matter of minutes they were handing their paperwork to a Chinese immigration officer. Uncle watched intently as the officer looked at his permit and Liu's pass. He waited for them to be passed back, but instead the officer picked up a piece of paper from his desk, read it, and said, "Could you come with me to the immigration office? There's something I need to clarify."

"Is there a problem?"

"No, I just need to sort out something."

Uncle hesitated, but he knew he had no other choice but to say, "Sure, I'll come with you."

Fong hadn't cleared Immigration yet and was close enough to hear the conversation. "Can I go with my friend?" he asked the officer.

"There's no need," the officer said.

"Maybe not, but I'd like to all the same."

"No, you can't. Is that plain enough?"

"There's no point in arguing," Uncle said to Fong. "I'll meet you at the taxi in a few minutes."

24

IT WAS A SHORT WALK TO THE ONE-STOREY BRICK office. The officer stood to one side to let Uncle enter first. Directly in front of him was a desk that ran from wall to wall. On either side of the desk were rows of benches on which sat several glum-looking men.

"Take a seat," the officer said.

Uncle did as he was asked and watched the officer go around the desk and into an office behind it. *Maybe they're calling Liu to make sure the pass is legitimate,* he thought, struggling to stay calm. Time passed slowly, five minutes seeming like fifteen. When the officer finally reappeared, he was accompanied by a man with a captain's insignias on his jacket. The captain caught Uncle's attention and motioned for him to join them. When Uncle approached, the captain said, "You can wait in my office."

"Wait for what?"

"I'm not in a position to answer your questions. You need to be patient."

Uncle walked into the office to discover that he and the captain would be the only occupants. The captain closed the door behind them and took a seat behind a desk. Uncle sat across from him.

"Can I use the phone to call Director Liu? I'm sure he can clear this up."

"Director Liu is in charge of customs. This is an immigration matter," the officer said. "Besides, I was told that you weren't to make any calls."

"Told by whom?"

"I don't think that matters."

"Can you at least give me some idea of what this is about?" Uncle asked.

"No."

"I am a citizen of Hong Kong."

"I can't comment on that or anything else."

Uncle took out his cigarettes and offered one to the captain. When he declined, Uncle lit his and took a deep drag. Two cigarettes later there was a heavy knock at the office door.

"Enter," the captain shouted.

The door opened and Uncle found himself looking up at four soldiers from the People's Liberation Army. Three of them held rifles against their chests. "What the hell is this?" he asked, his voice a mixture of anger and concern.

"My name is Lieutenant Ban," the soldier without a rifle said. "You are to come with us."

"Come where?"

"You'll find out when we get there."

"Then why would I come with you?"

"You don't have any choice," Ban said. "You either come peacefully or you'll be handcuffed, blindfolded, and led forcibly from this building."

"Am I under arrest?"

"You are being detained."

"Why?"

"We have our orders, and that's all I can say. I'm sure you'll find out more when we get to your destination."

"Which is where?"

"You aren't leaving Shenzhen, if that's what's worrying you," Ban said.

"There's a lot more than that worrying me," Uncle said, starting to rise from his chair.

Ban held out an arm and pushed Uncle back down. "Do we need to handcuff you or will you come quietly?" he asked.

"Can I make a phone call before we leave?" asked Uncle, trying one more time.

"No."

"I have a friend on the Hong Kong side of the border waiting for me. Can I at least let him know that I'm being detained?"

"No."

Uncle weighed his options. "You don't need to handcuff me," he said finally.

"Good. Then get up slowly from the chair and we'll escort you to the vehicles."

Lieutenant Ban led them from the building. Uncle walked behind him, a soldier at each side and one covering his back. Two jeeps were parked outside. "Get into the back of the second jeep," Ban said.

Uncle climbed in and was joined by a soldier. Ban and another soldier sat in front. "Let's go," Ban said.

They drove away from the border in the direction of the city centre. Uncle kept waiting for the jeeps to veer off the main road, half expecting he would end up at the compound of Quonset huts he'd been taken to before. But the vehicles kept moving in a straight line towards the city, which in some ways he found reassuring.

The city centre had changed so much in recent years that it was almost unrecognizable. It was a labyrinth of malls, streets lined with shops and restaurants, office towers, and apartment buildings. Uncle recognized some of the buildings, but not the grey stone monolith that proved to be their destination. He searched the exterior for an identifying sign but found none.

"We're getting out here," Ban said.

The soldiers from the first jeep had already piled out and stood on the sidewalk next to Uncle's. When he climbed out, they moved quickly to beside him.

"Follow me," Ban said, walking up a set of broad concrete stairs to the doors.

When Uncle entered the building, any questions he'd had about it were immediately resolved. Directly ahead, a ten-metre-high wall separated two banks of elevators. On it was a massive red star with a gold border and the words SERVE THE PEOPLE emblazoned in gold in its centre — the symbol of the PLA. The lobby was bare of furnishings but not empty, as soldiers were criss-crossing the marble floor. Without breaking stride, Ban led Uncle towards the elevators to the right of the star. The fact that he was in what seemed to be an office building and about to ride an elevator began to allay Uncle's concerns.

He didn't see Ban push the button, but when an elevator arrived, Ban stepped inside and the soldiers guided Uncle in after him. Uncle looked at the row of floor buttons and then watched as Ban reached for the bottom one, which read SUB-BASEMENT.

The elevator started its descent from the ground floor, past the storage floor and the basement, and then stopped. When the door opened, the soldiers directed Uncle into a corridor that had a low ceiling, dim lighting, and walls that were painted a dull gray. The air was surprisingly warm and slightly damp. Still, Uncle shivered.

"Lieutenant Ban, you've brought us another guest," a voice said.

Uncle turned to see a soldier with sergeant's stripes on his sleeves walking towards him with two other soldiers.

"This one is here at the request of General Ye," Ban said. "Here are his documents."

"I know. One of the general's staff called me a short while ago to say he'd be joining us," the sergeant said as he looked at Uncle's papers.

"Can we leave him with you?"

"Of course."

"Then we'll be off."

When Ban and his men moved away, the two soldiers took up positions next to Uncle.

"Who is General Ye?" Uncle asked.

"In my world you don't speak unless you're asked a question. And even then, restrict yourself to answering only the question that's been asked," the sergeant said. Then he spoke to the soldiers. "Take him to number ten."

"Just a second. I'd like to make a phone call."

"No phone calls."

"I want to contact my lawyer."

"No lawyers."

"As you can tell from my permit, I'm a citizen of Hong Kong," Uncle said. "Contacting my lawyer is a right."

"As I can also tell from your permit, you were born in China. As far as we're concerned, that makes you Chinese," the sergeant said. Then he turned to the soldiers and said, "Empty his pockets and take his belt before you put him in."

The soldiers each grabbed one of Uncle's arms and started walking. They were large enough that they could easily have carried him if he'd put up any resistance. Instead he went with them, taking in what he could of his surroundings. Any comfort he'd felt earlier was gone. The corridor was narrow, and past the elevator it was lined with steel doors without visible handles. At the bottom of each door was a small flap that was secured from the outside.

None of the doors were numbered, but halfway down the corridor the men came to a halt in front of one. While one soldier kept a tight grip on Uncle's arm, the other reached for a key he had on a chain around his waist. He unlocked the door and then said, "Fold your hands behind your head."

When Uncle did, the soldier quickly went through all his pockets, taking out his wallet, Zippo lighter, and cigarettes. When that was done, he pushed open the door. "In you go," he said.

Uncle stepped inside a room empty of light, except for that coming from the corridor. Through the gloom he saw that it was maybe three metres square, with a concrete floor and walls. It had a cot along one wall with a mattress but no other bedding. In the corner was a toilet that had no lid. There was nothing else in the room. He thought about asking the soldier for his cigarettes and lighter, but before he could the door was slammed in his face and the room plunged

into complete darkness. He slowly moved sideways to sit on
the cot. It was so dark that he couldn't see it, even though it
was close enough to touch. He sat down and held his hand
in front of his face. It wasn't visible. It was so quiet he could
hear himself breathe. The smell of urine filled his nostrils.

He calculated the time and then wondered how long it
would take for Fong to contact Liu and for Liu to engineer his
release. This wasn't a place he wanted to spend the night in.
Aside from the smell and the darkness, the mattress was so
thin that he could feel the cot's coils digging into his thighs.

He pulled himself fully onto the mattress and pressed
his back against the wall. *This China venture*, he thought, *is
getting increasingly complicated for me. What's at play here?*
He had no doubt that Peng had given the PLA the names of
every company and individual who had given him a bribe,
and it was possible they were targeting them as they crossed
the border. But why pick him out when he was leaving, not
entering? And why pick out him and not Fong? He had no
answer to the first question, and the only one he could think
of for the second was his Chinese origin.

The minutes dragged, or at least he thought they did,
because in the dark he had no real concept of time. Then
suddenly a slice of light came through a gap at the bottom
of the door. He saw a tray and part of a hand, and heard a
voice say, "Here's dinner."

The tray held a bowl of white rice and a cup of water. He
left the cot to take the tray, and as he did, the light disappeared and he was plunged back into darkness. He backed
up until he felt the cot against his legs and sat down with the
tray on his knees. The rice was lukewarm and sticky. He ate
it anyway and washed it down with the water.

Hours passed, and as they did his sense of unease began to grow. He started to wonder about Liu. How much influence did he actually have? It was the PLA who had put him in the cell. Did Liu have enough power to get him out of it? How much faith should he place in his silent partner? But he didn't have faith. What was another option? As his mind moved back and forth between optimism and the fringes of despair, he found that in the darkness every thought was heightened. It was as if depriving him of sight had sharpened his mind.

Another thing that was sharp was his need for a cigarette. Several times he reached absent-mindedly into his jacket pocket for his Marlboros, only to be brought back to the reality of their absence. On most days he smoked a full pack of twenty, and on days when he was under stress or studying the racing form, he could easily go through half of that again. He had been smoking since he was a teenager and had never been able to quit. Before coming to Hong Kong, lack of money had forced him to cut back for a few years, but he had never fully stopped. Now he began to feel what it would be like if he did try to stop. His mouth was dry, there was a knot in his stomach, and he was jumpy. He didn't know how much his situation was contributing to his edginess, but the physical craving for a cigarette was certainly part of it.

At one point Uncle had to pee, and he looked towards where he thought he'd seen the toilet. He knew that eyes could become accustomed to darkness, but his hadn't. It was as if all the light had been sucked out of the room, leaving behind an impenetrable blackness. He got up from the cot and stumbled towards the corner until his shins bumped into the toilet. He tried to centre himself over it and was relieved when he heard a splash as he peed. He found his way back to the cot and lay down. Surely he wouldn't have to spend the night in this place.

He wondered what time it was, and then thought about Fanling. Surely Fong had made it home safely. The meeting about Tai Wai New Village had been scheduled for eight o'clock. Had it been held? Was it still going on? Why hadn't he told Fong what he thought their response should be to the killing? *There's nothing I can do about any of that from here, and there's no point in thinking about it,* he thought, but he also knew it would be nearly impossible not to.

He wasn't sure if he actually slept, but it seemed he was awakened by a noise from outside. He sat up quickly, his ears straining to hear. Was it voices? Then he heard the sound of metal against metal and the door swung open. Even the dim corridor light forced him to blink as his eyes tried to adjust.

"It's time to have a talk," someone said. "Come out of there."

For a few confused seconds Uncle expected to see Liu standing in the doorway, but it was a PLA officer with two soldier guards lurking behind him. "Who are you?" Uncle asked.

"Captain Ma. I've been assigned to your case."

"What case?"

"There'll be no further discussion here. I need you to leave your cell."

Uncle slid from the cot and got to his feet. He felt a muscle tighten in his back, and stretched. One of the soldiers pointed a rifle at him. "You shouldn't make any sudden moves," Ma said.

"I can see that."

"Then let's go."

Uncle stepped into the corridor, his eyes beginning to adjust to the light.

"Follow me," Ma said and started walking down the corridor.

Uncle followed him, with one soldier by his side and the other behind. They went the length of the corridor to a set of double wooden doors. The captain pushed his way through them and then turned right. The soldiers guided Uncle through the doors and then led him into a room that was so brightly lit he had to shade his eyes.

"Sit there," Ma said, pointing to a plain wooden chair on one side of an equally plain table.

Uncle did as he was asked. Then Ma sat down across from him while the soldiers closed the door and took up positions on either side of it.

"Do you know why you're here?" Ma asked, placing his forearms on the table and linking his fingers.

Uncle looked directly across the table at him. He guessed Ma was in his early to mid-forties. He was clean-shaven and his hair was cut close to the scalp, accentuating a widow's peak. He was lean, of medium height, and his crisply ironed uniform was tight against his body. He was staring at Uncle but his attitude was one of disinterest, maybe even boredom. *How many times has he done this?* Uncle thought, and then said, "I have no idea why I'm here. I'm a citizen of Hong Kong. I would like to have my rights as a foreign citizen recognized and respected."

"You're in China, not Hong Kong," Ma said with a grim smile.

Before Uncle could respond, Ma pushed back from the table, stood up, and walked over to a table set against one wall. He picked up a jug of water and two glasses and placed them in front of Uncle. Then he went back and returned with a file folder, Uncle's cigarettes and lighter, and an ashtray.

"You can smoke if you wish," Ma said.

Uncle hesitated. "I'll wait," he said, not wanting to appear weak.

"And you can have as much water as you want," Ma said, reaching for the jug and pouring two glasses. Uncle picked up a glass and sipped.

Ma opened the folder, read silently for about a minute, and then leaned forward. "How well did you know Peng Da, the Director of Economic Development in this SEZ?"

"When I was deciding about making my first investment in Shenzhen, I met him in his office with Ming Gen, whose partner I became in his textile factory. The meeting was for the purpose of learning about the regulations that govern investments in the zone," Uncle said. "I met him again when we officially reopened the factory after re-equipping it. I don't remember any meetings after that, although we did talk on the phone when my company decided to make further investments in the warehousing sector. Again I wanted to make sure I was in compliance with various regulations."

"Did Peng Da ever ask you for money or anything else of value?"

"No."

"Did you ever offer him money or anything else of value?"

"No."

Ma raised an eyebrow and glanced down at the file. "What name should I call you?"

"As you can see on my permit, my name is Chow Tung."

"Yes, but it says here that many of your friends refer to you as Uncle. Is that true?"

"Some of my friends do."

"Hmmm. Well, Uncle, if you stick to the story you've just told me, this is not going to go very well for you," Ma said. "I know you paid Peng, and before we go any further, I need you to admit that."

"He asked for nothing and I gave him nothing," Uncle said briskly.

Ma looked past Uncle. "I'm finished here for now. Take him back to his cell," he said to the soldiers.

Uncle stood up.

"You can light a cigarette and take it with you if you want," Ma said.

"No, but thank you all the same."

"Then I'll see you later," Ma said.

Uncle left the room with the two soldiers. The one by his side gripped his arm with more force than Uncle thought was warranted, and the one behind prodded him with the barrel of his rifle. When they reached the cell, the soldier let go of Uncle's arm to put a key into the lock. As he did, the one behind put his mouth close to Uncle's ear. "Don't be stupid. Everyone talks eventually. Tell the captain what he wants to know now and you'll save yourself a lot of trouble."

"Thanks for the advice, but I've already told him everything I know," Uncle said.

The cell door opened, Uncle felt a hand on his back, and he was propelled through it back into the darkness.

25

UNCLE SAT ON THE COT, PONDERING HIS SITUATION.
Peng had talked, and there was no doubt that he had told them absolutely everything he could in order to save his life. The bigger question in Uncle's mind was whether Peng had told them only things he actually knew. Had he also elaborated on things he thought he knew? Perhaps he had even fabricated things he thought they wanted to hear. The answer to those questions wouldn't have any bearing on how Uncle responded to Ma, but it might give him a clue as to how determined and persistent Ma might be. If all he was doing was hunting down some of the people who'd bribed Peng, he might not pursue the issue as avidly if he was trying to connect Peng to Uncle as a way of linking Uncle to others. Ma's questions had been solely about Peng, and that was a positive sign — if anything positive was possible to find in those circumstances.

Whatever Ma's game, Uncle decided that the only way for him to react was to deny everything. There was nothing to be gained by conceding there was any truth in Peng's accusations. He would stonewall. As far as Uncle knew, there wasn't a single thing that directly connected him to Peng. It would be one man's word against another's, and since one of those men was dead, Uncle's word should prevail as long as he stuck to his story. It was with that thought that he lay down on the cot again, trying to ignore the coil springs and the idea that the mattress must be infested with living creatures.

He had just fallen asleep when he felt a burning sensation in his eyes. He opened them and then quickly turned his head towards the wall, away from the glare of the flashlight aiming at him from the door.

"The captain is ready for you again." Uncle recognized the voice as belonging to one of the guards.

"Is the flashlight really necessary?" Uncle asked.

"No," the guard said, but kept it focused on his face.

Uncle sat up with his forearm covering his eyes. "I can't see where I'm going."

The guard lowered the flashlight. "Move it," he said.

They walked down the corridor into the same room. Captain Ma was already there, sitting behind the table with an open folder in front of him. This time there was no jug of water or cigarettes in sight. "Take a seat," Ma said.

Uncle did, and then noticed there were two chairs, one unoccupied, across from him.

"Have you taken advantage of our time apart to rethink your answers to my questions?" Ma asked.

"There was nothing to rethink."

Ma looked down at the file. "Peng was quite specific about the nature of your investments and how much he charged you to facilitate their approval."

"I have no idea what you're talking about."

"He said you put cash into his Hong Kong bank account prior to his approving your proposals."

"For every one of our business proposals, we filled out the appropriate documents and submitted them through the proper channels. That's all we did. Peng never mentioned money and we certainly didn't offer or pay him any."

"So he was lying?"

"If he was claiming that we paid him anything, he most certainly was."

"As part of his plea agreement with us, he gave us access to his bank account and turned over all his bank records," Ma said.

"It couldn't have been much of an agreement, since he ended up dead," Uncle said.

"It was a difficult case, with complications that went beyond his corruption."

"I don't know anything about the case or his corruption."

"How much did you pay him?"

"Nothing."

"From what we've been able to piece together," Ma said, pausing to turn a page in the file, "it looks like more than two million Hong Kong dollars."

"We paid him nothing."

"According to Peng, you always deposited cash directly into his bank account, so there aren't any cancelled cheques or copies of wire transfers for us to get our hands on," Ma continued in a monotone. "That's unfortunate. However, what we've been able to do is match the timing of your cash payments with your investment proposals."

"I wasn't aware that Peng had a Hong Kong bank account."

Ma kept his eyes locked on the file as his right index finger traced a line across a page. "It appears that you were clever enough not to put the entire fee attached to any one proposal into his account at one time. Instead you made a series of smaller cash deposits over two- to three-week periods," he said. "Peng told us that's how you did it, but let me assure you that we didn't take his word at face value. We've done the math and we're satisfied that your total deposits match the fees he was charging for each proposal."

"I don't doubt your math, but how could I deposit cash or cheques into a bank account that I didn't know existed?"

Ma frowned. Uncle began to suspect that he was getting annoyed, but before Ma could respond, the door opened and another PLA officer entered the room. He walked over to the table and sat in the chair next to Ma. He was younger than the captain, and his uniform insignia indicated he was a lieutenant. He was taller and even thinner than the lean Ma; his face was drawn, and fixed with a scowl.

"This is Lieutenant Su. He'll be joining us until I finish with my questions, and then he'll be taking over for the rest of the night," Ma said to Uncle, and then turned to Su. "Mr. Chow, or Uncle, as he is more commonly called, has been telling me that he knows nothing about Peng's bank account or how his money happened to find its way into it."

The rest of the night, Uncle thought. *How is that going to work?*

"I've reviewed the file and the facts seem clear enough," Su said sharply to Uncle. "We have Peng's testimony and the corroborating bank data, which together give us sufficient cause to bring charges of corrupting a public official against you."

Uncle was taken aback by Su's tone. Was this just a good soldier, bad soldier routine, or was Su speaking for both himself and Ma? Uncle noted that Su showed no deference at all to Ma, his senior officer.

"I haven't seen the file, so I don't know what you're referring to," Uncle said softly. "And I hope that if you are indeed ready to press charges against me, you will allow me to get proper legal representation — representation I should have had by now."

"You are denying that you paid Peng?" Su asked.

"Absolutely. And we can talk for another forty-eight hours but that answer won't change, because it's the truth."

Su bit his lower lip and looked thoughtful. He turned to Ma. "Captain, you and I should discuss this. Why don't you ask your men to take this man back to his cell."

"Yes, let's do that," Ma said, and motioned to the guards. "Return him to his cell."

The guards lifted Uncle from his chair before he had a chance to stand. He hadn't realized they were that close to him, and he wondered if this had been prearranged.

"I want to contact a lawyer," Uncle said.

"Get him out of here," Su said.

The guards marched him to the door and then down the corridor. "You don't know when to keep your mouth shut, do you," one of the guards said to Uncle.

"I don't know why I should keep quiet when I haven't committed any crime," Uncle said.

"It will take a lot more than your saying you haven't done anything to convince those guys."

They reached the cell and Uncle braced himself, expecting the guards to throw him into it. Instead they simply unlocked the door and stepped back. Seconds later, Uncle's world was dark again.

He settled onto the cot, took several deep breaths, and tried to fend off the increasing sense that he was in the kind of trouble that could crush him. Ma's file was proof that someone had done their homework, and if they believed Peng, the conclusions they'd reached weren't unreasonable. It was true that whatever evidence they had was circumstantial, but that had never stopped a Chinese court from convicting an innocent man.

Uncle lay down on his back. He had no idea what time it was, only that it must be late in the night. What was going on outside those walls? Had Fong contacted a lawyer? Were the Lius exerting their influence? Who would get him released? As those thoughts tossed around in his head, he felt his palms getting sweaty and the knot in his stomach tightening. "Think about something else," he muttered to himself. But when he did, he thought of Wu and what was happening in Fanling. "Shit, I need to get out of here."

Normally when Uncle had trouble sleeping, he replayed horse races in his mind. It was a process that required him to recall a specific race and then focus on every detail surrounding it. As the details piled up, they took over his consciousness and gradually squeezed out whatever had been keeping him awake.

His greatest success that year had been the Hong Kong Gold Cup race in March at Sha Tin. He tried remembering the day. It had been cloudy and humid but it hadn't rained. The stands were packed with about ninety thousand people, and the lineups at the betting windows had been enormous. He had reserved a seat on the second level of the grandstand. He had spent hours upon hours handicapping the races, and focusing particularly on the Gold Cup — one of the three most important races of the year on the Jockey Club's calendar. As usual, the Cup had a large field of very good horses, but one really stood out — Co-Tack, who had won his previous four races. He was the favourite, but as much as Uncle hated betting on favourites, he couldn't get away from Co-Tack and his jockey, the amazing Tony Cruz.

Uncle had got his bet down early at short odds, and it had been a large one — twenty thousand to win and place. Then he settled into his seat, surrounded by the buzz of excitement that preceded every race and was especially heightened when a major-stakes race was about to be run. He remembered watching the post parade, his eyes locked on Co-Tack. The horse looked magnificent, its head held high, its steps confident, its coat shining but without a hint of nervous sweat. Cruz sat erect, his back ramrod straight, one hand on the reins and the other gently rubbing the horse's neck.

The race was 1,800 metres and for the first time was being held on Sha Tin's sand course. Uncle had binoculars that day, and he watched Cruz as the horse was loaded into the starting gate. He looked calm and in control. The horse, perhaps sensing the jockey's mood, went into the gate without any fuss and stood patiently as the other gates were loaded. Then they were off, the horses careering forward, the jockeys scrambling for position, trying to avoid each other and not lose the race in the first few hundred metres.

Uncle's binoculars never left Cruz. He had Co-Tack positioned mid-pack on the outside, and Uncle smiled. There was nothing more maddening than watching a horse get boxed in on the inside, full of run but unable to get past the slower horses in front of it until it was too late. But Cruz was a smart, experienced jockey and he had Co-Tack in what Uncle thought was the ideal position. He kept a tight rein on the horse until they were about halfway around the home turn, and then Uncle saw him loosen his grip and urge the horse forward with his hands. Co-Tack went from ninth to fourth in what seemed like just a few strides.

BOOM!

What the hell? Uncle thought, and then looked towards the cell door, where the noise had originated. The guard stood framed in the doorway, flashlight in one hand and a wooden baton in the other.

"Did I wake you?" the guard asked, lifting the flashlight so that it shone directly into Uncle's eyes.

"I'm not sure I was sleeping."

"They'll want to talk to you again shortly. I just wanted to make sure you're awake," the guard said, taking a couple of steps towards him.

"I am now."

"And one more thing," he said, now close enough to touch Uncle. "You need to answer their questions properly. They've got the goods on you and you're wasting everyone's time by lying."

"I'm not going to admit to doing something I didn't do," Uncle said.

"Sure, you didn't," the guard said as he swung the baton.

Uncle had sat up, resting on his right elbow, when the guard entered the cell. It was that arm the baton struck, hitting it above the elbow and causing Uncle to flop onto the bed. He shouted and reached for his arm.

"You're getting on our nerves," the guard said. "Think about where you are."

26

UNCLE COULD BARELY MOVE HIS ARM. IT WAS PAINFUL but he didn't think it was broken. That fact gave him little comfort, because obviously the rules governing his confinement had changed. How to respond? He shook his head. It was all or nothing. If he gave an inch, they'd want more. He had to stay the course.

Despite being in the sub-basement, it was warm in the cell. Uncle slipped off his jacket, groaning, as even that slight effort caused his arm to radiate pain. He lay down and put the jacket under his head as a pillow. He tried to retrieve his memories of the Hong Kong Gold Cup race, but they were gone. Instead he took deep breaths and then expelled the air in long, slow, lung-emptying *whoosh*es. He had taken about twenty such breaths when he began to feel light-headed, and then he slept.

He was sure he had slept but didn't know for how long when the door burst open, a flashlight found his eyes, and a guard screamed at him. Uncle turned his back to the door. He didn't hear the guard approach, but he did feel the baton as it struck his right shoulder blade.

"Look at me," the guard yelled.

Uncle twisted his body towards him, the entire right side of his torso throbbing.

"I want you to stay awake until the lieutenant sends for you. I'm going to check on you every half-hour. If you're sleeping, I'll wake you with these," the guard said, brandishing the flashlight and baton.

Uncle nodded, slowly pulled himself into a sitting position, and leaned his back against the wall.

"That's a good start," the guard said as he left the cell.

Time passed incredibly slowly in the pitch dark. It was a phenomenon Uncle hadn't noticed before, but with nothing to look at, not even a crack in the wall or a grain of rice on the floor, there were no distractions. It was just him and his imagination, and the longer he sat, the more active it became. *Maybe I could spin them a story,* he thought at one point. *It might buy me some time until help comes.* But as he tried to concoct one that wouldn't implicate anyone but Peng, he realized it was futile. Any story would only generate questions about details, and he wasn't sharp enough to invent clever answers. Besides, if they thought he was lying, that would only increase their certainty that he was guilty. His only chance was to maintain complete denial. Maybe they wouldn't believe him, but neither could they be certain that Peng had told them the truth.

The door opened. The guard passed the beam from the flashlight over the bed and into Uncle's eyes, then lowered it. Uncle thought he looked disappointed.

"When will the lieutenant want to see me?" Uncle asked.

"When he says," the guard replied.

Back in darkness, Uncle tried to calculate the time. It had to be midnight or later. He yawned and felt his eyes closing. Without thinking, he stretched his arm and flexed his right shoulder. The pain made him cry out, but it kept him awake, and that was his priority. He wanted no more to do with the baton.

The night dragged on, the door opening, the flashlight probing, and the guard's appearance providing a sense of time passing. Several times Uncle almost dozed off, but a quick stretch and flex brought him back. Eight visits later — four hours, if the guard hadn't lied to him — the flap at the bottom of the door opened and a tray was pushed through.

"Breakfast," a voice said.

Uncle slid from the cot and walked to the door. He started to reach for the tray with his right hand, but his arm and shoulder wouldn't obey. He picked it up with his left hand, moved carefully to the cot, and sat down. Breakfast, like dinner the night before, was a bowl of white rice and a mug of water. He suspected lunch would be the same. Overwhelmingly right-handed, he was so awkward eating with his left that several times rice fell off his spoon. When he had finished, he put the tray on the floor and felt the urge to have a cigarette. During the night he hadn't thought once about smoking, but a return to something as familiar as eating had triggered the need. *If they offer me a cigarette the next time they interview me, I'm going to take it,* he thought.

The door swung open and Uncle saw two new guards standing just outside. "You're wanted. Let's go," one said.

Uncle struggled to get his jacket on, and when he finally did, he noticed it was badly wrinkled. That bothered him, and he ran his left hand up and down the jacket front. He believed a man's appearance was a reflection of his character, and his image of being crisp and clean was something he valued.

"No one gives a shit about your suit," a guard said.

"I do," said Uncle.

"Don't make me come in there to get you," the guard said.

Uncle took one last tug at the bottom of his jacket. "What's the time?" he asked.

"Six-fifteen," a guard said.

He stumbled as he entered the corridor, and pain shot up and down his right side. He grimaced and struggled to regain his balance. The guards watched, not offering any assistance. When he finally righted himself, Uncle began to walk carefully and slowly, trying not to use too much of his upper body.

One guard went ahead to open the door to the interview room. Uncle entered to see Lieutenant Su sitting at the far side of the table.

Su nodded and then motioned at the water jug sitting on a separate table. "You can have some if you want."

"Thanks, I will."

"Take a seat. The guard can get it for you."

Uncle sat down gingerly. Su showed no indication that he saw his discomfort.

A guard put a full glass of water in front of Uncle. He took a sip, suddenly felt a thirst he hadn't been aware of, and drained the glass.

Su stared down at the file folder, ignoring him. Uncle saw that his passport was now on top of the stack of paper. Su opened it, glanced at Uncle, and then returned to the passport.

"You were born in China, in Wuhan," Su finally said.

"In a village near Wuhan."

"When did you leave?"

"Nineteen fifty-nine."

Uncle expected a comment about the Great Leap Forward. Instead Su asked, "How did you leave?"

"I swam across Shenzhen Bay."

"That was a popular exit point," Su said. "How fortunate we are to live in this era, in a time when people are proud to be Chinese and, instead of wanting to leave, are returning to invest in our country's future."

Where is this heading? Uncle thought. Gone was the aggressive, threatening Su of the previous night. Uncle had expected that mention of his illegal departure from China would generate some kind of negative response instead of something that was closer to condoning it. "I believe in what Premier Deng is trying to do. That's why I decided to invest in Shenzhen in the first place," he said.

"The problem, Chow Tung, is that you brought some of your less welcome and frankly nauseating Western capitalist habits with you," Su said, his tone sharpening.

It was a statement that Uncle knew he would be wise not to acknowledge. Then he thought of something and said, "Can I ask you a question?"

Su frowned.

"Who is General Ye?" Uncle asked, taking the plunge.

"Why do you ask that?"

"When I was brought here last night, one of your men mentioned that I was a guest of General Ye. Naturally I'm curious to know the identity of my host."

"That man's words should not be taken literally. General Ye is one of three divisional generals attached to Guangdong province. Guangzhou has the largest contingent and the most senior general, but General Ye's responsibilities here in Shenzhen are perhaps of even greater importance to the state. And as for the man's reference to him as your host — well, you could say that, given the general's responsibility for maintaining order in the zone, we are all his guests."

"Where is he from originally? Ye is not a common name in Guangdong."

"The general is from Xin county in Henan, a famous and revered place for us in the military. We call it the 'Cradle of Generals.'"

"There is a Ye Desheng on the Politburo Standing Committee. Are the two men related?"

"How do you know about Ye Desheng?" Su said, sounding surprised.

"When the twelfth Politburo Standing Committee was named, the newspaper I read every day listed all the members. His name was unusual enough for me to notice, and I've seen it mentioned several times since," Uncle said. "Are the two men related?"

Su hesitated and then said, "Yes, they are. Ye Desheng is the general's father, and he was a general in his own right. He was one of Mao's most trusted officers throughout the Long March and in all the years that followed, until Mao's death."

"I've heard that the sons of men who were Mao's key aides during the Long March have special advantages. In fact, I've heard them referred to as princelings."

"General Ye is no princeling," Su snapped. "He is a first-rate soldier who has risen through the ranks entirely on his own merit."

"I have no doubt that he has."

"Enough talk about the general. We're here to talk about you," Su said, tapping the folder.

"I've told you everything I know."

"No, you haven't, but I'm not going to argue with you about that," Su said. "Captain Ma and I spoke last night. We are agreed that there is already sufficient evidence to bring charges against you of corrupting a public official. If we do, you'll be in front of a judge within days and sentenced to what I assure you will be a very long prison term or a quick death."

Uncle noted the use of the word *if,* and knew that it was poisoned bait. Su was hinting at a deal, and Uncle wasn't going to admit to anything that might give him one. Besides, he remembered how Peng's deal had turned out. He looked across the table at Su and stayed quiet. As he did, it struck him that Su seemed awkward, almost uncomfortable with the negotiations that had begun without being declared. Maybe making threats was his comfort zone.

"You aren't the least bit afraid of prison?" Su said.

"Before I go to prison I have to be charged, tried, and found guilty. I have to believe that even in China an innocent man can be found innocent."

"You have nerve," Su said.

"I also have nothing to lose. China has already taken everything in my life that I valued. My grandparents, parents, and sister all died during the famine Mao created, and the woman I loved and was going to marry died swimming across Shenzhen Bay with me. What else can you take? What can you do to me that would be worse than what has already been done?"

Su looked down as if to examine the file, and Uncle knew he had rattled him.

"Would you like some more water?" Su asked when he raised his head.

"No, thank you."

"A cigarette?"

"No," Uncle said after a slight hesitation.

Su shrugged. "You're making this very difficult for yourself."

"That isn't my intention. Why would it be? All I can do is tell you the truth, and if that isn't good enough, then so be it."

"Let's not debate what is true or not true," Su said. "Do you have any interest in listening to an offer?"

"Lieutenant, I'm hardly in a position to say no, although I can't imagine what I might have to trade."

"We might be prepared to ignore the fact that you bribed Peng."

"Considering that I didn't, that isn't much."

"And, of course, if there wasn't a bribe then we would forego our right to prosecute."

"And in return?"

Su tapped the file folder, reached for a cigarette, and lit it. He blew smoke across the table at Uncle. "Are you sure you don't want a cigarette?"

"I'd love to have one but I won't, since it would only remind me of what I'm missing, and that would make my time in the cell all the more painful," Uncle said. "What I do want, though, is for you to tell me what you expect to get from me in exchange for your offer."

Su shuffled the papers in the file and then sat back, took a deep drag on the cigarette, and stared at Uncle. "We want to know about your business dealings with the Liu family," he said.

Uncle hoped his reaction was suitably calm as he shrugged and said, without any hesitation, "What business dealings?"

"Are you going to play the denial game again?" Su asked. "First you didn't pay Peng and now you don't do business with the Lius. What's next? Are you going to tell me you don't know them?"

"No, I do know them. Although to be accurate, I should say that I mean I know Liu Leji, the customs director," Uncle said. "I was initially introduced to him by Peng at a dinner we had to celebrate the opening of our first garment factory, but I didn't spend more than a few minutes chatting with him. Later I was introduced to him again through a mutual friend, Zhang Delun, who is a senior officer in the Hong Kong Police Department. I was having dinner with Zhang in Fanling and was complaining about the hassles involved in crossing the border. Zhang told me that an old friend of his, Liu, was director of customs, and that he'd talk to him to see if an accommodation could be made for me. In Hong Kong it isn't unusual for friends to use their *guanxi* to help other friends."

"How did Liu and Zhang become friends?" Su interrupted.

"They met at university in Hong Kong. They were class-mates for a couple of years."

"And this Zhang brought you together?"

"Yes, he arranged a dinner in Fanling. I explained my dilemma to Liu and he said he would arrange passes for me and one of my employees, Fong."

"Did you pay him for the passes?"

"Of course not. He was doing a favour for a friend of a friend. It was *guanxi* and nothing more."

"And since then, how much time have you spent with him?"

"None that I can remember, though I may have seen him now and then in passing at restaurants. But that's not unusual in Shenzhen, where there aren't many good restaurants to frequent. I mean, you often see the same businessmen and government officials together when you go around the city. It is almost unavoidable."

Su looked down at his file. Uncle wondered if he had a list of questions or was just winging it.

"Listen, Lieutenant, I don't know what kind of stories Peng was spinning in an attempt to save his own skin, but suggesting that I'm in business with the director of customs is ludicrous."

"What makes you think Peng has anything to do with this?"

"Who have we been spending all our time talking about? I'm assuming he invented a story about a business connection between Liu and me."

"And did he also invent a story that you're partners with Liu's wife, Meilin, and his aunt, Gao Lan, in numerous warehouse businesses?"

"If that's what he was claiming, then yes, he did invent it," Uncle said, more quickly than he would have liked, struggling to ignore the cold chill that ran through his body. *How much information does the PLA have, and how did they obtain it?* he thought.

"So you don't know either of these women?"

"No, I don't know them."

Su nodded. "I wasn't expecting you to be truthful about this. The most natural first reaction is to lie, and I suspect that's what you'll continue to do until you come to grips with the reality of your situation," he said. "So here's what we've decided to do. We're going to give you twelve hours to think about what you're going to tell us the next time we meet.

If you are forthcoming about your relationship with the Lius, then the offer I've made will still be valid. If you are not, then we'll get you in front of a judge as quickly as we can and ask for a minimum sentence of twenty years in prison. And who knows, the judge may not think that is sufficient."

"I heard that Peng made a deal with you people. How did that turn out for him?"

"His deal wasn't with us. I assure you, we keep our word," Su said. "If you confirm that you are in business with the Lius and provide us with details, you will be released and sent back to Hong Kong."

Uncle closed his eyes. He was tired, and the verbal sparring with Su was starting to wear on him. "I don't need twelve hours to make a decision. I know nothing, and that won't change in twelve hours, or twelve days," he said finally.

"No, we insist that you enjoy our hospitality for at least that long."

27

THE ROUTINE HAD BEEN THE SAME EVERY TIME UNCLE
left his cell and made the short walk to the interview room.
He was escorted by two soldiers acting as guards, then the
same two guards took up posts by the door in the room, and
when the interview ended, they took him back to his cell. But
this time when Uncle stood up and walked to the door, one
of the guards left his post to speak to Su. Uncle stood with
the other guard until his colleague rejoined him.

"You've really pissed off the lieutenant," the returning
guard said to Uncle.

Uncle didn't respond and instead turned in the direction of the cell. The soldiers flanked him. They were both
at least six inches taller than Uncle and weighed about
a hundred pounds more. He shuffled along, hoping they
wouldn't try to hurry him or squeeze him between them.
The pain from his shoulder and arm wasn't subsiding; if
anything, it was getting worse. But they let him walk at
his own pace and didn't lean on him or yank on his arms.
He was grateful for the small kindness, even if it wasn't
deliberate on their part.

When they reached the cell, Uncle felt emboldened enough to ask, "Is there any chance of getting some light in there?"

"No," the guard barked. "And there's also going to be no sleep. Those are our orders. The lieutenant wants you to spend your time thinking."

The door closed behind Uncle as soon as he stepped through it. He found the cot and sat down. What had been a bad situation an hour before was now infinitely worse. He hadn't expected the Liu family to enter the conversation, but, looking back at the previous interviews with Ma and Su, he realized that was where it had always been headed. They had just taken their time getting to it, and he'd been stupid not to anticipate it. They didn't give a fuck about Peng. He was relevant only as leverage to get to the Lius. *But why do they care so much about the Lius?* he thought.

Uncle recalled his talk with Su and was satisfied with the way he had conducted himself. He had given nothing away — at least, nothing he could remember. He had mentioned Zhang Delun, but if Su and the PLA had a way to check the connections between Liu and Zhang and Zhang and Uncle, both would be verified, and that would be a good thing. If they looked into the ownership of the warehouses, there wouldn't be a trace of a Liu. Financially, they wouldn't find a record of a single dollar changing hands. It was true that Gao Lan and Meilin had visited the warehouses, that Fong met with them quite often, and that there had been those lunch meetings. Was it possible the PLA had been tailing them? But, even if they had, what did it prove?

This was most likely Peng's doing, he thought. Peng might have been grasping at straws, desperate to find anything that would deflect attention from him. He couldn't have known for certain that the Lius and Uncle were connected, but he had sensed enough to make that claim. Was that all it took to get the PLA interested and involved?

"What a fucking mess," Uncle said. The recognition that there was nothing he could do to help himself gnawed at him. He was completely dependent on Liu or Fong to do something that would extract him from this hellhole, and the thought frustrated and angered him in almost equal measure.

The cell door opened and a guard he hadn't seen before stuck his head inside. When Uncle nodded at him, the guard nodded back and closed the door.

"I need to stay awake," Uncle muttered, and stood up from the cot. He was still in total darkness, but the frequent openings of the door had allowed him to check out the cell in its entirety, and he had a picture of it in his mind. He held out his good left arm and walked in the direction of the door. When his hand touched it, he stopped, turned, and walked towards the back wall. It took six medium steps to reach it. "If I keep moving, I won't sleep," he said aloud.

For the next hour or so he shuffled between the door and wall, resting twice on the cot when the pain in his shoulder became too much to handle. He kept time by counting the number of times the door opened, and he was happy every time it did. But the minutes still dragged and, as his visits to the cot became more frequent, he knew it was going to be difficult to last twelve hours without sleeping. He asked himself if grabbing half an hour of sleep was worth getting struck with the baton. As he weighed the pros and cons, the door swung open again. That surprised him, because he was sure only about ten minutes had elapsed since the last visit.

Two guards pushed their way into the cell, and Uncle could see at least two more standing in the corridor. "Get to your feet," one of them said.

"Am I going somewhere?" asked Uncle.

"Yeah. There's been a change of plan."

Uncle stood up.

"Turn and face the wall and put your hands behind your back."

Uncle's head filled with questions, but everything about the guards' manner told him they weren't going to answer them. So he did as he was told, wincing as his right arm went behind his back. The guard moved directly behind him, grabbed his left wrist, and attached a metal handcuff.

"What the hell — " Uncle started to say, but his words turned into a groan as his right wrist was cuffed.

As Uncle tried to adjust his body to lessen the pain in his shoulder, the guard said, "Stay still and keep your head straight."

A few seconds later Uncle's world turned black once more as a mask was slipped over his eyes. "Now turn around. We'll walk you to the door," the guard said.

Uncle turned and felt their hands grab his arms, and then he was propelled forward. When they reached the corridor, he started going to the right but was pulled back.

"Other direction," the guard said.

Maybe because he'd been counting his steps in the cell, Uncle found himself doing the same thing as they walked down the corridor. After 112 steps the guards stopped. Uncle heard a door opening and then he was forced to walk again. A door closed behind them and he heard a jumble of voices as the guards talked to each other. Uncle strained to hear what they were saying but couldn't make it out. All he could be sure of was that there were more than two of them and maybe as many as five.

"Get on your knees," an unfamiliar voice said.

"What?"

Hands grabbed him by the shoulders and started pushing him down. Uncle resisted.

"Get down on your own or we'll break your fucking knee-caps," the voice said.

Uncle lowered his left knee to the ground and then slowly and gingerly did the same with his right.

"Your lack of co-operation has become a problem," the voice said. "Our superiors have had enough of you."

Uncle heard the shuffle of feet, and then something cold and metallic was held to the base of his skull. He knew it was a gun, but he couldn't believe they'd fire it.

"If you have any religion, now is the time to make your peace," the voice said.

"I don't have any religion, but if the plan is for me to join my ancestors, my family, my loved ones, the time can't come soon enough," Uncle said in a steady voice.

"Oh, we have a brave little man here," the voice said. "I'll tell you what I'll do, little man. I'll take five bullets out of this gun and leave one. Then I'll spin the barrel and start firing. If you're lucky, you will live for an extra thirty seconds or so."

Uncle said nothing but lowered his head as if making it an easier target to hit. He heard the men talking to each other, and then the gun was again placed at the base of his skull.

There was a click and the voice said, "One." Uncle counted silently to five and then there was another click. The voice said, "Two." Five seconds elapsed between each of the first four clicks, but after the fifth, the gun was pressed harder and held longer. Uncle had stayed still the entire time, confident that the gun wasn't loaded but accepting that if it was, there was nothing he could do about it anyway. If he was meant to die at the hands of the PLA in a quasi-prison, then so be it. He'd see his family and Gui-San that much sooner.

He heard a sixth click and again didn't react.

"You knew we weren't going to kill you, didn't you," the voice said.

Uncle didn't reply.

"But the next time you're brought down here, we will. This was to give you a taste of what you can expect if you aren't more co-operative. We know there's been talk about a prison term, but that's not going to happen. You co-operate or you die."

"Say something," a different voice demanded. "We want to know that you understand."

"Co-operate or die. What's not to understand?" Uncle said.

"You little prick," someone said.

"Kick him," another shouted.

As those words reverberated in Uncle's ears, a boot was driven into his lower back and he toppled forward onto the ground. He twisted to one side to try to regain his feet, but he was kicked again, this time in the groin. He groaned and tried to pull himself into a fetal position, but the kicks were coming at him from all sides. The last thing he heard before he passed out was someone saying, "We'd better not kill him."

28

UNCLE AWOKE FEELING LIGHT-HEADED, WITH NO IDEA where he was or what had happened to him. He felt a tightness on his arm and realized he was hooked up to an IV. He thought he might be in a hospital, but what hospital had iron bars on its windows? He tried to lift himself up so he could get a clearer view of his surroundings, but a sharp, biting pain ran down his entire back, ending that effort. He closed his eyes and was soon asleep again.

When he woke the second time, Uncle wasn't alone in the room. A nurse stood next to the bed changing the IV bag.

"Where am I?" he asked.

"Good, you've come to," she said. "I'll let the doctor know as soon as I'm finished with this."

"Where am I?"

"You're in a military hospital."

"But there are bars on the windows."

"You are in a secure area of the hospital," she said carefully. "Now let me get the doctor."

She left, and Uncle began to piece together the events that had brought him there. He remembered Captain Ma,

Lieutenant Su, questions about Peng, more insistent questions about the Liu family, a black cell, and finally the guards who had treated him like a football.

A voice interrupted his memories. "Mr. Chow, you are finally awake."

"And you are?" Uncle asked.

"Doctor Song," said the man in the white coat as he entered the room.

"You're with the PLA?"

"No. This is a military hospital but I'm not formally attached to the PLA. Although I have to add, that doesn't mean I don't have admiration for them," Song said as he approached the bed.

"How badly am I hurt?" Uncle asked.

"You have several broken ribs and a fracture in your right shoulder blade, and your internal organs have taken quite a beating. Nothing life-threatening, though."

"How long have I been here?"

"This is your third day. We kept you sedated until we had a complete picture of your situation," Song said.

"When can I leave?"

Song smiled. "Not so fast, Mr. Chow. We need to make sure your health is stable. Then, of course, there's the question of how the PLA prosecutor's office decides to proceed."

"What does the prosecutor's office have to do with this?"

"You're in a secure part of this hospital for a reason. You are being held as a suspect in some offence that I haven't been made privy to."

"I'm being held for an offence I didn't commit, and when I refused to confess, some PLA goons kicked the crap out of me."

"Unfortunately, none of that is my area of responsibility," Song said. "I've been told to call a Captain Ma when you're able to talk and can be safely moved."

"Moved to where?"

"I have no idea."

Uncle shook his head. "This is crazy. Can I at least make a phone call?"

"That isn't my decision. Actually, I've been told that you shouldn't be allowed to communicate with anyone outside the hospital."

"How about moving me? When will that be safe?"

"I don't know yet, but please don't have any concerns that I'd put you at risk."

"At risk? Turning me over to Ma and his thugs is risk enough."

"Please don't involve me in your situation," Song said.

"It seems to me that you're already involved."

"I'm a doctor looking after a patient, nothing more than that. Now I want to check your blood pressure and see how your ribs are coming along."

Uncle sighed. "Go ahead."

He was allowed to get out of bed later that day to go to the bathroom. It was a difficult and painful exercise and he was grateful to lie down again. He had been helped by a rather stout nurse who looked as if she could have carried him if necessary. "You have to keep moving," she'd told him. "The more you move, the more quickly you'll adjust to the pain."

"I'll do that, I promise," he said. "But tell me, do you think you could make a phone call for me?"

She frowned. "I was warned about you. Don't try to get me in trouble."

"One phone call."

"I can't."

Uncle asked both her and the doctor again the next day, and the day after, and their answers were always the same. Except on the third day the doctor said, "I think you're ready to travel."

"Where am I going?"

"I don't know, but I told them that I need you back here after they've finished talking to you."

"What if they don't bring me back?"

"Don't be ridiculous," he said, without any conviction.

The following day, the stout nurse helped Uncle get dressed. His suit and shirt, to his surprise, had been cleaned. Then he was put in a wheelchair and taken downstairs. His second surprise was that he was rolled into an ambulance, where a medical attendant and two PLA soldiers waited for him. He couldn't see where he was going, but he was certain it was to the building where he'd been held. It was a twenty-minute trip, which didn't tell him anything, but when the ambulance stopped and he was rolled out, he saw that he was indeed back where his nightmare had started.

The medical attendant pushed him into the building, with the soldiers walking alongside. They took the elevator to the sub-basement. Uncle was convinced he was going to be put back in a cell, but instead they turned left and rolled him in the direction of the room where he'd met Ma and Su. Two soldiers with rifles held against their chests stood in front of the door. When they saw Uncle, they lowered their guns and opened the door.

Ma and Su were both inside, sitting next to each other at the table. But this time they weren't alone. Four soldiers armed like those in the corridor stood inside the door, and along the wall three PLA officers sat in chairs. Two of the officers had the same insignias on their epaulettes as Ma, so Uncle assumed they were captains. The third officer was older and more portly, with a thick grey moustache and a head of silver hair. There were two gold stars on his epaulettes.

A soldier rolled Uncle to the table and then stood off to one side.

"Thank you for joining us," Ma said.

"How could I refuse?" Uncle replied with a small smile, conscious that every eye in the room was focused on him.

"I'm pleased to see that you haven't lost your sense of humour," Ma said.

"It's one of the few things I haven't lost, but I'm sure you'll try to find a way to separate it from me."

Ma pursed his lips. "The events of a few days ago were regrettable. It isn't how we typically manage our affairs. The men who were involved have been disciplined."

"Is that an apology?"

"It is an explanation."

"Are you trying to tell me those men acted entirely on their own, that they weren't given orders?"

"Orders can be misinterpreted, and in this case they were."

"That's enough chat about who did what to whom and why. Let's get on with the reason we're here," a loud, authoritative voice said.

Uncle looked at the silver-haired man and in that instant knew who he was. "General Ye," he said.

"Get on with things," Ye said to Ma, ignoring Uncle.

"Yes, sir," Ma said, and then turned to Su. "Do you want to start?"

Su nodded and opened the file folder in front of him. "Mr. Chow, the last time we spoke, I explained to you that we have more than sufficient evidence to bring charges against you for corrupting a public official, namely Peng Da, a director in the Shenzhen Special Economic Zone," he said. "I also explained that we are prepared to forego those charges if you will co-operate with us in an investigation into the business practices of various members of the Liu family, including Liu Leji, who is currently director of customs for this zone. Will you confirm that's what you were told?"

"I do have memories of being told that, and also that I'd be freed and permitted to cross the Hong Kong border if I told you what you want to know."

"That is correct."

"I have several problems with that particular conversation," Uncle said. "The first is that you also told me I had twelve hours to consider my position, but only a few hours later I was dragged from my cell, handcuffed and blindfolded, had a gun put to my head, and then was kicked into unconsciousness. It makes me wonder if I can trust anything you say."

"As Captain Ma has explained, those men acted wrongly."

Uncle turned to look at Ye. "I didn't think the chain of command in the PLA was so loose," he said. "It is General Ye I'm speaking to, isn't it?"

"It is, and you have my word that any deal you strike with Ma and Su will be honoured. So stop fucking around and tell them what they want to know."

"That's my second problem. I don't have anything to tell them. I'm not doing business with the Liu family and I have no knowledge of any business in which they might be involved."

"We have been told otherwise," Su said.

"You intimated to me that it was Peng who made those claims. Given the situation he was in, I think he would have told you anything you wanted to hear to save himself."

Ma touched the file. "It says in here that you own and operate three large warehouses with a local resident named Ming Gen."

"He's also my partner in two garment factories."

"We are aware of that, but we're more interested in the warehouses," Ma said. "Is Ming an active partner in those warehouses or simply listed because the regulations require it?"

"He's kept busy by the garment factories, so he doesn't have any direct involvement with the warehouses. He treats them as a passive investment."

"Are the warehouses profitable?"

"Very."

"Has Ming received his portion of those profits?"

"We made a decision to retain the bulk of the profits inside the companies for the purpose of reinvesting, so profit distributions to my company and Ming have been minimal."

Ma leaned towards Uncle. "Will you make that banking information available to us?"

Uncle paused. "Under the right circumstances I'd be prepared to instruct my bank to provide all the statements from the first day the warehouses were incorporated. I have nothing to hide."

"What circumstances?" Ma asked.

"I'd have to be on the Hong Kong side of the border."

"Why should we trust you to do that if you were in Hong Kong?"

"Trust seems to be in short supply on both sides," Uncle said. "The difference is that if I renege, I have businesses worth hundreds of millions of dollars that you can go after. If you renege on me, I'll probably end up dead."

"You have an inflated view of the power we yield," Ye said.

"I think not, General."

"And all this talk about your partner Ming," Ye said, ignoring Uncle's comment. "It's a distraction and nothing more. We know you're in business with the Liu family. From the day you opened the first warehouse, the customs department has been directing business your way."

"General, the SEZ had a shortage of warehouse space. We built our warehouses to meet a need. They are modern and the most efficient in Shenzhen. Why wouldn't the customs department refer business to us?"

"That's convenient bullshit," Ye said. "Ma, tell the man the other information you have."

"Yes, General," Ma said. "We have learned that Liu Leji's wife, Meilin, and his aunt, Gao Lan, have been a constant presence in the warehouses. When we sent officers disguised as potential customers to speak with the warehouse managers, they referred to the women as two of their bosses."

"And the aunt flies in from Beijing to do this, isn't that right," Ye said.

"It is," Ma said, and then turned back to Uncle. "How do you explain that?"

"I can't, because I know nothing about it."

"I'm losing my patience," Ye snapped to one of the officers sitting next to him. "Captain Lin, explain to Chow one last time what his options are."

The officer seemed surprised by the request and appeared hesitant, but finally he stood up and walked over to Uncle. He was tall, at least six feet and several inches, and towered over Uncle in his wheelchair. He looked down at him. "As the prosecutors have outlined, there is irrefutable evidence that you bribed Peng and are therefore guilty of corrupting a public official. But General Ye has decided that, because the Liu family's indiscretions are a much greater danger to the stability of the state and the future of the special economic zones, he is prepared to waive the bribery charges and return you to Hong Kong — if you will admit that the Liu family is a silent partner in your warehouse businesses and has been actively promoting them for your mutual benefit."

"And if there is nothing to confess?"

"There is a confession to be made. It's only a question of whether or not you're prepared to make it," Lin said. "And if you are not, then Captain Ma's department will bring charges against you and you'll receive a swift trial and sentencing."

"Assuming I'm found guilty," Uncle said.

"This is nothing to joke about," Lin said.

"I know that, and believe me, I'm not taking this lightly," Uncle said. "But how much time do I have to make a decision? Another twelve hours?"

"One minute," Ye said.

Uncle shrugged. "Then in that case the answer is no. I won't confess to something that isn't true."

Ma looked at the general. "What will we do with him?"

"How soon can you have the bribery charges brought before a judge?"

"If you use your influence, we might be able to do it by late tomorrow."

Ye turned to the other officer sitting next to him. "You make the calls and then coordinate with Ma," he said.

"Yes, sir."

"What will we do with Mr. Chow in the meantime?" Lin asked.

"Put him in a cell," Ye said.

"I was told I'd be taken back to the hospital," Uncle said.

"We have to call for an ambulance. We can't have you sitting around just anywhere while you wait," said Ye.

"Sir, would you object if I accompanied Mr. Chow to the cell?" Lin asked. "I would like one last chance to persuade him to see things our way."

Ye hesitated and then said, "I think you'll be wasting your time, but go ahead."

29

TWO SOLDIERS ACCOMPANIED LIN AND UNCLE DOWN
the corridor, where they were met by more guards.

"Mr. Chow is to be put in a cell until his ambulance
arrives," Lin said. "I'll be going in to talk with him, so turn
on the lights."

The guards walked them further down the corridor,
opened a cell door, and stepped back. One of the soldiers
rolled Uncle inside. "This is twice as big as the one I was in
before," he said as he looked around.

"Close the door," Lin said to the guard.

After the door had closed, Lin said to Uncle, "Do you
mind if I sit?"

"Do what you want."

Lin sat on the cot and whispered to Uncle, "Come closer."

Uncle started to ask why but stopped. He moved so close
that his chair was bumping against Lin's knee. Lin reached
into a breast pocket, took out a slip of paper, and passed it
to Uncle. "Read this," he said softly.

Uncle opened it and read, *You can trust this man.* It was
signed by Liu Leji. "What's this about?" he asked.

"Try to keep your voice down. There could be ears at the door," Lin said.

"I need to know what this is about," Uncle repeated, as quietly as he could.

"I'm here as a friend," Lin said.

"I'm supposed to believe that? How stupid do you people think I am?"

"Your skepticism is justified. Leji said I should tell you that at your last meeting with his aunt, she asked you to start calling her Lan. That's a rare compliment from Ms. Gao."

Uncle caught Lin's eyes. The other man didn't turn away. *I either trust him completely or I don't trust him at all. There can be only one source for the story about Ms. Gao, but there's no room for error and there's no halfway measure.* "What are they going to do with me?" he asked.

"I don't think they'll actually send for an ambulance," Lin said.

"They'll keep me here?"

"At least for a little while. They're desperate to connect you to the Lius," Lin said, his voice so soft that Uncle found himself almost leaning into his face. "All they have right now are Peng's accusation that you and the Lius are in business together, and one warehouse manager — not several — who told them he thinks some of the Lius have made visits to his warehouse."

Trust or no trust, this is the time when a commitment has to be made. "Peng knew nothing about our arrangement," Uncle said, his decision made. "He was just guessing, and probably inventing all sorts of things."

"He was guessing because they were grilling him about Liu Leji. They wanted him to provide dirt on Leji, and that was the best he could do. He didn't offer up the information spontaneously. They kept hammering at him for something, anything, until he gave them that."

"Why are they going after the Lius, and why am I getting dragged into it?"

"You've been caught in the middle of a political war. Do you know that General Ye's father is a high-ranking member of the Politburo Standing Committee?"

"I do."

"His father is General Ye Desheng, and he was and still is a Maoist," Lin said. "Not everyone on the Committee is pleased with the direction in which Premier Deng is taking the country. Several hardliners want to keep things as they were during Mao's chairmanship, and Ye Desheng is their leader. They want to roll back Deng's initiatives, and they're particularly focused on eradicating the special economic zones, which they regard as capitalist snakepits that will poison our socialist society. They can't target Deng directly so they're doing the next best thing — going after his closest friend and lifelong ally, Liu Huning. If they can topple Liu, they'll weaken Deng. Who knows, they might even be able to get him removed, or at least get him to reverse the economic course he's set the country on."

"And they think they can get rid of Liu Huning by proving what?"

"They need to find enough evidence to charge Liu Leji with corruption. Ms. Gao and Meilin are only secondary concerns because, frankly, a great many high-ranking officials have wives and children who don't have government jobs and are involved in businesses. Leji's position as director of Customs makes him a prime target, though, because if he aided or profited from the warehouse businesses, it's a clear-cut case of corruption. And if he is charged, there's no way that Liu Huning can avoid being tarred with the same brush. That family is one unbreakable unit, and nothing happens within it that Huning hasn't approved — or so everyone believes."

Uncle became quiet as he tried to make sense of what he was hearing. He knew he wasn't as alert as he would like to be; the questions in his head were jumbled and coming randomly. He picked one and asked, "What role are you playing in all this?"

"Nothing I planned on, I assure you," Lin said. "I've been on General Ye's staff for four years but I've known Leji my entire life. He was raised by his uncle, who was a comrade of my father, and our two families lived side by side in the same compound in Beijing. The only difference between Leji and me is that his father returned from a labour camp at the end of the Cultural Revolution, and mine didn't."

"But you're on Ye's staff."

"He doesn't know how close Leji and I are. Besides, I'm a loyal soldier and I've been pleased to do General Ye's bidding until now," Lin said. "And truthfully, he has been loyal as well. I've never heard him utter a word of political dissatisfaction. This is a new experience for me. I'm assuming that he's being directed by his father."

"You mentioned the political manoeuvring in Beijing. How can you know that's what's behind all this?"

"Leji told me. He was warned by his uncle a few months ago that some members of the Politburo Standing Committee were eager to discredit him, with Ye Desheng leading the charge. Knowing how close the Ye family are and that General Ye was in Shenzhen, Liu Huning asked Leji to keep his eyes and ears open. When Peng was first arrested, I don't think Leji was that concerned, but when Peng was turned over to the PLA for further questioning, after he had already agreed to plead guilty, Leji began to suspect an ulterior motive. It was then that he contacted me. I did some discreet poking around and discovered that General Ye had personally assigned Captain Guan to interrogate Peng and had instructed him to focus on what Peng knew about Leji's business dealings. I told Leji. Maybe I shouldn't have, but friendship has to count for something. When I did, he told me about what was going on in Beijing. By the way, did you recognize Guan when you saw him in the room with the general ?"

"No."

"He's the man who put the gun to your head and threatened to kill you."

"I never saw his face. I was blindfolded."

"Guan is a good enough soldier, but when he's left unrestrained, he can be an animal. The general turned him loose on Peng, and then on you. Peng told them everything they wanted to hear. Of course, they put the words into his mouth," Lin said. "I have to say you have frustrated them to an extraordinary degree. They can't understand why you won't do a deal with them. I mean, even if you weren't in business with Leji, it wouldn't cost you anything to tell them what they want to hear, the way Peng did. The general can't figure out if you're being honourable, stubborn, or just plain stupid, but he does think you are brave. I was with him when Guan told him about taking you from your cell and the beating they applied. The general asked him to repeat how you handled that farce of the gun in the back of your head. When Guan told him, the general said, "I don't think we're going to break this man. It's hard to break a man who isn't afraid to die."

"That shows how little they know about me."

"They actually don't have much interest in you, other than trying to connect you to the Lius in any way they can. It was the same with Peng. All the general cares about is getting enough dirt — verified or not — to be able to bring charges against Leji."

"What are they going to do with me now?"

"You have to accept that your life and well-being don't matter to them."

"That's obvious enough, but from a practical viewpoint where does it leave me?"

Lin shook his head. "My fear is that they will turn you over to Guan again, and this time the gun will be loaded."

Uncle and Lin sat quietly for several minutes, pondering Lin's last comment. Uncle was the first to speak. "Can you make some phone calls for me? My people need to know where I am and what's going on."

"Your people know. Leji has been in touch with them many times since you were arrested at the border crossing. They've been giving him a difficult time."

"How so?"

"You have very loyal colleagues, Uncle. There's been talk of trying to break you out, but Leji has refrained from telling them exactly where you are, in case they might actually try. As you can imagine, it would be a monstrous mistake."

"Did Leji tell you that we're triads?"

"He did, and I told him I would forget that he'd told me. This entire affair is complicated enough without adding your criminal affiliations to the mix."

"It may be complicated from where you're sitting, but from where I am it's quite simple. I talk or I don't, and either way, I suspect, the result will be the same as what befell Peng."

"This isn't the time to despair," Lin said, resting a hand lightly on Uncle's knee. "I've been keeping Leji fully briefed and he's been passing the information to his uncle in Beijing. The family knows you haven't said a word, that you haven't betrayed the trust they put in you, despite everything you've had to endure. Strings are being pulled in Beijing, favours are being called in, and old alliances are being re-formed. Leji told me that his uncle is focused on getting you released."

"That's encouraging. I don't mean to sound ungrateful, but at what speed? I've already been in PLA hands for days. How much longer can this go on? How long before I get another visit from Guan?"

"We need to buy some time," Lin said.

"How much time?"

"I don't know, but every hour is precious."

"What are you suggesting we do?"

"You and I have to negotiate a deal."

"What kind of deal?"

"We need to pretend you're willing to co-operate, and then drag out negotiations for as long as we can."

"Will the general have the patience for that?"

"He isn't a patient man, but if he thinks he has a chance to help his father bring down the Lius, I'm confident he'll go along with it — at least for a while."

"Then talk to him. Buy me some time," Uncle said.

"I need a starting point. I have to tell him what you're prepared to admit and what you want in return."

Uncle hesitated. Lin was smooth, maybe too smooth. Was this a trap? Had Lin suckered him in somehow? Despite his earlier decision to trust him, he decided to proceed slowly. "Why don't you get the general to make the first move. Tell him I'm prepared to co-operate but I need absolute assurance that I'll be able to leave here and return to Hong Kong without any delay or retribution. Tell him I'm still not confident that he'll keep his word."

"Telling him you don't believe he'll honour his word would be the ultimate insult, so I'll skip that. I'll find a way to rephrase it. Maybe I can just emphasize that you need an iron-clad guarantee before you're prepared to share information with us."

"Okay. And tell him it has to be something specific, something binding," Uncle said. "I don't want to deal in generalities."

"That has the added benefit of maybe stretching out negotiations a bit."

"Let's hope it does."

Lin stood up. "I'd better get started on this. They'll be wondering what I'm up to."

"When you leave, tell the guards outside to keep the lights on and their hands off me."

30

THE LIGHTS WERE LEFT ON AFTER LIN LEFT THE CELL, and Uncle was able to wheel his chair over to the toilet. Trying to stand was difficult and painful, so he eventually gave up and peed from a sitting position. He made a bit of a mess, which he thought was a perfect reflection of the situation in which he found himself. As bad they were, though, things weren't as dire as they'd seemed an hour before. If Lin was genuine — and believing he was was the only real option Uncle had — then he might be able to buy enough time for Liu Huning. But buy enough time to do what? Was Uncle simply a pawn in a power struggle in Beijing? When all was said and done, was it possible that he might be considered disposable by both sides?

"Gui-San, I think I may be joining you soon," he said suddenly. "It isn't the way I wanted to do it, but the choice isn't mine. Things are in such disarray here, I'd like a chance to sort them out. Please understand that. The Chinese army has decided I'm the instrument they can use to destroy the Liu family, and in Fanling, God knows what's going on with the Tai Wai gang threatening us. If I survive, it will mean

I've protected the Lius and I can get back to Fanling. But if I have to leave this world here, my love, I'll be so happy to see you again."

Uncle heard a noise and rolled the chair towards the door. He flexed his legs. He could move them easily enough and they didn't hurt, but his back ached from top to bottom and his ribs screamed in pain when he turned the wrong way. He had no idea how long it would take for everything to mend, but right now that was a secondary concern.

A few seconds later Uncle heard footsteps coming down the corridor. He pushed the chair away from the door and waited. When it opened, Lin appeared first, and right behind him was the man Uncle now knew was Guan.

"The general has agreed to negotiate with you, but he wants Captain Guan to be a party to the negotiations," Lin said.

"I don't know Captain Guan and I have nothing against him," Uncle said, careful to disguise the fact that Lin had told him who he was, but also wondering if Lin actually had Ye's trust, "but I'd feel more comfortable continuing to negotiate one-on-one with you."

"You're hardly in a position to tell the general how negotiations will be conducted," Guan said.

"You couldn't be more wrong. I am in exactly that position — unless of course the general isn't serious about negotiating," Uncle said. "So let me be clear. I want Captain Lin to be my sole point of contact."

Guan's body stiffened. Uncle suspected that if Lin hadn't been in the cell, a punch, or worse, would have been delivered.

"We'd better go back and talk to the general," Lin said.

Uncle saw that Guan wanted to argue. He thought for a second about provoking him, then logic took over. "Tell the general I'm not trying to be difficult. I simply don't want to be negotiating with a team. I find that your style is conducive to productive conversation," he said to Lin.

"Let's go," Lin said to Guan, and turned to leave the cell. Guan stared at Uncle and then reluctantly followed his colleague.

Uncle shifted in his chair. This was going to be more difficult than he had imagined. Guan obviously had Ye's trust. Even if Lin came back alone, Uncle sensed that sooner or later he'd be dealing with Guan again. Ye wasn't going to give Uncle an assured path to Hong Kong without something in return. He almost hoped the general would make it difficult by refusing to commit to a clear-cut release, but what if he didn't? What if Ye gave him a deal with an ironclad guarantee? Uncle shook his head, and he began to feel tired as the complications accumulated in his head. The bottom line, he thought, was that even if he believed he could get back to Hong Kong, he couldn't betray the Lius, and there was no story he could spin that would work around that fact. No story would mean another visit from Guan.

Uncle changed position on the chair again and felt pain radiating down his back. He closed his eyes and the pain gave way to total weariness, his body suddenly sapped of all energy. When he opened his eyes, things were so blurred he couldn't make out the cell door. He leaned forward and then said, "Shit," as he tumbled to the floor.

Uncle heard the sound of people talking. When he opened his eyes, he expected to find himself in the cell. But he seemed to be back in the hospital, and the voices he was hearing were those of Doctor Song and Lin, who were standing by a window not far from his bed. Lin was doing most of the talking, one of his hands gripping the doctor's shoulder, his face only inches away from Song's. Uncle couldn't make out what Lin was saying, but he could hear the urgency in his voice.

"Hey," Uncle said. When no one responded, he said as loudly as he could, "Hey."

They turned and looked at him with grim faces.

"What happened?" Uncle asked in a raspy voice.

"Ah, you are returned to us," Song said.

"What happened?"

"You had a sudden drop in blood pressure, most likely caused by excessive stress," the doctor said. "And when you collapsed onto the floor, you hit your head and concussed yourself. As you can see, you're back in the hospital."

"My head feels cloudy."

"I've sedated you quite heavily."

"You've been out for more than twelve hours," Lin said. "I've been trying to convince the doctor here that you should be prevented from receiving visitors for another twenty-four hours. We don't want another low-pressure scare."

"What will Ye do if I'm out of circulation for that long?" Uncle asked.

"I think that's a conversation we should have later," Lin said. "All that matters right now is that we safeguard your health."

"I agree," Song said, and turned to Lin. "I think you're correct. Another twenty-four hours under my care would be entirely appropriate for Mr. Chow."

"I'm pleased you see it that way," Lin said.

"Good. In that case I'll leave you two alone for a few minutes, but I have to suggest that you don't spend too long, Captain. I don't want the patient getting overtired."

Lin walked over to the bed but didn't speak until the door had closed behind Dr. Song. "That was a very convenient fall you took," he said.

"It wasn't deliberate. I suddenly felt weak, and the next thing I knew I was heading for the floor."

"I know. Song made it quite clear to me and to Ma — who was here earlier — that it was a medical issue that caused it. Still, we shouldn't be ungrateful."

"So we have another twenty-four hours?"

"Only if General Ye decides to listen to the doctor. But I'm sure Song will be persuasive."

"How can you be so confident?" Uncle asked.

"The doctor will be paid handsomely, but only on the condition that he buys us that time."

"Is twenty-four hours going to be enough?"

"Well, who knows what kind of shape you'll be in by then. Maybe I can buy some additional time. One thing is certain, though. This time the doctor won't agree so readily to your being physically moved from the hospital."

"That won't necessarily stop Guan and the others from coming here," Uncle said.

"True, but the general has agreed that Ma and I should handle the negotiations with you. I'll let Ma know we can't begin for at least another twenty-four hours, and when we do, you and I will have to stretch it out as much as we can," Lin said.

Uncle closed his eyes. "I can hardly think about that right now. I ache all over, and even talking for this small amount of time has tired me out."

"Get some more sleep," Lin said.

Uncle nodded, and then his head rolled slowly to one side.

31

SLEEP WAS RARELY PEACEFUL FOR UNCLE. MOST NIGHTS he suffered from terrifying, sweat-inducing dreams. There were two recurring scenarios. They could come to him separately, but on particularly bad nights they could follow one another, leading him from one predicament to the next, and occasionally they would even blend, forcing him to make choices that would leave him shaking when he woke.

The most common dream was of being in the Bay of Shenzhen, trying to swim the four kilometres that separated the brutality of China from the freedom of Hong Kong. He had obviously made it, but three of his companions hadn't, and one was the woman he loved and had intended to marry, Gui-San. He hadn't seen her drown. He had been lying on a wooden door they were using as a raft, nauseated and feverish after ingesting a bellyful of the bay's filthy water. She had been on her own in the water, and Uncle still couldn't forgive himself for not having been at her side. Before they began the swim she had made him promise to be there, and he had failed her. In his dream he was almost glued to the door, clinging to it as if it was life itself, and it wasn't because he was ill.

It was fear that kept him there. He could hear his friends and Gui-San thrashing in the water around him, crying for help, but he kept his head down, pretending he didn't. The dream was never clear about her actually dying, but he always woke filled with a depth of shame that never seemed to diminish.

There was no shame attached to his second dream, just anger and desperation born from hopelessness. As he had told Liu Leji, his grandparents, parents, and sister had all starved to death. It had been slow, painful, and inevitable, and although he had done everything he could to find work and food, he had failed them as well. But it wasn't from lack of effort; his dream had him travelling from Wuhan to their village with a basket filled with fruit and vegetables. It was a futile trip, because he was prevented from getting there at every turn. He was robbed; he slipped and the basket tumbled down a cliff; animals ate the food while he slept by the side of the road. On and on it went, the food always disappearing and Uncle never reaching the village.

But if he dreamt while he was sedated at the military hospital, Uncle wasn't aware of it. In fact, he was hardly aware of anything. He did wake several times, but only for what seemed like a few foggy minutes before he relapsed into sleep. Twice he heard muffled voices, the words indistinct, and he shrugged them off. Then came a voice calling his name loudly and insistently. He tried to ignore it but it wouldn't go away, and finally he opened his eyes.

"I'm sorry, Mr. Chow, but it's time you woke up," said Dr. Song.

Uncle shook his head as he slowly realized where he was. "We have to stop meeting like this," he said.

Song smiled. "Good. So you know who I am?"

"Of course, Doctor."

"Captains Ma and Lin have been coming here three times a day for the past two days. I didn't want them to talk to you until I was sure you could be coherent," Song said. "Now, for the record, what is my name?"

"Doctor Song."

"Where are you?"

"In a military hospital in Shenzhen."

"Perfect," he said. "Now I'm going to have the nurse remove your catheter and IV, and then we'll help you to the bathroom. When you've washed, we'll send for something light for you to eat."

"I've been sleeping for two days?"

"Off and on. I thought sedating you for that long was called for."

Called for or paid for? "What happens after I've eaten?"

"I'll call Captain Lin."

It took an hour to get Uncle from the bed to the bathroom and back and then fed a bowl of chicken broth and a plate of plain noodles.

"How are you feeling?" Song asked when he was done.

"I'm okay. I can walk, albeit slowly, and the pain in my back isn't so severe."

"How is your head? I can give you some extra painkillers if you need them."

"I think I'll manage."

"Are you ready for me to phone the captain?"

"Do I have a choice?"

Song hesitated and then said, "He asked me to call when you were awake and alert. I don't think I should ignore his request."

"Call him," Uncle said, then lay back on his pillow and wondered what, if anything, had happened during the previous forty-eight hours that might have had an impact on his situation.

Song was gone for quite some time, and Uncle imagined he was having a problem contacting Lin. That thinking changed when a nurse entered the room carrying Uncle's clothes. "Am I going somewhere?" Uncle asked.

"I don't know," she said. "I was told to bring your clothes here and help get you dressed."

"I can manage on my own. You don't need to stay," Uncle said. "When is Doctor Song returning?"

"Soon," the nurse said as she laid the clothes on the end of the bed. "Now, if you change your mind about needing help, just press the buzzer on the wall to your right."

Uncle didn't move until she had left the room, and then it was only reluctantly. Why did they want him to get dressed? The last time it had been to take an ambulance ride to hell. He carefully swung his legs over the side of the bed and lowered himself to the floor. He felt surprisingly clear-headed and his legs were stable. He took several slow, careful steps to the end of bed, slipped off his hospital gown, and started to dress. He managed to get on his shirt, trousers, and suit jacket with only a few pauses to let the pain subside, but he knew he'd never be able to put on his socks. He thought about calling the nurse and decided it wasn't worth it. He crossed the room and cautiously eased himself into the room's only chair to wait for whoever would come through the door.

"How are you feeling? The doctor says you're making a decent recovery," Ma said as he entered the room.

"I haven't been awake long enough," Uncle said. "I was expecting to see the doctor."

"He'll be by a bit later."

"And where is Captain Lin?"

"He'll be here in a minute; he's looking for some extra chairs. We don't want to stand over you while we talk."

"You want to talk to me already?"

"You sound alert enough to me."

"Why did you want me to get dressed?" Uncle asked.

"We want this to be as professional as possible under the circumstances."

"Circumstances I didn't create."

"Let's not waste our time going back over what has already happened," Ma said. "General Ye has been incredibly patient while you recover."

"I have chairs," Lin said from the doorway.

Ma took a chair from his colleague and put it down next to Uncle's. Lin placed his on the other side and sat.

Uncle turned to Lin. "Do we really have to do this now? I would like more time to gather myself."

"Doctor Song says you're in good enough condition to talk to us."

"I said I want to deal with you alone."

"The general has decided the two of us will represent his interests," Lin said. "He hopes that your past experience with Captain Ma will make that acceptable."

"At least I know him, which is more than I can say about Guan," Uncle said. "Does this mean the general still wants to reach some kind of settlement with me?"

"Yes, he does, but we don't have an infinite amount of time to get to that settlement. You know what he wants. This will boil down to what you're prepared to give him," Lin said.

Since Lin had arrived in the room, Uncle had been trying to detect in his voice or manner any sign that events in Beijing had moved favourably in his direction. Lin's attitude was entirely professional, low-key and detached. "Before I start giving him anything, I need certainty that I will be able to resume my life in Hong Kong, intact both physically and mentally."

"The general has given his word," Ma said.

"I'm not taking anyone's word for anything," Uncle said. "I want certainty."

"How can we give you that?"

"One of you could cross the border with me. When I'm safe, when I have two feet planted in Hong Kong, I'll tell you what I know."

"Why would we trust you do that?" Ma asked.

"I'll give you my word. Why should it be worth any less than the general's?" Uncle said.

"He would find that highly insulting."

"Then don't tell him I said it," Uncle said. "You can tell him instead that I'm the one with everything to lose, and when you think about it, that is the truth. If I try to play the general for a fool, I'll make an enemy of the most powerful man in Shenzhen. How would that work out for me? At the least I assume he could make my businesses disappear and that my partner Ming could find his garment factories taken from him. Why would I throw all that away?"

"He does have a lot at risk," Lin said to Ma.

"When did you come up with this idea?" Ma asked.

"I'm not sure. Maybe around the time I was trying to figure out how to stop the general from killing me even if I told him everything I know."

"The general would not and will not kill you," Ma said, his voice rising.

"I'm sure Peng was told the same thing."

"There's no reason to bring up Peng," Lin said.

"He's my only point of reference when it comes to judging how the general conducts business."

Lin leaned towards Uncle. "Let's focus on the future, shall we?"

"That's fine, but my future has to include me safely returning to Hong Kong."

"We understand what you want, but we aren't in a position to agree to it."

"I expected you would have to talk to the general, so while you're doing that, you can also tell him that I have another demand," Uncle said.

"Which is?" Ma asked.

"I want a letter or memorandum or whatever from him indemnifying all my businesses from actions that the PLA or any branch of the Chinese government might take against them," Uncle said. "I don't know how to word such a thing, so I'll leave that to the general."

"Why do you want that?" Ma asked.

"What if the general isn't pleased with what I have to say and decides to come after me?" Uncle said. "I'm not predicting he won't be pleased, but I'm a cautious man, and not entirely trusting."

"Even if he agreed to do it, how could you enforce it?"

"I don't know, but I'd take my chances."

"What do you think?" Ma asked Lin.

"Is that a hard condition?" Lin asked Uncle.

"Yes."

"Then we have to present it to the general," Lin said to Ma. "He can always say no. Truthfully I think it will annoy him, but there is a possibility he'll go along with it."

Ma turned to Uncle. "Do you have any other conditions?"

"No."

"Good, because I think that's enough as it is."

"So what happens now?" Uncle asked.

"We'll leave you here and go talk to the general," Ma said.

"When can I expect to see you again?"

"Depending on how the general reacts, you may not see us," Ma said, and then paused. "But in all likelihood you will, and probably quite quickly. The general is eager to get this resolved."

Uncle ignored the veiled threat. "In the meantime, am I allowed to leave this room? Can I finally make a phone call?"

"No and no," Ma said.

32

UNCLE EXPECTED LIN WOULD LINGER, BUT HE DIDN'T, and that left him uneasy. It was one thing for Lin to act detached; it was quite another for him not to acknowledge, even in the subtlest way, that things outside the hospital walls were still ongoing. Had Liu Huning lost the battle in Beijing? Had Lin decided that the safer side to be on was General Ye's?

"How are you feeling?" Dr. Song said as he walked through the door. "Your visitors didn't upset you too much?"

"I've been better."

"Let me check your pulse and blood pressure," Song said, reaching for Uncle's arm. A moment later he nodded. "Both are close to normal, but it might be a good idea for you to return to bed."

"No, I think I'll sit up for a while."

"All right, but let us know if there's anything you need."

Uncle nodded. "Could you answer a few questions for me?"

"That depends on the questions."

"I can see through the window that it's light outside, but I don't know the actual time. What is it?"

"Four-twenty."

"And one more thing. How many other people are there in the secure area of the hospital?"

"None. You are our only patient."

"You mean prisoner."

"As far as the medical staff are concerned, you are a patient," Song said.

"As nice as that sounds, it doesn't change the fact that I'm here against my wishes."

"That isn't our decision to make."

"Doctor, what would happen if I tried to leave?"

"The medical staff wouldn't intervene, but the two armed guards standing outside your door most certainly would."

Uncle leaned his head against the back of the chair and closed his eyes. He was trapped and no one was coming to his aid. That thought and a gnawing sense of desperation began to creep into his mind. He fought against it, trying to find the inner core that was his retreat in times of crisis, the place where no one could touch him.

"Are you sure you don't want to return to bed?" Song asked. "You look pale."

"Yes, maybe I will," Uncle said. "But if you don't mind, I'll just lie on top with my clothes on."

Uncle groaned as he started to rise from the chair, and the doctor reached for his arm to help him stand up. He wavered when he finally got to his feet, and for a second he thought he was going to fall, but gradually his legs became steady. "My back hurts like hell," he said.

"There isn't much we can do for it. It will heal, but it will take time."

Uncle shuffled to the bed and eased himself onto it.

"I assume the officers will be returning," Song said.

"Yes, but I have no idea when."

"If I'm not here when they do, I'd like to wish you the best of luck."

"That sounds ominous," Uncle said with a slight smile.

"Most of the visitors to this part of the hospital don't leave as happy men."

"Let's hope I'm the exception."

"Let's hope you are," Song said, and then started towards the door.

Uncle watched him leave and then heard what he thought was a deadbolt locking. How long would he have to wait for Ma and Lin? Or would it be Guan who showed up? He folded his arms across his chest, his fingers intertwined. If he didn't move, the pain in his back lessened, but nothing could keep his mind from doing somersaults. He began to struggle with a potential problem he hadn't foreseen when he had agreed to Lin's suggestion that they negotiate as a way to buy time. What would he do if General Ye agreed to all his conditions?

He would go to Hong Kong, that much was clear, but for the rest it was an incredible muddle. Once he got there, if he told Ye the truth about the Liu family, they'd be completely vulnerable and at risk. Was Liu Huning close enough to Premier Deng to be able to protect his wife, son, and daughter-in-law? Could he protect himself? Uncle had no way to know, just as, he admitted, he had no way of knowing if Ye would honour an agreement to leave the gang's businesses intact. It was possible, he thought, that all he might get from doing a deal with Ye was his freedom. Was that worth destroying the Liu family and possibly Ming, and losing a large majority of the gang's financial capital? Even if it was possible, it was far from being certain, he reminded himself.

On the other hand, if he got to Hong Kong and then continued to insist that he knew nothing about the Liu family's activities, and if he swore they had no financial interest in the warehouses, he might be able to shield them. But he was one hundred percent sure Ye would then unleash the full force of the PLA against Ming and all the gang's businesses. They'd have no chance of surviving, and neither he nor Fong would ever again be able to set foot in China.

So, sell out the Lius and hope to be able to hang on to the gang's businesses, or stay true to his partners and watch years of work and capital accumulation disappear? "Fuck," he said, angry at himself for not having thought things through when Lin had suggested they start negotiating. He had been tired, battered, and weak, but that was no excuse for being sloppy.

His earlier despair returned. What if Ye wouldn't do a deal? What if they took him back to the cells? What if it came down to him and Guan? At least it would be a resolution, he thought, because he knew he'd never give in to him, and if he didn't, he would die. "I should have been dead twenty years ago," he whispered. "There's nothing Ye or Guan can do to match the pain of knowing I've stolen that time from Gui-San and my friends."

He closed his eyes. When he opened them, the room was dark, and Uncle realized he had slept. Sunset came around six-thirty, but beyond that he had no idea what time it was. He turned and pressed the buzzer on the wall. A moment later the door opened and a nurse entered.

"I've been sleeping again. Could you tell me the time, please?"

"It is almost ten o'clock. We've been checking on you. You missed dinner but we didn't want to wake you. Would you like something to eat now?"

"Yes, please."

"And would you like to put on pyjamas?"

"Not right away. I'd like to eat sitting in the chair."

"Do you want some help getting to it?"

"No, I can manage," he said.

It took him a few minutes to get out of the bed, gather himself, and get into the chair. As soon as he felt settled, his mind began to process the fact it was ten o'clock. That meant it was about five hours since Ma and Lin had left to speak with Ye. He hadn't expected them to be gone that long, but his problem was that he had no idea if that was a good thing or a bad thing.

The nurse returned carrying a tray, which she placed on Uncle's lap. He looked down at a bowl of rice, a baked chicken leg, and a small serving of bok choy. Quite suddenly his appetite grabbed him. He felt as if he hadn't eaten proper food in days, and then realized that was actually the case. He ate quickly, barely tasting the food, and then drank a glass of water. As soon as he finished, the door opened and the nurse reappeared. He found that odd, and wondered for the first time if he was being watched. Then he thought about the conversation he'd had with Lin and dismissed the notion. Lin would never have been so frank if the room was bugged.

She took the tray and then looked down at Uncle's feet, still in hospital slippers. "Would you like me to help you put on your socks and shoes?"

"Do I need them?"

"I think you do. We've been told you're leaving us."

33

UNCLE SAT ALONE IN THE ROOM, STARING AT THE closed door. Who was going to open it? Who was coming to get him? He struggled to stay calm. Regardless of who it was, there was nothing he could do to change it. Had a firm decision been made? It would be naive to think that he was leaving the room to have more conversations, so yes, he was sure a decision had been made, but what had General Ye opted to do?

What felt like fifteen minutes passed, and then another fifteen. Whoever was coming to get him wasn't in any hurry. Uncle tried to convince himself that was a positive sign, but the counterargument swirled in his head just as strongly. His mood shifted back and forth. He was on an up cycle when he heard voices outside the door. He stopped breathing as he strained to listen. Then the door opened and a PLA officer walked into the room. He was closely followed by four armed soldiers and Dr. Song, who was pushing an empty wheelchair.

"I am Lieutenant Bai," the officer said. "You are to come with us."

"Where are we going?" Uncle asked.

"You'll find out when we get there. So no more questions, please," Bai said, and then stood to one side.

Dr. Song stepped towards Uncle. "I want to check your vitals before you leave."

"Do you know where they're taking me?" Uncle whispered as Song leaned towards him.

"No," Song said quickly.

As Song did his work, Uncle noticed that Bai didn't take his eyes off either of them. What did he think, that Uncle was going to leap to his feet and make a run for the door?

"Everything is normal," Song said after taking Uncle's pulse.

"Fine. Now help him into the wheelchair," Bai said.

A soldier rolled the chair over to Song.

"Do you need help to stand?" Song asked Uncle.

"No, I can manage." He pushed himself to his feet, groaning from the effort.

"Turn to the side," Song said. Uncle did and Song placed the chair against the back of his legs. "Now you can sit," he said.

After Uncle had eased into the chair, Song snapped the footrests into place. "He's all yours," he said to the lieutenant. "But try not to jostle him too much. His back is still a problem."

Bai nodded and then said to one of his soldiers, "You push him, but keep it slow and steady."

When the chair was pointed in the direction of the door, one of the soldiers took up a position in front and the others stood on either side. The lieutenant walked past them and led the way from the room.

"Be well," Uncle heard Song say as he was wheeled into the corridor.

The soldiers walked so close to the chair that they were virtually all Uncle could see until he reached the elevator, where yet two more soldiers stood holding the door open. They rolled Uncle into the elevator and then all of them bundled in after him. On his previous trip from the hospital to the cells, they had taken him to the lobby and put him in an ambulance at the front entrance. This time the elevator went past the lobby and stopped at a parking level. *They don't want me to be seen leaving,* he thought, and felt his anxiety spike.

When the elevator doors opened, Uncle found himself looking directly into an ambulance. It had been backed up to within ten metres of the elevator, its rear doors were open, and a ramp ran from the ambulance to the floor. Two medical attendants stood by the ramp.

"Roll him in," Bai said to them.

One of the attendants walked over to Uncle and replaced the soldier who had been pushing him. A moment later the wheelchair was inside the ambulance, along with both attendants and two soldiers. Bai was still outside but now held a walkie-talkie in his hand. "We've got him and we're ready to leave," he said into it.

Uncle could hear a voice replying, but the static was so bad he couldn't decipher what was being said. Whatever it was, it seemed to satisfy Bai, because he gave the walkie-talkie back to a soldier and then walked up the ramp into the ambulance. "We can go now," he said to the attendants. One of them turned and rapped on the small glass window that separated them from the driver. A few seconds later, the ambulance kicked into gear.

Uncle was facing forward, the window in front of him dominated by the driver's head, leaving just enough space on each side to allow him a glimpse of the outside world. When the ambulance left the garage and drove onto the street, he tried to identify the surrounding buildings but didn't recognize anything. Despite the late hour, traffic was still heavy, and they made slow progress through the streets. Uncle wondered why the ambulance didn't put its siren on, and then just as quickly answered his own question. They had him under control; there was no need to rush.

They had driven for what Uncle guessed was fifteen minutes when he noticed the lieutenant checking his watch. "Do you have a deadline to meet?" he asked.

Those were the first words anyone had spoken since they had left the hospital, and they seemed to startle the soldiers.

"No, but we're getting close to our destination, so I'm going to have to blindfold you," Bai said. "I'll leave your hands free, but if you make any attempt to remove the blindfold I'll handcuff you."

"You won't need the cuffs," Uncle said, instantly alert to the unspoken need for secrecy the blindfold represented.

"I hope not," Bai said, taking a mask from his jacket pocket.

Back in darkness, Uncle began to dissect what he'd just learned. Bai had said they were close to their final stop. The last trip to the cells had taken about twenty minutes, and that was in good traffic. This time traffic was heavier and he didn't think they'd driven for that long. Could it be that they weren't going back to the cells? And what about the mask, why was it needed? If they were going to kill him, what did it matter if Uncle knew where they were? It made no sense at all, and Uncle felt his spirits lift ever so slightly.

They drove for a few minutes more before the ambulance came to an abrupt stop. Uncle expected the back door to open, but instead the vehicle made a right turn and started down a hill. It stopped again for several seconds, then made a left turn, followed by a series of turns. Uncle heard a car honking and then the ambulance horn sounded in reply. They stopped. He heard a shuffling of feet around him and the back door opening. There was a clang, which he assumed was the ramp being put in place. Someone grasped the wheelchair handles, spun the chair around, and pushed Uncle towards the door. The chair was tilted back as it went down the ramp.

"They're waiting for you on the second floor," a voice said. "I'll let them know you're on your way."

"Yes, sir," Bai said.

The wheelchair was lifted over a step, went through what Uncle guessed was a door, and then was rolled along a corridor that echoed the sound of the boots striking its floor. Uncle guessed it was concrete or stone of some kind, like the corridors linking the cells. *This isn't so good,* he thought. They came to a stop. "We're taking the service elevator. Push the button," Bai said to one of the soldiers.

Service elevator? Where the hell are we?

No one spoke while they waited, until the silence was broken by the sound of the elevator door opening. Uncle was pushed inside for a ride that was over almost as soon as it began. As they exited, another unfamiliar voice said, "Well done, Lieutenant. Take him to Room Six, at the end of the hall. You can't miss it; we have guards at the door."

"Yes, Colonel," Bai said.

Uncle was on the move again, but this time on a surface that made no noise, which confused him. The men walked for about a minute before they came to a halt.

"You can leave the visitor here," a voice said. "We'll take care of him."

Visitor?

"My instructions were to deliver him to General Ye."

"I represent the general, so that's exactly what you've done."

"Yes, sir."

"And you can take off his mask. There's no need for it anymore."

Light hit Uncle's eyes like a camera flash. He blinked, and gradually his vision started to adjust to the powerful overhead lighting. When things came into focus, he saw Bai standing next to a tall, lean, middle-aged man with single stars on his epaulettes. There were at least ten other soldiers in the area and flanking the door to Room Six.

"Where am I?" Uncle asked.

"If they'd wanted you to know that they wouldn't have asked the lieutenant to blindfold you," the tall soldier said.

"Who are *they*?"

He raised an eyebrow as if he couldn't believe Uncle had asked the question. "That isn't for me to say."

"Well, at least tell me who you are."

"I'm General Wa, a member of General Ye's staff," he said, and then pointed to the door. "You are to wait in there until they're ready for you. Can you walk or do you need the wheelchair?"

"I'll stay in the chair."

"Very well," Wa said, and turned to Bai. "Take him inside and then you can return to your post."

A soldier standing next to Wa stepped forward and opened the door with a simple turn of the handle. Bai pushed Uncle through into a room that had a large table surrounded by twelve chairs in the middle. Along the walls on both sides were credenzas with nothing on them, and on the walls were various paintings of waterfalls. This was a meeting room or a small corporate boardroom, Uncle thought as Bai pulled a chair back from the table and rolled Uncle into its place. Then, without a word, the lieutenant turned and left. Uncle looked around the room. There was only the one door. As with the credenzas, there was nothing on the table, and no sign of a phone. Uncle wheeled himself over to a credenza and started opening drawers in the hope of finding something that would help him figure out where he was. They were all empty. If this was a meeting room it certainly wasn't used very often. He had just looked through the last credenza and wheeled himself back to the table when the door opened.

"Sorry for this inconvenience, but I think you might find that it's worth it," Captain Ma said as he strode in.

"Can I assume from that remark that the general has agreed to my terms?" Uncle asked.

"Not entirely," Lin said, following Ma into the room.

"Actually, not at all," Ma said, as both he and Lin sat down at the table.

"So where does that leave me, apart from confused?" Uncle asked.

"We've just left the general; he's here in the hotel," Lin said. "When we met with him earlier to outline your conditions, he was furious. He said no to everything, and even withdrew the offer not to proceed with bribery charges against you in the Peng case. I think it's fair to say that his attitude was completely hostile."

"I concur with that assessment," Ma said. "He basically said that you would either co-operate or spend the rest of your days in a cell — or worse. The 'worse' part wasn't defined, but we understood what he meant, as I'm sure you do."

Uncle's mouth became dry and his palms sweaty. It was a strange combination, which was compounded by his inability to sort out what Ma and Lin were actually trying to tell him. "So why am I here and not in a cell? I've already said no to that kind of proposition, and I'm not going to change my mind. I won't tell the general what he wants to hear about the Liu family if it means lying."

"I thought you were prepared to speak about your relationship with them from the Hong Kong side of the border," Ma said.

"You're reading too much into what we discussed earlier. All I said was that I'd tell you what I know. And what I know — and would have sworn to — is that the Lius are not now and never have been my partners in anything. That's a fact that doesn't change, whether I'm in Hong Kong or here."

"I know that was your position, and I relayed that to the general," Lin said.

Uncle looked at Lin, trying not to hide his surprise. Whose side was Lin really on?

"That was when he got most angry," Lin continued. "But eventually he began to calm down, and as one meeting merged with another, he began to retreat."

"Retreat? What does that mean?"

"It means no cell," Lin said.

"No charges," added Ma.

"And you're free to return to Hong Kong anytime you wish," Lin said with a broad grin.

"You've completely lost me," said Uncle. "What's happened?"

"Shall I tell him or will you?" Lin asked Ma.

"I think it should come from you," Ma said.

"Liu Huning is in Shenzhen. In fact, he's on the top floor of this hotel," said Lin. "He met with General Ye earlier tonight, and then again after the general had an opportunity to speak with his commanding officer and his father, Ye Desheng, in Beijing. We weren't party to any of those conversations, but we were told their outcome."

Uncle sat dumbfounded, his head full of questions that were almost too complicated to ask. When he did get one out, it was simply, "You were told by whom?"

"The general. He said it's now obvious to him that some of his subordinates were taken in by Peng's desperate attempt to salvage his situation," Lin said. "He said there's no evidence that Liu Leji or any member of the Liu family has been involved in improper activity, and that those subordinates should never have believed Peng's lies."

"Some officers will be reprimanded. I'll probably be one of them," Ma said. "And apologies will be made to Liu Leji for any embarrassment this wrong-headed investigation may have caused."

"You might be struck by the cynicism of it all," Lin said. "But for us it's just how things are done."

"That's how things are done everywhere," Uncle said. "It makes no difference if you're in the military or not. Those with the most power prevail, and they're the ones who get to write the story."

"Shall we finish writing yours?" asked Lin.

"What do you mean?"

"There's someone on the top floor who would like to meet you."

34

MA WALKED WITH UNCLE AND LIN TO THE SERVICE ELE-
vator and then left them there. "He isn't actually a bad guy,"
Lin said. "He just follows orders a bit too precisely."

Uncle didn't respond, and watched from his wheelchair
as Lin pushed the button for the thirty-second floor.

"You're quiet," Lin said.

"I'm in shock."

"That's understandable. I'm sorry we sprung it on you that
way, but we didn't have a choice."

"Why couldn't I have been told something before I left the
hospital?" Uncle said. "When I got into the ambulance, I was
convinced I was heading back to the cells, and I was almost
equally convinced that it would be the last trip I'd ever make."

"As I said, I'm sorry. The truth is that the general hadn't
completely changed his mind about pursuing the Liu family until an hour ago. He was certainly leaning that way,
and from what I've been told, his father was quite insistent
that he bring an end to it, but nothing was final," Lin said.
"Would you have preferred to be told at the hospital that all
was resolved in your favour, only to find that wasn't the case

when you got here? In our minds, that would have been more crushing. So we decided to wait until we were certain. "

"Who are *we*?"

"Liu Leji and his uncle have been actively involved."

Uncle nodded but said nothing as the elevator reached the thirty-second floor. When its doors opened, he found himself facing two armed soldiers.

"He's with me," Lin said from behind Uncle, and then rolled him into a corridor lined with more than a dozen soldiers.

"This is like an armed camp," Uncle said.

"The floor is occupied by VIPs," Lin said. "Mr. Liu's suite is at the far end."

They passed two other suites, each with soldiers at the door, before they reached their destination. A soldier stood aside to allow Lin to knock. Seconds later it was opened by a young woman in a blue cotton dress, who smiled at Lin and stepped back into the suite. Lin pushed Uncle into a sitting room containing a number of richly upholstered sofas and chairs, plus coffee and end tables. Uncle was taken aback by the size of the room; it was bigger than his entire apartment.

"Mr. Liu is in the conference room," the woman said, motioning to a closed door to their left. "I'll let him know you are here." Uncle watched her knock on the door, wait for a few seconds, and then poke her head inside.

"You can go in," she said when she reappeared.

The first person Uncle saw when they entered was Liu Leji. He walked towards them, a broad smile splitting his face and both hands reaching out. "My dear Uncle, how wonderful to see you," he said.

Uncle held out his hands for Liu to grasp and felt a surge of emotion. As the two men paused with their fingers intertwined, Uncle saw that they had captured the attention of everyone else in the room. Five people were sitting around a rectangular table with chairs for eight. Two were women and three men, but only one looked old enough to be Leji's uncle. "It looks like we're interrupting a meeting," Uncle said, noticing the notepads and a whiteboard filled with numbers.

"You are, but that doesn't matter," Leji said. He turned towards the older man, who sat at the end of the table. "This is Chow Tung. This is Uncle."

Liu Huning stared at Uncle and, even from the far end of the room, Uncle could feel his intensity. "I need to speak to this man alone. We can continue our business later," Huning said to the man nearest him.

"Yes, sir," the man said as he stood up. The others at the table followed his example and they left the room.

"Captain Lin, you can leave as well," Huning said.

"Yes, sir," Lin said. "I'll wait outside in case I'm needed."

"Come closer," Huning said to Uncle.

Uncle rolled his chair towards Huning, who was rising to his feet. He was tall, close to six feet, Uncle guessed, but stood so erect that he gave the impression of being taller. He was completely bald and, combined with a face that was long and narrow, it made him look gaunt. He wore an olive-green polyester Zhongshan suit — a "Mao suit," as it was more commonly known, even though it had been introduced by and named after Mao's rival, Sun Yat-sen — with its distinctive tunic jacket's buttoned-up collar and four pockets.

Huning left the table to meet Uncle halfway. He held out his hand and the two men shook. The older man's handshake was firm, and it seemed to Uncle to be full of purpose and determination.

"We're so glad to see you. How is your health?" Huning said. "We understand that your jailers were most unkind."

"I'll mend," said Uncle.

Huning nodded and pursed his lips as if weighing what Uncle had said. Then he turned abruptly and sat down on a chair facing Uncle, the men's knees almost touching. "Come and sit with us, Leji."

"My aunt and my wife send you their very warmest wishes," Leji said as he joined them.

"His aunt — my wife — is quite taken with you," Huning said, not unkindly. "She likes serious men."

"They've both been worried about you," Leji said. "I spoke to them fifteen minutes ago to let them know you've been released. They were both relieved."

"Have you spoken to anyone else? Lin told me that my friend Fong has been anxious."

"I spoke to Fong as well. He wanted to rush directly here, but I told him not to do anything until we'd talked," Leji said, then looked at this watch. "It's very late, and I think it's probably best if you stay here tonight. We've booked a room in this hotel for you. We can call Fong from there and make whatever arrangements are necessary to get you back to Hong Kong tomorrow. We won't feel completely comfortable until you're across the border, and I feel an obligation to get you there. Fong can meet you on the other side, if that's okay with you."

"That sounds just fine."

"Leji told me Fong said your men were prepared to storm the building where they were holding you," Huning said. "It would have been a stupid thing to do, but it speaks well for their loyalty."

"I'm sure your nephew has told you that I'm a member of the Heaven and Earth Society," said Uncle.

"He has."

"Loyalty to our brethren and their families is something we prize above all else," Uncle said, pleased that Huning knew he was a triad and seemed to accept it.

"We aren't your brethren, but you showed tremendous loyalty to us as well, or at least to our partnership," Leji said.

Uncle glanced at Huning and tried to gauge whether he was uncomfortable with that frank admission of their relationship. The older man was instead focused on Uncle, and seemed interested in his reply. "We made a deal. I gave you my word and you gave me yours. You've never gone back on your word and I had no intention of going back on mine. Everything we've done has been based on trust, and I never want you to regret placing it in me and my organization."

"Captain Lin said they did their best to break you," Huning said.

"I don't think there's any reason to go into the details," said Uncle.

"He said that in addition to the beatings, they put a gun to your head and pulled the trigger six times, with the promise that one of those bullets would find you."

"I didn't believe the gun was loaded, and if I was wrong, it would have been rather late for me to correct that error in judgement. So, either way, my fate was determined."

"They did that to me too, you know," Huning said, his hand resting lightly on Uncle's knee. "During the early days of the Cultural Revolution, the Red Guard used intimidation as a prelude to re-education. Many people were beaten, and some killed."

"Like Premier Deng's son?"

"Yes. He was thrown out a fourth-floor window. They probably wished it was Xiaoping himself, but men like us still had enough friends and allies that we were protected from the very worst of the abuses. They thought keeping us out of sight for three or four years in a factory or labour camp would eliminate the threat we represented, especially given how old we were when we were allowed to return to Beijing. We were both in our sixties."

"But weren't you then purged again?"

Huning smiled. "You know something of our personal histories."

"I wanted to understand what Premier Deng is trying to do in Shenzhen and in the other special economic zones, so I did some reading."

"Xiaoping has been trying for years to introduce a system that marries the very best of communism with individual self-interest. In economic terms, he believes in practising socialism at the macro level and capitalism at the micro, though of course we never use the word *capitalism*. I've been at his side, through good and bad, for fifty years. We were removed from office three times, the first time peacefully, then rather more forcibly during the Cultural Revolution and later, when the Gang of Four tried to grab power after Mao's death," Huning said. He tapped Uncle on the knee. "So when you were talking earlier about trust and loyalty, I've learned it first-hand, working with the man who is now our premier. I know how to recognize it and to value it. What I'd like to do with you is find a way to reward it. Is there anything I can do for you?"

"Make sure I get back to Hong Kong," Uncle said.

"That's assured. There must be something else I can do."

Uncle paused. What could someone in Huning's position deliver? "There is one thing, but it may be a great deal to ask," Uncle said finally.

"What is it? If I can't do it, I'll tell you."

"Well, I have a very good friend and colleague named Xu," Uncle said slowly. "He is part of my organization in Fanling, but for the past few years he's been working with factories in Xiamen, to their benefit and ours. But his heart is in Shanghai. That's his ancestral home, and he still has a house there in the French Concession. He would like to return. Can you make that possible?"

"He is triad?"

"Of course. But, as you must know — otherwise, I assume you wouldn't be permitting your wife and son to do business with us — we avoid practices that are exploitive or call negative attention to ourselves."

"So you're telling me that you want your man Xu to conduct business in Shanghai?"

"We are businesspeople."

"Regardless of your business, that might be difficult to arrange."

"I thought that might be the case."

Huning held up an index finger. "I said it would be difficult but I didn't say it was impossible. I need to make a phone call, which I'll do from my bedroom. The two of you stay here until I come back."

"Your uncle is an impressive man," Uncle said after Huning left the room.

"He's a survivor."

"How old is he?"

"He's eighty-two, a few years older than Premier Deng."

"He seems to be in excellent health, but how much longer does he expect to keep working?"

"He doesn't think of it as work. It's service to China, and as long as Deng Xiaoping is premier, I can't see my uncle leaving his side. They finally have the power they've sought for decades to implement the programs this country needs, to advance into the next century and to restore our proper place in the world as a major power — if not *the* major power," Leji said. "Interestingly, the past few days have affirmed and strengthened their position, and we may have helped that happen."

"What do you mean by that?"

"Ye Desheng, General Ye's father, was loosely linked to the Gang of Four and is an advocate of Maoist egalitarianism. He is opposed to Deng Xiaoping's reforms, but not openly. My uncle thinks he's been hoping the reforms fail, but as the years have passed, their success has become more and more obvious. Our guess is that Ye decided he couldn't wait any longer. He saw this as an opportunity to test his strength within the Politburo Committee by attacking us through his son."

"Us?"

"Me, you, my aunt, and my wife. They wouldn't dare mention my uncle, but everyone understood the implications if the rest of us were brought down," Leji said. "So, if they had broken you and you had implicated us, my uncle would have been the next target, and after him, who knows? It might even have been Deng Xiaoping."

"What made Ye back down?"

"Political reality. He quickly learned that Premier Deng stands squarely behind my uncle, and that none of the other Committee members want to risk offending the Premier," Leji said. "Then there's the small matter of their having nothing they could use against my family, because you wouldn't give it to them."

"What will happen to Ye Desheng?"

"Nothing. He claims he had no idea what his son was doing."

"And the general?"

"General Ye could not be more apologetic. But then, it was made clear that if he wasn't, he'd be commanding troops in Mongolia," Leji said.

"So they'll stay in the positions they have?"

"There's nothing to be gained by humiliating them, except creating lifelong enemies."

Uncle smiled. "That isn't much different from the way we deal with potential enemies."

The door opened and Liu Huning stood in the entrance. "Leji, push Uncle's wheelchair, will you. We're going down the hall to pay a visit."

"Sure," Leji said without hesitation.

"Where are we going?" Uncle asked.

"I don't know," Leji said as he took the chair's handles.

Liu Huning was already in the hallway by the time they reached the suite's exit door. Leji sped up to catch him.

Watching Huning from the rear, Uncle would never have guessed his age. He took long, limber steps and swung his arms energetically. The soldiers lining the corridor snapped to attention as he passed, and two officers saluted him. Huning walked past the elevator. He seemed to be headed to the other end of the hallway, where a group of ten or more soldiers had congregated.

"He's expecting us," Uncle heard Huning say as he drew near.

Uncle watched an officer — a colonel, he thought — knock on the door and then slowly turn the handle. Huning stepped inside and then turned to wait for Uncle and Leji.

"He doesn't have a lot of time, but if your favour is to be granted, he's the man who can do it. So whatever he asks you, answer quickly and answer truthfully," Huning said as Uncle and Leji reached him.

They entered a suite that was identical in every way to the one they had just left, except that the living area was occupied.

"Xiaoping, this is the man I told you about," Huning said.

He sat in an upholstered chair, his head resting against the back and his feet dangling above the carpet. He wore a navy-blue Zhongshan suit buttoned to the neck. His face was wreathed in smoke; he held a cigarette between two fingers and the ashtray to his right was filled with butts. As Uncle drew closer he recognized the distinctive haircut, with the sides shaved halfway up his head, the hairline that had receded to the middle of his scalp, and the tuft of hair — still black — that looked like a bird's plume.

"My friend Huning tells me that you are originally from Wuhan," Deng Xiaoping said.

Uncle lowered his head, not sure what else he should be doing to show respect. "I'm from a village near Wuhan. My family had a farm there."

"But you left?"

"We lost the farm during the Great Leap Forward, and

then, one by one, my family members died. There was nothing left for me."

"That was a difficult time for so many of our people. One reason I've kept coming back is that I never want to see it repeated."

"No, sir," Uncle said.

"And now you've come back as well," Deng said. "Huning tells me you have invested very heavily in Shenzhen."

"And I've encouraged friends to do the same in the other special economic zones."

"Why?"

"Whether I like it or not, Hong Kong and the People's Republic are going to be reunited. As a businessman I can choose to resist it, ignore it, or adapt to it. After reading about what you're trying to do here, I decided to adapt. I decided to commit and I persuaded my friends to do the same."

"But Huning tells me you now want to spread your efforts outside of the zones."

"My best friend — a man who means as much to me as it appears Liu Huning means to you — was driven out of Shanghai twenty years ago. He has a house there, and he's never sold it because he's always dreamed of returning to it. When Liu Huning offered to grant me a favour, it was the first thing that came to mind."

"What is your friend's name?"

"Xu Bo. His family lives in Fanling, in the New Territories, but he's been spending much of the past few years in Xiamen. Like me, he believes in the future of the special economic zones, and I can tell you honestly that he has already contributed to that city's economic well-being."

Deng stubbed out his cigarette and immediately lit another. Uncle noticed that his fingers were heavily stained yellow, with shades of black. "Why did he leave Shanghai?" Deng asked.

"He is triad, as am I."

"From what Liu Huning has told me, though, you are a businessman first."

Uncle drew a deep breath. "First and foremost I am always a member of the Heaven and Earth Society. But I have chosen to conduct myself and to devote my organization to doing business in a way that is honest, legal, and sustainable. I guarantee that Xu would operate in a similar manner in Shanghai."

Deng looked at Huning. "What do you think? Is this a Pandora's box?"

"No, I don't think so. This is a man requesting a favour for a friend. That's how I see it, nothing more than that."

Deng stared at Uncle. Uncle looked back into his eyes without blinking.

"You have done us a service here in Shenzhen — in fact, several services," Deng said. "Have your friend contact a man named Tsai Lian in about a week. Tsai is deputy party secretary in Shanghai, and he's also the nephew of a close friend of Huning and me. If your friend's house is still standing, Tsai will do what he can to help him recover it. Beyond that, what Tsai and Xu decide to do is their business."

"I can't thank you enough for this," Uncle said, his voice catching as emotions he hadn't anticipated flooded through him.

Deng nodded and then turned to a man who had been standing off to one side with a notebook in his hand. "Did you get the details?"

"I did, sir."

"Call Tsai tonight."

"Yes, sir."

Deng turned back to Uncle. "We're finished here. Good luck to you," he said.

35

LIU LEJI PUSHED UNCLE FROM THE SUITE. THEY HADN'T gone ten metres before Uncle blurted, "I wasn't expecting that."

"Which part, meeting Premier Deng or the fact he was so accommodating about Xu?"

"All of it."

"I wasn't expecting any of it either, though I have to say, from my family's point of view, any favour granted was warranted."

"Do you think he can actually make it happen for Xu?"

"There isn't much that man can't make happen," Liu said as he rolled the wheelchair towards the elevators. "You have a suite several floors below. We've been told that physically you shouldn't try to do too much on your own, so we've arranged for one of the nurses from the hospital to tend to you."

"I appreciate that."

"There's beer and water in the room and the nurse will order any food you wish."

"And there will be a phone, like you said? I'm quite anxious to speak to Fong and some of my other men. There was an issue pending when I was arrested at the border that has been weighing on me."

"When I spoke to Fong earlier, he said he'd stay at the office until he heard from you. We'll call him as soon as we reach the room."

They rode the elevator down five floors. When they exited, Uncle was surprised to see armed soldiers standing directly across from the doors. "Are there soldiers on every floor?" he asked.

"I asked the same question," Liu said. "There are men in the garage, in the lobby, on the roof, and on the top five floors."

Uncle's suite was to the right of the elevators, at the far end of the hall. Liu stopped when they reached it and knocked sharply on the door. A middle-aged woman who looked vaguely familiar to Uncle opened it, smiled, and moved to one side.

"The nurse's name is Fenfang," Liu said. "I met her earlier. She said she looked after you for a brief time at the hospital."

"That's entirely possible, but I have only a vague memory of my time there," Uncle said.

"I'm pleased to see you here," she said.

"No one could be more pleased than I."

"Would you like some water?" she asked.

"Director Liu told me there's beer. If there is, I'd rather have one of those."

"I'll get it right away," she said. "And how about the director?"

"I'll have one as well," Liu said, rolling the wheelchair into the suite. "There's a phone on the desk and another in the bedroom. Which one do you want to use?"

"We'll call from here. Will you dial for me?"

"Sure. I have the number written down," Liu said, reaching into his pocket for a slip of paper and then pushing the wheelchair next to the desk. He dialled with some deliberation, waited for a few seconds, and then said, "Fong, your boss is with me and eager to speak to you."

Uncle took the phone. "Hey. It looks like I'll be coming home tomorrow."

"He's coming home tomorrow," Fong shouted, and Uncle heard a chorus of animated voices in the background.

"Who's there with you?"

"A handful of forty-niners. Xu was here too until about an hour ago."

"Xu came back from Xiamen?"

"He was worried sick about you. And we also had the Wu situation to deal with."

"I couldn't stop thinking about Wu. What happened?"

"He's crawled back into his hole in Tai Wai. I don't think we'll have to worry about him for a while."

"How did you handle the death of our man? How did you get Wu to back off?"

"Xu flew in from Xiamen first thing the morning after the killing for an executive meeting," Fong said. "Wang wanted to go to war. He wanted an eye for an eye, and no one could really blame him, since it was one of his best young men who died. But Xu and Yu counselled caution. They both said our primary objective had to be ending or at least blunting Wu's aggression, and that taking one of his men's lives in return would only extend and increase the violence. Aside from getting momentary revenge, neither of them saw any good coming from that. We'd only lose more men, have our businesses disrupted, and force the police to get involved."

"That was wise of them. And I'm sure you shared those views."

"I sided with Wang at first, but they won me and the rest of the executive over. In fact, they even persuaded Wang to let them pursue their strategy."

"What was the strategy?"

"The Fanling and Tai Wai gangs are about the same size. Xu said we needed to bring a larger gang to our side, not just to voice support but also willing to go to war beside us if it came to that," Fong said. "He called Tse, whose gang is bigger than ours and Tai Wai's put together. Tse committed to us and then went further, by calling Wu and all the other Mountain Masters. He told them he was aligning with Fanling and would bring down anyone who messed with us."

"He and Xu have built a nice relationship."

"Maybe they have, but Tse made it clear he was supporting us because of you," Fong said. "He said he's made more worry-free money in the past year than ever in his whole life, and it was your plan to go into the special economic zones that made it happen."

"Did he know I was being held in China?"

"Yeah, we had to tell him, but Xu explained that it was a bureaucratic problem that would get sorted out in a few days. They have enough of a relationship, I guess, that Tse believed him, or at least didn't question him. Tse's bottom line was that he wants you left alone to come up with new ways of making money."

Uncle heard a soft voice behind him and turned to see Fenfang offering him a Tsingtao beer. Liu already had his. He took the bottle, tapped Liu's, and drank.

"Is everything okay in Fanling?" Liu whispered.

"It appears I've been worrying about nothing," Uncle said.

"That's a nice thing to discover."

"Isn't it," Uncle said, taking another swig. He leaned back in the wheelchair, the phone still pressed to his ear. "Fong, unless there's something urgent you want to tell me, I don't need to hear anything more. So if there isn't, I'll pass the phone to Liu and you can sort out how I get back to Hong Kong tomorrow."

"Sure, boss, give the phone to Liu," Fong said.

36

February 1984
Yuen Long, New Territories, Hong Kong

IT WAS SEVEN A.M. WHEN UNCLE BEGAN THE HUNDRED-metre uphill climb that led to the Ancestor Worship Hall on Fo Look Hill in Yuen Long. In one hand he carried a small folding stool, in the other a paper bag that contained two oranges, loose tea, incense sticks, a whisk, and a cloth. It was almost four months since he'd been arrested and interrogated in Shenzhen, and only now was he able to walk without excessive pain. Still, he took his time going up the hill, taking care not to step on anything that might cause a sudden twist or turn. The path was flanked by hillside covered in shrubs, gorse, and wildflowers. On some visits he stopped to pick some of the flowers, but on this day he headed directly to the Worship Hall.

The remains of his fiancée, Lin Gui-San, were interred there — or at least his memories of her were. Her body had never been recovered from Shenzhen Bay, so Uncle had filled an urn with sand from the beach, pressed into it the jade bracelet he had intended to give her on their wedding day, and placed it in a niche with a picture of her.

As he neared the summit of the hill, he saw that the hall was empty of people. He preferred being alone there and always came early enough for that to be a possibility.

The building faced northeast, so it overlooked the sea and caught the morning sunlight. It was about thirty metres across and fifteen metres deep, with a red tile roof and sweeping curved overhangs. The front was completely open to its surroundings, and this openness and the wonderful sightlines contributed to its feng shui. A small stream ran along one side and a fountain gurgled near the entrance steps. It was a place that welcomed *qi,* promising peace and tranquility to the people being memorialized there.

Uncle reached the hall and climbed the five steps that led inside. He walked past the statue of a seated Buddha and another of a Taoist god. He approached the hall's back wall, which was a mass of small alcoves and niches, each devoted to a loved one. The niches were small and could accommodate only an urn and some small mementos. Most of them also contained a photo of the deceased.

Gui-San's niche was on the left side of the wall at about chest height. Uncle stopped in front of it, unfolded the stool, and put the paper bag on top of it. He then opened the bag, took out the small whisk broom, and approached the niche. He reached into it, removed the urn, and placed it gently on the ground. The two oranges he'd left on his previous visit were now dry and shrivelled. He took them out, and the small bowl of dry tea leaves that had been left with them. The niche was now empty except for a photo of Gui-San taken in Wuhan on her twenty-first birthday. Uncle had had it enlarged and laminated and had affixed it to the back wall. Under the photo, gold lettering read:

LIN GUI-SAN

BORN IN CHANGZHAI, HUBEI PROVINCE, 28 OCTOBER 1934

DIED NEAR HONG KONG, 28 JUNE 1959

FOREVER LOVED

FOREVER MISSED

Uncle swept the floor of the niche with the whisk, returned it to the bag, and took out the cloth. He wet it in the fountain and returned to the niche. He wiped away the dust and grime that had collected on the photo and the floor of the niche, and then he bent down carefully and cleaned the urn. When that was done, he put the urn back into the niche and then placed the two oranges and fresh tea in the small bowl next to it.

He turned and went back to the stool. He put the whisk and cloth back in the bag and extracted six sticks of incense. Facing the niche, he lit them with his faded black crackle Zippo lighter — the lighter that had belonged to Gui-San's father and was her most prized possession. He placed three sticks into slots in the front of the niche and then held the others between his palms. He raised his hands to his chest, lowered his head, and began to pray. He prayed until the sticks began to burn his flesh. Then he stopped, put what was left of the incense into a receptacle, and sat on the stool facing the niche.

"This was the first year I didn't visit you on your birthday. I'm so sorry that I couldn't make it. I hope it never happens again," he said to her. "I was in Fanling but I had trouble walking. In fact I needed Fong's help to get from my apartment to the office every morning. I guess I could have asked him to come here with me, and I thought about it, but this is our personal place, and I want to safeguard the privacy it gives us.

"There, that's said. I feel a bit better now. It was bothering me because I could imagine you wondering where I was, and I could imagine you worrying about me, and that's the last thing I want. Although, to be entirely honest, it wouldn't have been misplaced to worry about me. I was in a difficult place and a difficult situation. There were times when I thought I was going to die and I felt despair, but whenever I did, I thought of joining you, and the blackness lifted."

Uncle felt his eyes moisten, and rubbed them. He reached into his pocket, took out his pack of Marlboros, and lit a cigarette. He took a puff, blowing the smoke to one side, away from the niche. "Aside from the possibility that I could die, the experience affected me in one other important way," he continued. "I don't know if you were pleased when I told you a few years ago that we were going to invest in China. I told you I had my doubts initially — some of them were emotional, because of my hatred for the Communists, but practically I was also concerned about the security of our investments. There's no law in China, or maybe I should say there's a legal system that can be changed to suit whatever circumstance the government decides is important on any particular day. I thought that by aligning myself with people who made decisions for the government I would be able to protect us. What I didn't factor in strongly enough was that those people could change and become the problem."

He paused, ground the cigarette butt under his heel, and put it in the paper bag. "Peng was foolish. It's one thing to accept payment for services rendered, but it's another to flaunt the fact that you have lots of money in front of people who don't. The government went after him, and I'm sure he told them everything he'd ever done. I thought we were still safe, though, because there must be dozens, if not hundreds of people like us who paid him bribes, and it would have been self-defeating for the officials to prosecute people who were investing in the zone. But then politics intervened and the PLA was brought into the picture. I'm certain Peng mentioned my name and linked it to the Liu family, and I became a target because of that connection.

"I've mentioned to you before that Liu Leji's father, Huning, is a member of the Standing Politburo Committee. What I didn't know is how close he is to Deng Xiaoping and how unhappy some Committee members are with the direction Deng is taking China in. I found out quickly enough, when the PLA picked me up," he said. "They wanted me to confirm that I was doing business with the Lius. If I did, they promised to send me back to Hong Kong and leave my businesses alone. I didn't believe them, but even if I had, I would never have been able to bring myself to do it. I can't think of anything worse than betraying a trust that's been placed in you, especially when it's done not blindly but after a lot of thought, and with full knowledge of how horrendous the consequences could be if that confidence was ever betrayed. I knew I'd rather die. But obviously I didn't. My luck held, Gui-San, and an amazing thing happened."

He lit another cigarette, took two quick drags, and then put it out. "I stopped smoking for a while when I was being held in China. It wasn't voluntary, but it did wean me physically from the urge to smoke. I even managed to avoid it for a few weeks after my return to Fanling. But then I went to dinner with Fong and Xu, and when Fong offered me a cigarette, I took it. It was almost a reflex reaction, and so was stopping to buy a pack of Marlboros on the way back to my apartment. Now I'm smoking as much as I ever have," he said, then paused. "I don't know why I just mentioned that. I was talking about something amazing, wasn't I. Well, it did involve Xu, so at least there's a bit of a connection.

"Xu is leaving Fanling with his family, and I hope it's for good. I know that sounds like I'm happy he's leaving, but I'm not. I'm happy for him. His dream has always been to go back to Shanghai, and now he can — openly, with the approval of and even some help from the Communists. How did that happen?" he said, and smiled.

"I met Premier Deng, and we talked man-to-man. He's small, Gui-San — in fact, you're taller than him — and he looks like a strong wind might blow him over. But there's a strength to him that I couldn't have imagined. He has survived everything the Communists have thrown at him, yet there's no bitterness or anxiousness to him. He's a man who is certain about the rightness of his path, who will keep pursuing it regardless of the opposition, and who radiates confidence and a calmness that says he will inevitably prevail. I'll never like the Communists, but I don't hate them as much as I used to. And I can admire and respect a man like Deng without having to agree with everything he represents. Strangely, that's what Liu Huning said to Deng about me.

"So our Chinese ventures are intact and are now expanding. I've tried to be careful, to be cautious, but we're getting to the point where we're in so deep we might never get out. That should frighten me but it doesn't, because I think — like Deng — some things are inevitable. The clock is ticking towards the day China will reclaim Hong Kong, and there's no resisting the tidal wave that will come when it does. I want to be ready for that wave, to be positioned to not just survive it but to prosper from it. Setting up businesses in China was the first step, making alliances with people in power was the second, and returning Xu to Shanghai is the third, and possibly the most important for the Heaven and Earth Society," he said.

Hearing noises behind him, Uncle stood up. "There are people coming up the hill. I should let them have as peaceful a time with their ancestors as I've had with you," he said. He stepped towards the niche, kissed the tips of his fingers, and pressed them against the photo of Gui-San. "I love you. I'll be back next month. I want to stay close to home for a while."

He picked up the paper bag, folded the stool, and turned towards the exit. The morning sun drilled into his eyes and he was forced to cover them with the back of his hand. "What a beautiful morning to spend time with your loved ones," he said to the man and woman approaching.

ACKNOWLEDGEMENTS

Writing about Shenzhen in the early 1980s is not an easy task. What was essentially a collection of villages with a population of 35,000 is now — forty years later — a city with about eighteen million inhabitants. That growth began in 1980–81, but really exploded in the mid-to-late '80s. For the purposes of my plot, however, I've started it sooner. I have been true to Premier Deng's economic strategy for Shenzhen and the other special economic zones; all I've done is make it more successful in a quicker fashion.

I am sure that some readers will find the idea that a director of customs would start his own warehouse business and direct customers to it a bit far-fetched. I admit that it seems outlandish but in truth, when I was doing business in Shenzhen, the customs department was running its own customs brokerage house, and the military was directly involved in any number of businesses.

Now, my thanks.

To my first readers, and then the advance-copy readers — you are all appreciated to the utmost degree: my wife, Lorraine, Robin Spano, Catherine Rosebrugh, John Kruithof,

Ashok Ramchandani, Caleena Chiang, Christina Sit, and Carol Shetler.

To Doug Richmond, my editor, and Maria Golikova, the managing editor, at House of Anansi Press. I have been blessed with great editors from the beginning of this journey. They never fail to make a book better.

To my agent, Bruce Westwood, for his support and steadfast care when some days it must seem more sensible to sit at the farm with a glass of wine.

And to everyone who took the time to email me or talk to me at some event. When as a writer you sit alone for hours and days on end, you can forget that there are people out there who are eager to find out where your stories go. Keep the emails coming; they never fail to motivate me.

IAN HAMILTON is the author of thirteen novels in the Ava Lee series and two novels in the Lost Decades of Uncle Chow Tung series. His books have been shortlisted for numerous prizes, including the Arthur Ellis Award, the Barry Award, and the Lambda Literary Prize, and are national bestsellers. BBC Culture named Hamilton one of the ten mystery/crime writers from the past thirty years who should be on your bookshelf. The Ava Lee series is being adapted for television.

COMING SOON
from House of Anansi Press

Uncle will return in . . .

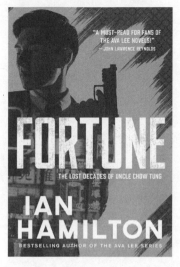

(January 2021)

NOW AVAILABLE
from House of Anansi Press

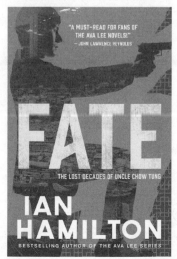